THE BOY WHO WASN'T THERE

A Roger Harper Novel

JAMES G RILEY
BERNADINE RILEY

ABOUT THE AUTHORS

James and Bernadine live in Florida with their dog, Barkley. They have nine wonderful grandchildren; six girls and three boys. James taught math and economics whilst living in England. In California and Arizona, he worked as a banker, stockbroker, and insurance agent.

As well as being a homemaker, reflecting her passion for education, Bernadine spent five years serving on a school board. At one time, she owned a gift and book store. Furthermore, she likes to quilt, cook and solve puzzles.

For more information visit:
https://jamesgriley.com

Email: **jamesandbernadine@jamesgriley.com**

g goodreads.com/jamesgriley

a amazon.com/author/jamesgriley

f facebook.com/jamesgriley.author

instagram.com/jamesgriley.author

pinterest.com/jamesgrileyauthor

ALSO BY JAMES G RILEY

OTHER ROGER HARPER NOVELS

(Book 1) The Man Who Would Cheat At Cards

ISBN: 978-1-944108-04-5

SAMPLE REVIEW

★★★★★

Wonderfully written and cleverly intense.

A delightfully well-written thriller with incredible detail to description. I was thoroughly impressed from start to finish. The poker scene was well crafted and intense. A must-read for anyone looking for action and thrills

Co-written with Bernadine Riley

(Book 2) The Man Who Would Stop A Clock

ISBN: 978-1-944108-09-0

SAMPLE REVIEW

★★★★

An intriguing plot

I wondered before I started just how the title of the book would be relevant to what is at once a thriller, a mystery, and a who-done-it. Certainly, the way it was done is very clever. This is a great story and very well told.

(Book 3) The Man Who Could Not Cheat Time

ISBN: 978-1-944108-14-4

Sample Review

★★★★★

Gripping story, tightly plotted and very well written!

This is very much a murder, thriller story. Roger Harper's character development, although it is a book 3, was intriguing as it played and was shaped with the other "international" characters of the book.

There are also plot twists that make you think of what the ending will be, but the way in which everything was pulled together was very good. The tension is really turned up a notch in the final third of the book. Overall, it was a very good read and it kept me in my seat, wanting me to read more.

————

A Special Agent Allen Richardson Mystery

Lab Rats

ISBN: 978-1-944108-08-3

Sample Review

★★★★★

Warning this may test your imagination

Talk about imagination. Jim tested mine with Lab Rats. The plotline is unique, and his characters come to life. His description of the caves is outstanding - I thought I was there and somewhat claustrophobic :) Great read.

————

Conundrum (A Quest For King Arthur § Book One)

ISBN: 978-1-944108-05-2

SAMPLE REVIEW

★★ The premise was good

I believe that the author shows promise. The story threads come together in the last quarter of the book.

Amulet (A Quest For King Arthur § Book Two)

ISBN: 978-1-944108-07-6

SAMPLE REVIEW

★★★★★ I highly recommend it

James G Riley opens his second novel in a series with a well-written summation of his first book for those not familiar with Part One. His novel is clever by every measure. It's a retelling of a classic tale, with a twist involving time travel and bi-located settings in the years 2016 and 546. We get the pleasure of reacquainting ourselves with the classic characters in King Arthur's world, as well as being introduced to their modern-day counterparts thrust into the past. The details of the adventures are vivid. Riley thoroughly researched his material. His writing is transportive, educational, and entertaining throughout. *Amulet* is worth the read for anyone loving the concept of time travel and the challenge to solve riddles to advance the storyline.

Merry Dance

ISBN: 978-1-944108-12-0

SAMPLE REVIEWS

★ ★ ★ ★ ★

JAMES G RILEY

MERRY DANCE
A COLLECTION OF
SHORT STORIES &
POEMS

Mystery and fantasy for all ages

Every story was a surprise. Jim's imagination is off the charts. You will enjoy each of these stories for their uniqueness. Delightful.

★ ★ ★ ★ Entertaining short reads

This charming collection of fanciful stories and poems is the perfect antidote to a long wait in a doctor's office. It will likely amuse and pique the curiosity of readers trapped on a boring train or plane ride. The author doesn't always solve the paranormal problems he presents, but pondering them will make for an entertaining short read.

———

DISCLAIMERS

———

ACKNOWLEDGMENTS

Authors' portrait photograph by Amanda Rose Day

———

DEDICATION

To Our Grandchildren

"Why do my brothers mourn? why do my daughters weep? that a young man has gone to the happy hunting-grounds?"

— *James Fenimore Cooper   (The Last of the Mohicans)*

———

PROLOGUE

A YOUNG FIRST NATIONS BOY WAS DEAD; KILLED THESE SEVEN DAYS past. Steeped in sorrow, a shroud of dark gray cloud enveloped the Douglas Mountain Range. The memorial ceremony began with the tribal elders stomping their feet to the beat of a drum as they encircled the bonfire. With spears and clubs last used in anger during the Frazer Canyon War of 1858, they gestured toward the sky. Children, thinking it was a game, threw sticks into the flames causing firefly sparks to shoot into the air. Women wept.

Dressed in the scarlet uniform of the Royal Canadian Mounted Police, a lone figure watched from the cover of the coniferous forest. With the alleged perpetrator long gone, his superiors pressuring for a speedy conclusion, the last line of his report would read:

Accidental death. No further action required.

Nevertheless, out of respect, the Mountie remained at the settlement to witness the funeral rites of the Native American Indian.

Presenting an offering to the boy's spirit as it journeyed to the afterlife, a young girl tossed elk meat and salmon from a cedar-wood platter into the fire. Next, she pulled an eagle's feather from her headband. Pausing between mesmeric twists and turns, she pointed the feather north, south, east, then west. The ingénue called on *Sisiutl*, the supernatural three-headed serpent, to avenge the boy's death. So ardent were her cries, despite being but ten years of age, the elders marked her as a future shaman.

An unexpected clap of thunder rumbled between the mountain peaks and echoed along the U-shaped valley. Taken as a portent, the ceremony ceased abruptly. Without delay, the funeral party formed into two columns. Four men lifted the pallet supporting the blanket-wrapped corpse onto their shoulders. In silence, the procession then proceeded along the winding trail leading to a plateau near the top of a nearby hill.

Doing his best to remain concealed, the Mountie followed. A witness to the boy's burial, he was surprised when the interment was not in a box supported by two tall mortuary totems. Then again, his understanding of native customs relied on the clichéd history of early traders' first contact with indigenous communities.

As the mourners departed, once more thunder reverberated along the valley. Rain followed, a drenching downpour, marking the end of a melancholic day.

The to-be shaman slept fitfully that night, plagued by prophetic visions and vivid dreams. One foretold of strangers arriving from far away, carried on the wings of a giant bird, come to redress the festering wrong, restoring harmony and prosperity to the land. She told no one, yet somehow she knew the dead boy's spirit would approve.

Forty-eight hours later, upon returning to Vancouver, the Mountie duly completed his one-page report. Hastily reviewed by an Inspector, rubber stamped

CASE CLOSED,

it would find its way to the RCMP's basement archives, forgotten, left to collect dust. Not forgotten, however, by those who dwelt near the abandoned township of Port Douglas. Soon to become part of an oral tradition, the tribal elders told stories of a ghost spirit, that of a young boy, who protected the remnants of a once-thriving First Nations reserve.

CHAPTER ONE

ROGER HARPER, NOT ONE TO SIT AROUND FOR LONG PERIODS, exhibited his unease by constantly fidgeting. So much so that he earned a rebuke from his wife, Julia. "For goodness sake, will you stop fiddling with your collar, sweetie?"

"I don't know why you insisted I wear a suit and tie," he replied, as they waited for their appointment to complete the transfer of title to property left by her late father.

"Because, Roger, first impressions count, that's why. Any other complaints?"

"Why have we arrived here so early?" was the second comment.

"Being late for an appointment is impolite. You, of all people, should know that. How often have I heard you carping when you're at the receiving end? Besides it's not as though you are here to have a tooth pulled."

"Seems like it, honeybee. They couldn't have installed more uncomfortable chairs if they had tried."

"Occupy yourself, Roger. Look through the illustrated book on Canada that is on the table. Maybe you'll learn something useful about the country?"

Before Harper could object, Julia reached forward, picked up the book, and handed it to her husband. For her part, she removed an iPad from her handbag and immersed herself in the ebook she had previously started.

Both occupied, the couple sat in silence until the outside door opened and a smartly dressed woman, a few years younger than Julia, entered. After checking in with the receptionist, she made her way to the waiting area. A brief nod to the couple by way of greeting, she took a magazine from a rack in the corner, before taking a seat.

"That's what I mean, Roger," Julia told Harper in a low voice. "One dresses appropriately for a business meeting."

"If you say so, honeybee," was the despondent response.

"Don't sound so downcast, Roger. Like me, you should be excited about our family adventure to Port Douglas and staying in a lakeside cabin. Maybe, I'll get a chance to meet up with my sister before we leave?"

"We can find time to do that, Jules. However, right now, it's the kids I'm concerned about. Do you think they are okay, with Federico looking after them?" The person Harper was referring to he had met in Cuba nearly two years ago. They had become close friends.

"Of course. If you are worried Federico may have trouble changing Ophelia's pull-ups, Olly and Spencer are both capable of doing that. After all, they will be teenagers next year."

"I guess so. What's the novel you are reading, honeybee?"

"A romance. A middle-aged couple finds love while on vacation. You can read it after I'm done."

"No thanks. Not my cup of tea."

"Figures."

"What does that mean, Jules? I can do romantic. I've already arranged for a mariachi band to serenade us on the cabin's veranda."

Julia laughed. "With a personal chef barbecuing steaks, and a waiter serving wine, I suppose."

"You've got it, honeybee. Just the two of us, under the stars, dining together."

Another laugh; more a snort. "I'm guessing that idea won't go down well with Olly and Spencer. But it's the thought that counts." Julia squeezed Harper's hand. "Have you found anything interesting in the book you're browsing?"

"There's a chapter on some of the differences between the U.S. and Canada. In the States, for example, we have a federal oil reserve. In Canada, they stockpile maple syrup."

"I did not know that," Julia confessed.

"Furthermore, they buy milk in plastic bags, while we do more online shopping than they do."

"I prefer the latter, but if I ever visit a Canadian supermarket I'll bear that in mind."

"Do you think we'll find any supermarkets in Port Douglas?" Harper asked.

"Hardly, but let's not allow that to distract from our holiday." Julia glanced at her wristwatch. "Not too long before we meet with the attorney."

"Good," her husband acknowledged. "I've finished with this book. I'll close my eyes for a few minutes and wait until we are called."

Julia went back to reading her romance novel. Short-lived, Harper whispered, "Hey, Jules. The smartly dressed lady; are you aware that she's your half-sister?"

Julia looked up in surprise. "How do you know that, Roger?" Then realization came to her. "You didn't?"

"I did." Harper could not suppress a cheesy grin.

Julia responded with a frown. "I've told you before, Roger. It is rude to get inside people's minds. Don't do it again."

"Sorry," her husband replied. "I'll behave."

"Promise?"

"Scout's honor." However, the whispering continued. "Aren't you going to introduce yourself? It would be remiss not to."

"All right. Come on then."

Julia stood up. Dragging her husband by the sleeve, she when up to the other women.

"Excuse me for asking, but your name wouldn't be Dalia Walker, would it?"

"Why yes? How did you know?"

"Lucky guess," Julia fudged.

"Wait a second." Ms. Walker's eyes lit up. "You must be Julia Harper. Well, I never." Julia enthusiastically nodded back, a broad smile on her face. "Come here, sis. Give me a hug."

Harper waited twenty seconds or so, before politely coughing.

The two ladies broke their embrace. Both had to wipe tears from their eyes.

"Sorry. My bad. Allow me to introduce my husband, Roger."

"Roger, please to meet you."

Offering his hand, he responded without explanation, "Just Harper."

"I think we deserve more than a handshake, don't you, Harper?" his sister-in-law countered, following up with a generous hug. "And you must call me Dee. Everyone does."

The door to an inner room opened and a well-groomed gentleman stepped out, introducing himself as Ellis Davis.

"Ladies. I see you have already met. Splendid. Simply splendid." Glancing at Harper, he added, "You, sir, I assume, are party to these proceedings."

"This is Roger," Julia chimed. "He belongs to me."

"Roger, hmm. My son is also named Roger."

"Please call me Harper. No offense to your son, but, unless it's my wife, I hate anyone using my first name."

CHAPTER TWO

THE READING OF JULIA AND DEE'S LATE FATHER'S WILL, TOGETHER with the conveyancing of his home near Port Douglas, seemingly took forever. Intertwined with the order of business, the lawyer skillfully extracted snippets of information about the people sitting in front of him. Additionally, Ellis Davis reciprocated the exchange, divulging to the trio that he was a widower, his son Roger was married, and he had four grandchildren. Furthermore, when he learned that Julia and her family were planning to visit the lakeside property, the primary reason for making the three thousand-mile flight, he went into extraordinary detail, elaborating on the need to travel in a suitable vehicle and to take adequate supplies with them.

Julia could not make up her mind whether this was a ploy to increase the billing since Davis was charging by the hour, or genuine pride in his family. Her husband, on the other hand, instinctively gravitated towards the latter, confident the gentleman was exhibiting a genuine interest in his clients.

It was almost an hour before the threesome left the lawyer's office. All agreed the experience had been exhausting. Notwithstanding, Harper, heeding the lawyer's advice, left Julia and Dee to chat while he made a phone call to the rental company. Since Davis had explained many of the so-called roads in the immediate vicinity of Port Douglas were little better than hiking trails, Harper tried to upgrade his reservation from a standard motor home to one with all-wheel drive. Told none were available, he added a second vehicle as backup.

Off the phone, he returned to find his wife alone, waiting. Having asked to go with them, Dee had left to pack a suitcase. Harper, preemptively removed from the decision-making, nonetheless agreed. Moreover, when told his newly found sister-in-law was to stay at the same hotel overnight, to facilitate an early getaway in the morning, he amiably nodded his head, wondering if he might negotiate a party discount.

———

Having taken a shower and readied herself for bed, Dee sat at the dressing table of her hotel room brushing her hair. She reflected on the evening.

During the meal, Julia's half-sister gave an abbreviated version of how her mother had raised her as a single parent. In truth, she knew few details about Chance Norton, none of them good.

However, Dee was more expansive when it came to her career at the University of Vancouver.

An Associate Professor of Anthropology, she was delighted to learn the property she now co-owned was but a short distance from several First Nations reserves. With her students still on summer break, upon hearing the Harpers had already planned a trip to Port Douglas, asking if she might accompany the group was a natural progression.

Julia spoke about her childhood and the launching of her career as a nurse. Nothing was said about how she and Roger met or her husband's occupation. Instead, the narrative jumped to Oliver, their older child, who was born in Dubai. There the family lived until Harper was invited to the UK to assist the Government in investigating a suspected terrorist plot. All very hush-hush; they could not talk about it.

From England, Harper took a temporary assignment in Cuba, while Julia stayed with a relative at a plantation-style home on the outskirts of Savannah, Georgia. Except for mentioning that was where their daughter, Ophelia, was born, again the details were scant.

In contrast, Federico Ramírez talked at length about his formative years in Brazil and his exploits as a journalist. Eventually settling in Cuba, he set about researching the life of Fulgencio Batista, a prerequisite to writing the former President's biography.

"Cuba; that must be when the pair of you met," Dee concluded, but neither the Brazilian nor Harper chose to elaborate.

Lastly, there was Spencer, whose parents were missionaries in Bolivia. Harper and Julia were acting legal guardians. A couple of months older than Oliver, they were a perfect foil for each other. Occasionally they fought like cat and dog. Other times they colluded together. The boy, a puzzle finder, thriving on riddles and unsolved mysteries; the girl, quick with her camera, assisted by gathering supporting evidence.

Putting down the hairbrush Dee moved to the bed. The alarm set, she turned off the bedside light, and settled down to sleep. Apart from the occasional sound of voices in the corridor, all was quiet.

Strange, Dee thought to herself. *I learned so much about the older children; the adults not so much. Every time I thought of a follow-up question, it drifted out of my mind. Why was that? Too much wine, maybe? No. I only had one glass. What then?*

The answer, if one existed, did not present itself that night, for within ten minutes Dalia was sound asleep.

CHAPTER THREE

EARLY THE NEXT DAY, A FRESH SOUTHERLY BREEZE TEMPERED THE 81°
heat, causing small puffs of cumulus cloud to form and scurry across
the otherwise clear blue sky. An hour later, these fragmented forma-
tions had gathered together and grown vertically, blanketing much of
the heavens. Unconcerned by the change in the weather, two vehicles,
a Winnebago motor home and a Land Rover Safari, drove north along
Highway 99.

The Land Rover headed the mini-convoy, with Harper driving. His
grief-stricken friend, Federico, sat in the passenger seat, staring glumly
out of the nearside window, hardly noticing the landscape of coniferous forest, ignoring their silent protest against the encroachment of
human occupation.

Thus far, their conversation had been sporadic and lacked
substance. Consequently, Harper chose to expand on the topic shared
with Julia the day before. He began by pinpointing things peculiar to
Canada. "Did you know that it is illegal to kill a Sasquatch in British
Columbia? It's true," Harper professed. "Written into Canadian law."
After getting no response from the Brazilian, he concluded, "I suppose
you think that's not important?"

"It is if you are a Sasquatch."

Harper chuckled. "There *is* someone at home in that noodle of yours, after all."

"Leave me alone, Harper, I am not in the mood."

"Come on, cheer up. This road trip has to be a thousand times better than being cooped up in a cell at the Guantanamo Bay detention camp. Don't you agree?"

"I suppose," was the terse reply.

"I helped you escape, and you were able to return to Havana. Yes or no?"

"Yes. And I was reunited with Karmina, for a short time." There was a pause. "But now she is dead," he added plaintively.

"She did a very brave thing, Federico. She managed to free us from the clutches of that mad scientist, Doctor Daniels."

"And because of that she's dead," Federico repeated. "Dead. Dead. Dead."

Harper elected to try a sterner approach. "Snap out of it, old son. Your moping is upsetting the weather."

"The weather? What do you mean? There's nothing wrong with the weather, unless you have some objection to fluffy clouds. If you ask me, they look awe-inspiring. The shape of those over there, for example," Federico pointed out, "reminds me of *Christ the Redeemer* statue in Rio De Janeiro. At the top, see how the cloud spreads out like Our Savior's arms."

"I understand what you're saying," Harper conceded. "And up ahead, those look like the face of Popeye. With a little imagination, you can make out a pipe and rings of smoke. Did you watch Popeye cartoons, when you were a kid, Federico?"

"Occasionally. I remember my mother telling me that Popeye the Sailor Man really existed. He was a retired sailor, regularly involved in barroom brawls, who sustained a permanent injury to one eye. Hence the nickname *Pop-eye*."

"I didn't know that," Harper acknowledged. "You're quite the talking encyclopedia, Federico, when you climb out of the doldrums. Any more nuggets of nonsensical information you care to share?"

"Popeye's girlfriend, Olive Oyl, is based on an actual person too." Far from done, the Brazilian continued by cataloging the origins of more cartoon characters. Bugs Bunny, Tom and Jerry, Road Runner. The list went on and on.

Harper wished he had never asked. Losing interest in the one-sided soliloquy, he allowed his friend's voice to fade into the background noise of the vehicle's engine.

————

The occupants of the following vehicle, the RV, unaware of the Brazilian's profound revelations, had yet to resort to fact swapping to bolster their frame of mind. Dee driving, with Julia sitting beside her, their conversation focused on the newly acquired property on the west shore of Little Harrison Lake.

Julia wondered how the house was constructed, to which Dee replied, "Lumber. If it followed the traditions of a pioneer community, definitely lumber. Don't get your hopes up, sis. We'll probably find a two-room ramshackle of a cabin with raccoons renting loft space."

"That's why I insisted Roger hire this motor home. If all else fails, we and the kids can bunk in here. The macho menfolk can either sleep under the stars or doss down in the back of the Land Rover."

Dee snickered. "Given a choice, I prefer a mattress to hard ground."

"Me too," Julia agreed. "I don't think either one thought of bringing an airbed."

"If push comes to shove, they can always share accommodation with the raccoons." Dee concluded, unsympathetically.

————

The blaring horn of a passing car jolted Harper into realizing Federico was now talking about soccer, specifically the past performance and future prospects of Brazil's team in the World Cup.

Harper, more into American football, nevertheless remarked, "You know, Federico, one day soon, you might meet an attractive woman. Who knows, you could end up married and have eleven children. Enough to form your own soccer team?"

Federico was silent for a moment, thinking. "What if some of these children turn out not to like football?"

"Then keep having babies until you have eleven that do," Harper countered with a snicker.

"Karmina didn't want to have kids of her own. Did I ever tell you that, Harper?"

"No, you didn't," his friend replied softly.

"I think that's the reason I never asked her to marry me."

Spotting a giant billboard ahead, on the right side of the road, Harper could not help but change the subject. "Would you look at that?"

LAST FUEL STOP FOR FIFTY KILOMETERS

"It's got to be an attempt to bamboozle people into stopping for gas. Has to be." Before Federico could offer an opinion, Harper's cellphone rang. The Brazilian answered.

"Tell Roger to pull into that gas station," Julia instructed. "Dee and I need to use the restroom."

CHAPTER FOUR

HARPER LEANED AGAINST THE SIDE OF THE WINNEBAGO MOTOR home, watching his wife and sister-in-law walk towards the gas station store. Distracted by the sound of feet clomping down the vehicle's steps and onto the gravel forecourt, his niece began sprinting towards the brightly painted totem pole thirty yards to his right.

"Spencer, where do you think you're going?" he shouted.

Camera in hand, "To take some pics, " was the reply, the speaker not turning her head or pausing in her stride. "Be back in a jiffy."

Seconds later a King Charles Spaniel shot after its owner, yapping away, enjoying the chase.

The Brazilian, who was standing next to Harper, asked, "Do you think the dog will be okay, not being on a leash?"

"Sure, Federico. The mutt is named *Shadow* for a reason. It never strays far from its mistress's side."

"I hope you're right, Harper. You'll catch hell from Julia if anything bad happens."

More heavy footsteps accompanied the twelve-year-old boy as he exited the vehicle and made to follow his cousin.

"Olly, stop!" his father commanded. "You are to stay in the RV."

"But Dad," the boy protested, "I want to see what Spencer is doing. There's no harm in that, is there Rico?"

"I suppose not," the Brazilian replied, having no children of his own, not realizing that to divide is to conquer.

"Very well," Harper reluctantly agreed. "Make sure you both stay in sight of the vehicle, that's all."

"We will," Oliver promised. As he made to leave he briefly paused. "By the way, Dad, Ophelia is awake. I think she needs her diaper changing."

The boy turned and scampered off.

"I am thinking it's a job for you, *daddy*" his friend teased. "Five minutes ago you were extolling to me the virtues of marriage and raising a large family. Show me how easy it is to change a pull-up diaper."

"How did you cope yesterday morning when Jules and I were with the lawyer?"

"Spencer helped out. Now it's your turn." The Brazilian moved his left hand and pinched his nose. "Rather you than me."

"You are enjoying this aren't you? One day, *amigo*, this may well be your job." Before mounting the Winnebago's steps and going inside, Harper added, "Come into my changing room and I will be happy to give you a firsthand demonstration."

"You could have waited for me," Oliver protested. "I was sure my dad was going to say no, that is until I got Rico on my side."

"You're here now, Olly, that's the main thing." Spencer continued to photograph the totem she had spotted, with her digital camera.

"What bird do you think that is, at the top of the pole?" the boy asked.

"An eagle, I think."

"And below that?" Oliver quizzed.

"Looks like a whale, although I can't see why Indians would want to carve one. We are so far away from the ocean." Spencer readied herself to take another photograph, but upon pushing the shutter release nothing happened. "Bother. The camera's batteries are dead."

"No worries," her cousin replied. "I have spares in my fanny pack. Just like a Boy Scout, I am always prepared."

In less than a minute, batteries replaced, Spencer began photographing the back of the pole. Oliver watched until he suddenly realized the dog was no longer with them. "Where's Shadow? He was here a moment ago."

"Chasing a rabbit, I expect," Spencer answered, seemingly unconcerned.

There was a streak of movement in the boy's peripheral vision. "Enough with the camera, Spencer. I've just spotted Shadow. He's somewhere behind those scrapped cars to your left. Come on, follow me, before he shoots off somewhere else."

———

"There. That wasn't too difficult," Harper declared having swapped out his two-year-old daughter's pull-ups.

Picking Ophelia up, he began to bounce her up and down on his knee. She started to giggle with delight.

Federico, before the subject reverted to making babies, glance out of the RV's side window, wondering when Julia and Dee might return. "The women are taking their time."

"When it comes to powdering noses, who knows how long it takes. Relax. Say, do you have any chewing gum?"

"Not on me. There's some in the Land Rover. Stay here while I fetch a packet."

Harper nodded, as he resumed keeping Ophelia amused.

No sooner had the Brazilian exited the Winnebago than he bounded back up the steps. "Oliver and Spencer are no longer by the totem pole. Hurry. We need to find them before Julia gets back."

"What about Ophelia?" Harper asked.

"Well, you can't leave her on her own. Bring her with us, of course. So much for *you* being an expert in raising children."

———

Following the sound of the dog's barking, the two older children took a well-worn path that cut a swath between the tall grass.

"Shadow," Oliver called.

The noise stopped.

"Shadow, where are you?" Spencer cried.

No dog appeared.

"Leave those rabbits alone and come here right now."

Oliver was amused. Spencer sounded just like his mother when she was cross with him.

"What are you grinning at, Olly? It's not funny. We need to find him." Spencer was near to tears.

"We will," the boy assured her. "Shadow," he shouted, "I have a treat for you." He pulled a bag of sweets from his fanny pack and waved it in the air.

No response.

"Shadow," Oliver called again, holding the bag higher.

A few seconds later, the spaniel appeared out of the bromegrass and came racing towards them.

"There you are, Shadow." Spencer patted the dog on the head when he reached her. "What have you been doing?"

The pooch wagged its tail excitedly, sprinted back in the direction it came, halted a few yards away, and barked.

"You want us to follow?" Spencer asked.

Shadow yapped in reply, and led the way.

Pushing through the tall vegetation, they reached a log lying horizontally, short pieces of timber set at a right angle underneath to prevent it from touching the ground. Except it was not just any log. It was an ancient totem pole. The cedar had weathered to a silver-gray, pitted in places through termite damage. It too had images carved into the wood. However, compared to the one standing on the gas station forecourt, some were different.

"Say, Olly, come and take a close look at this. There some writing carved near the base."

Oliver walked nearer and crouched down. "Not in English, though."

"Of course not. It's an Indian totem pole, after all. I'll take a close-up photo, and later ask Aunt Dee to translate for us."

"Good idea. Don't forget."

Spencer continued clicking away with her camera. Meanwhile, Oliver wandered farther into the overgrowth.

Having finished photographing the second totem, Spencer looked up. Oliver had disappeared. However, before she could call out, Shadow barked once more, drawing the girl's attention to another felled cedar tree. Stripped of its bark, someone had begun carving a replica of the original.

The girl cautiously climbed onto the bole and began taking more photographs, oblivious of the ensuing panic back at the gas pumps.

CHAPTER FIVE

As Julia Harper crossed the forecourt, heading back to the parked vehicles, she commented to her half-sister, "I can't believe the guy in the store charged us five dollars just to use the restroom. That's outrageous."

"Beggars can't be choosers," Dee replied. "There was nothing we could do except pay up and smile sweetly."

Reaching the row of gas pumps, Julia glanced at the nearest. "At least gas prices are reasonable."

"Look again sister dear. That is per liter, *not* per gallon. Multiply by 3.8 and you'll figure out what I mean."

"Wow! That's nearly twice what we pay in Savannah. The whole setup is loathsome."

"If you are low on gas, as I said a moment ago, beggars can't be choosers."

"I wonder if Roger topped up the gas tanks?" Julia asked. Then, realizing apart from themselves, no one was in the vehicles, she continued, "By the way, where is Roger?"

"Over there, by the totem. The three children, and Federico, are with him." Dee waved. "They've seen us and are on their way back."

"Good," Julia responded. "The sooner we leave here the better.

Remind me, Dee, not to stop at this place on our return journey. Furthermore, the owner of the store was kinda creepy." With, an involuntary shiver, she added, "Reminds me of the Bates Motel."

"Trust me when I say, as long as you stay away from showers, especially those with bloodstained curtains, you will be okay." Dee laughed.

————

Since Julia presumed the children were accompanied at all times, nothing was said about Oliver and Spencer's misadventure behind the derelict cars. Instead, Harper and Federico returned to the Land Rover, which again took the lead.

"Shouldn't you have told Julia about us losing sight of the kids?" the Brazilian asked.

"And endure the earthly equivalent of the wrath of God? No thank you. What's that phrase? Ah. I remember. *Ask no questions and you'll be told no lies*. If you ever get married, you will realize there are times when it's best to say nothing."

The Brazilian shook his head in disapproval. "I'd tell my wife everything. We'd have no secrets."

"Suit yourself," Harper responded curtly. "But mark my words, there will come a day when you'll learn the hard way."

"You're a born skeptic, Harper. Do you know that?"

"I'll take that as a compliment. I had a good teacher."

"Who was that?" Federico asked.

"Myself." Once more, Harper laughed.

"A born skeptic who tells pathetic jokes, if you ask me."

————

In the Winnebago, Oliver occupied the rear-facing bench behind his mother. Strapped into a booster seat, next to her brother, Ophelia slept.

Sitting opposite, dining table in between, Spencer leaned forward and whispered to her cousin, "You disappeared. Where did you go?"

"I saw a young boy standing at the edge of a group of trees, so I followed. I'm pretty sure he's a Canadian Indian."

"Wearing moccasins on his feet and a chief's headdress, I assume?" Spencer taunted.

"Of course not, silly. He isn't old enough to be a chief."

"Why the low voices, you two?" Aunt Dee asked. "Something you can't share?"

"Not really. Olly is telling me about an Indian boy he saw in the woods behind the totem pole."

"It's disrespectful to call people of the First Nations Indians. It is important you both remember that now and as you grow up. Are you sure he was from the First Nations, Oliver?"

"He spoke to me in a strange language. Let me think a second. His first words were *Nauka nim Cooley Itswood*."

"You have a good memory, Olly. The boy was speaking *Chinook Wawa*, which is a language developed two hundred or so years ago, between European traders and the First Nations people, so that they could speak to one another."

"Do you know what he was saying, Aunt Dee?"

"I sure do, Spencer. The boy was introducing himself. *My name is Running Bear*. Anything else you can remember, Olly?"

"When I asked him what he was doing at the gas station he replied, *Wuk nauka kentek*, or *Wuk nauka kemtek*. I'm not sure about the first and last word."

Do you mean, *Wik nayka kemteks*? Dee asked.

"Yes, that sounds about right," Oliver acknowledged.

"The young boy was saying he didn't understand you."

"Oh, I see."

"You should have tried sign language, Olly," Spencer suggested.

"I would have, but that's when Dad called us, saying we needed to return to the van. Perhaps if we go back, I could try again?" Oliver suggested.

"We need to keep going, and make sure we arrive in Port Douglas well before nightfall," his mother countered. "I don't want to be searching for the house in the dark."

"Don't look so glum," Spencer commented. "Maybe you'll see him again?"

"When?" Oliver asked.

"On the way back."

There was a quick exchange of glances between the two sisters, Julia shaking her head. Oliver did not notice, facing toward the rear of the vehicle.

"I'll play you a game of cards," Spencer volunteered.

"Okay," the boy replied. "As long as you don't cheat."

"I never cheat," Spencer responded, indignantly.

"Children, be nice, please," Julia implored. Again looking at Dee, she silently mouthed, *The joys of parenting.*

CHAPTER SIX

THE JOYS OF PARENTING ALSO INCLUDED FEEDING TH! E TROOPS. Fortunately, as they approached Pemberton, Harper spotted the sign for a fast-food restaurant nestled in a plaza named Hartzell. After he called Julia on his cell phone, the two vehicles easily found parking spaces. Within minutes the group was seated at a table and the waitress took orders for sodas, burgers, and fries.

Five minutes later, their food arrived.

Between taking bites out of a burger bun, Julia spooned peach-flavored yogurt into Ophelia's mouth. *I'm glad we decided to make the trip,* she thought to herself. *Meeting Dee in person, and her deciding to join us, is a bonus.* Inwardly she smiled. *I'm sure we'll be best friends for life, once we get to know one another.*

Meal over, everyone exited the restaurant. The two older children spotted another totem, farther into the shopping center. Dee did not take too much coaxing, agreeing to accompany them and explain the meaning of the carvings.

By contrast, Julia wanted to visit the bookshop two stores down.

Her husband was mandated to join her, leaving Federico uncertain as to whom he should go with.

"Go join the others, *amigo*, and learn all about First Nations culture," Harper suggested. "Or you can join Julia and me in the book-shop. You may get some ideas for the novel you plan to write. Either way, don't stand there gawking like a fish out of water."

Julia unsure of what Harper was alluding to dragged him inside.

"What was that all about, Roger?" she asked.

"Nothing really," he replied.

"Didn't sound like nothing to me."

"If you must know, Jules, I'm trying to stop Federico from dwelling on the death of Karmina. There's nothing wrong with that, is there?"

"I suppose not. Mind you, Roger, this is a side of you I've not seen before." She slid her arm around his waist and gave him a quick peck on the cheek, before starting to peruse the bookshelves.

On the other hand, Harper, having watched the Brazilian slowly gravitate in the direction of Dee and the older children, continued staring out the window.

———

"What type of bird is that at the top of this totem, Aunt Dee?"

"A thunderbird, Spencer. It represents a supernatural creature prominent in Xa'xtsa First Nations myths. Allegedly, it produces thunder by flapping its wings and lightning by opening and closing its eyes. Individuals who had been struck by lightning and survived often become shamans, for they had received the power of this sacred bird."

"What's a *shaman*?" Oliver asked.

"A shaman, sometimes called a medicine man, is a person who acts as a medium between the visible world and an invisible spirit world. They are also known to practice magic or sorcery for purposes of heal-ing, fortune-telling, and control over natural events."

Oliver followed up with, "Like the gypsy woman at the fairground?"

"My turn," Spencer protested before Dee could reply. "Below the thunderbird, is that a beaver?"

"Very good," her Aunt responded. "The giveaway is the two buck teeth, but if we walk around the back of the pole I expect we will see its oversized leathery tail."

"Why choose a beaver?" Oliver asked.

"As a totem animal, the beaver represents accomplishments achieved through cooperation. A trait valued by the First Nations people."

Methodically the anthropologist worked her way down the totem, explaining to the children the meaning of each carving. At the base stood a stylized but recognizable figure of a man standing upright. Dee thought the carving might depict a deceased chief or high-ranking member of a tribe.

Federico, not particularly enthralled by the conversation, wondered if he would have made a better choice visiting the bookshop. He was relieved when Dee suggested that they should return to the vehicles. However, Oliver and Spencer begged they be allowed to spend a few minutes in the native arts and craft store immediately behind the pole. Reluctantly, the Brazilian followed.

———

"Stop gazing at the shoppers outside, Roger. Come over here and see if any of these books interest you."

Harper, not in the mood to peruse bookshelves, aimlessly wandered the store. Ophelia, head resting on her father's shoulder, showed a similar disinterest in reading. Julia, on the other hand, had amassed quite a selection before she went to the sales counter. History, legends, traditions; all focused on British Columbia.

"You must be into aboriginal culture, ma'am," the owner assumed, as she started ringing up the prices of the assorted publications.

"Our family will be staying at Port Douglas for a couple of weeks. These will give me something to read in the evenings," Julia replied.

"Camping?" the proprietor asked.

"Heavens, no. I like my creature comforts too much. My sister and I have just inherited property on the western side of Little Harrison Lake. We are on our way to check it out."

"There is only one residence on that side of the lake. You must be talking about the *Book House*."

Surprised, Julia admitted, "I never knew it was called the *Book House*. How unusual."

"To be honest that's not its real name. It is what my husband, Alfred, and I call it. Chance Norton, who lives there, is a frequent customer in our store. Comes in three or four times a year and snaps up almost everything about the area, that Alfred has acquired at auction. My husband is a book broker, don't you know."

There was a long pause and then, realizing Julia's earlier remarks about inheriting the property, she continued, "Lordy, Lordy. Here I am going on about Chance in the present tense. I wondered why I hadn't seen him lately. You are his daughter, I presume. How rude of me. Please accept my condolences."

Julia smiled awkwardly, not wishing to divulge that her late father had left her mother when she was very young, and she could not remember him.

The storeowner did not notice, as she was reassessing Julia's selection. "If I remember correctly, Chance already purchased everything here. You will probably find copies in the Book House library. However..." She reached under the counter and produced a scuffed leather portfolio. "Alfred picked this one up at a flea market in Vancouver with Chance specifically in mind. It's someone's collection of photos taken around the turn of the twentieth century and later. Amongst them, you will find shots of the former sawmill when Port Douglas was an active logging camp."

Julia picked up the album and quickly leafed her way through the pages. As well as the sawmill, she found pictures of a steamboat full of passengers, confirming that Douglas was a launch point for travel down Harrison Lake. Handwritten notations were to be found below the majority of photographs. The last one read:

Traveling to Agassiz and Hammersley to pick hops
and berries.

"Truly fascinating," Julia concluded. "How much to purchase?"

"No charge," the owner insisted. "A little gesture on my part for being so insensitive about Chance's passing."

With thanks, Julia, Harper, and the toddler left the store. The others were waiting near the vehicles, cones of ice cream in their hands.

"Did you find anything interesting about the totem pole?" was Harper's first question.

Dee immediately launched into a monolog of how the plaza totem, although adopting many of the features of native poles, was not strictly authentic. "The sort of thing one might find in a Hollywood film production," was how she described it.

She continued by cataloging clan poles, used to depict families and lineages. Dee moved on to monument poles, at the entrance of homes, which delineated family histories. Welcoming poles came next, and as their name suggests, were erected to welcome visitors. Legacy poles commemorated important historic events. Last but not least, the social science lesson concluded by describing mortuary poles which honor the deceased. "*Haida* mortuary poles include a box at the top where the ashes of the chief or high-ranking member are placed. Isn't that interesting?"

Harper was no longer in the audience to answer. He had lost interest at monument poles and had slunk off to purchase ice cream. He returned in time to hear Spencer extolling the virtues of a copper pendant she wore around her neck, the engraving depicting an eagle.

From a printed card, she read, "*The eagle symbolizes grace, power, and great intellect*. Great intellect; that refers be me," she added, with a giggle.

"Self-praise is no recommendation," Oliver responded. "You taught me that, didn't you, Dad?"

Everyone turned to face Harper, who was feeding Ophelia a mini spoonful of ice cream out of a quart tub. "If you say so, Olly. I can't remember," he replied. "Anyone want more ice cream? I can share."

"Give Ophelia to me, Roger. At times, you are a bigger baby than she is."

Handing over the child, he added defensively. "Just asking, that's all. Did you buy anything from the gift store, son?"

"Aunt Dee bought me a dream catcher. Isn't it cool, Mom and Dad?"

Closer inspection revealed the handcrafted object consisted of a round willow hoop, woven with a loose web of yarn, ornamented with a central amber bead, and feathers hanging below the hoop.

"And what do you propose to do with that, Olly,?" was the follow-up question.

"Catch dreams, of course."

Ask a stupid question and you'll get a stupid answer, Harper thought to himself.

Oliver continued, "We didn't buy you anything, Mom and Dad, because we weren't sure what you'd like."

"That's all right, Olly," Julia assured him. "We came out of the bookstore with an album of old photographs. You and Spencer can look at it later."

"That's great," the boy replied. With genuine enthusiasm, he continued, "Have either of you noticed, Aunt Dee purchased something for herself. Guess what it is?"

"Give up," Harper answered almost immediately.

Julia looked, not sure until her sister touched one of her earlobes.

"Earrings. How unusual. What are they made of?"

"Porcupine quills and seed beads," Dee informed her.

"Aren't they lovely, Roger?"

"Can't say I would wear them, personally," he answered. "Are they something you fancy Federico?"

"No. I bought this." The Brazilian produced a three-inch diameter glass paperweight. "And before you ask, Harper, what you're seeing inside represents spiraling strands of smoke. The large, flattened bubble, in the center, depicts a smoke-ring message, or signal."

"You've got that right, *amigo*. The message reads *it's time to leave*." Harper looked up. "Those clouds overhead are decidedly blacker than they were an hour ago. I think there may be a storm coming."

CHAPTER SEVEN

Twenty minutes after departing the shopping plaza, the two vehicles turned right, leaving Highway 99, and proceeded along the SHUCK-ch trail. Originally the primary route to the Cariboo goldfields, now relegated to a forestry service road, the convoy continued south, weaving its way through clusters of potholes.

The two older children, both sitting on the same forward-facing bench in the RV's dining area, were indifferent to the shaking and jolting from the uneven surface. They were engrossed in the photo album acquired by Julia at the bookstore.

Dee took the opportunity to ask her sister, "What's with Harper calling Federico *amigo* all the time?"

"Stems back to the time they were in Cuba together, where, as you probably know, the locals use a distinctive version of Spanish. He's the only close friend Roger has. At one time, before he met me, he hung around with a guy named Kirt Mitchell. Mitchell went by the nickname of Midnight because he stayed up all hours playing poker. They fell out and parted company after a big poker tournament where they won millions of dollars."

"Really?" Dee aware this was an opportunity to build on the meager information divulged the night before, asked, "Tell me more."

"Midnight tried to keep all the prize money for himself. He betrayed Roger by drugging him and having him flown by helicopter to a modified oil rig in the Gulf of Mexico. That's where Roger and I met. I had been tricked into being the medical nurse to a group of men who were being held prisoner and experimented on with psychedelic drugs."

"Wow. That doesn't sound very kosher."

"You're right, Dee. However, with the help of a small group of inmates, Roger managed to acquire a satellite phone. He called in favors from some of the other poker tournament players who had left him IOUs. One of them rescued us using a submarine."

"That reads like the plot of an adventure novel," Dee told her.

"With a happy ending, I'm pleased to say. Roger and I got married, shortly after."

A loud sound cut into the sisters' conversation, as Spencer slammed the photo album closed with a groan of disappointment. Having quickly turned the pages, the pair had finished scanning a hotchpotch collection of postcards and prints.

The Illecillewaet Glacier as it appeared in 1909, the notation read. *Asulkan and Asulkan Glaciers in 1894*. The mining communities of Quesnel Forks and Barkerville portrayed prospectors panning for gold. *The Post Office at Rossland circa 1906*. Vancouver's *Streetcars, 1890*. *Provincial Parliament Buildings, Victoria* taken in 1910. *Horse-drawn hose-and-ladder fire engine, 1894*. Oxen-drawn wagons hauling lumber. Snow-covered mountainscapes. Shopping parades with vintage cars. Pedestrians sporting Edwardian attire. So on, and so on.

"That's that then," Spencer declared. "A complete waste of time, don't you agree, Olly?"

"I decided that after the first half-a-dozen pages. Much of the time I've been looking out the window. They sure have big lakes in this part of the world."

"That is Lillooet Lake," Julia told him, having overheard her son's remark. "I take it neither of you are interested in the period photographs."

"Nope. Most are a reddish-brown color," Oliver declared. "Here. Look for yourself," he added offering the album for his mother to take.

Julia, with one arm, reached out without turning her head. Like two runners passing a baton, mother and son did not quite connect. The scrapbook dropped onto the dining table with a thud, pages spilling open. Fortunately, only one photograph dropped out, ending on the floor of the vehicle. Spencer closed the book and passed it forward.

Oliver picked up the wayward print. "That's Running Bear," he exclaimed. "I'm certain, it's him. He's with a girl about the same age."

Spencer asked to see. "And that totem pole in the background is similar to the one behind the gas station. Hold on a minute and I'll show you."

The girl retrieved her digital camera, turned it on, and found the series of snaps.

"The top carving is identical, for sure. A bird with a long beak."

"That would be a raven," Dee interjected. "The raven, in the Pacific Northwest, symbolizes being responsible for the land, bringing water and fire to the earth. Any other carvings you recognize, Spencer?"

"A wolf, and below that there is a frog. It *is* the same pole or an exact copy."

"Let me see, please," Julia asked, taking the print with care.

"The boy at the gas station can hardly be the same person in the photo, Olly."

"Why not, Mom?"

Julia turned and faced her son. She smiled, trying to break the news gently. "Because on the back of this print is a date. 1959. Do you want to look for yourself?"

Before Oliver could answer, a flash of forked lightning lit up the sky, accompanied by the rumble of rolling thunder. Rain followed as a cloudburst, making it practically impossible to see the Land Rover.

Harper, driving the lead vehicle, commented to Federico, "Didn't I say there was a storm coming?"

"You did," the Brazilian agreed. "But slow down before you run us off the track. *Entende* [Understand]?"

CHAPTER EIGHT

NINOHTE METAWAN WÊPINAMÂTOWIN [WANT TO PLAY A GAME]?

The phrase drifted into Morning Star's mind, as she was washing dishes in the kitchen sink. Turning to face the room, she already knew there would be no one to see. Nonetheless, she replied, "*Sôskwâc? Niya otamiyowin [Right now? I'm busy]*."

Ehai, sîmâk [Yes, now].

The elderly woman turned back to the sink. Placing the last plate on the drainage rack, she looked out of the window. "*Mekwâkimowan* [It's raining outside]," she reminded the other.

Pihci mêtawêwikamik mâka [Then use the recreation room], was suggested.

Morning Star, *Wâpanacahkos* in her native tongue, knew continued dissent would only prolong the pleading. Therefore, she dried her hands on the dishtowel, put on her raincoat, boots, and hat. Picking up a hurricane lamp, she made for the door.

The rain beat down as the wind roared. Stoically *Wâpanacahkos* made for the nearest building. Similarly made from timbers, as was her own cabin but four times the size, it was formerly the community's meetinghouse. As the sole remaining resident of the town she used it as a storeroom for her crafting supplies. Once inside, with the hurricane lamp lit, the room took on an eerie netherworld appearance of silhouettes and shadows, caused by the haphazard placement of boxes and bric-a-brac. The center of the room was uncluttered, however, save for a ping-pong table that had one corner sagging because of a broken support.

"Okay, I'm here," Morning Star announced, in her native tongue. "You can show yourself, *sôskwâc* [without further delay]."

In response the rafters groaned.

She picked up one for a pair of ping-pong paddles. Memories of years past came flooding back. Playing with her childhood friend before he died, they often met in this very room. He always won, she remembered. When she protested, calling him *wayesihtwâwin* [a cheat], he just laughed. Nothing she would do or say threatened their friendship, not until that fateful day when the relic was taken.

"I don't have time for this," Morning Star protested. "I have things to do."

"*Piko ka-tôtaman natohtawik* [You need to listen to what I have to say]." The figure of a boy, nine years old, emerged from the shadows. Dressed in a one-piece tunic stitched together with narrow leather strips, wearing moccasins, he looked exactly as she remembered him all those years ago.

The elderly woman smiled. "It's been a long time, *Maskosis* [Bear Cub]. What brings you here today?"

"You will have guests arriving before dusk. The new owners of the lodge across the lake. They bring their *kistôtew* [family]."

"How many?" Morning Star asked.

"Seven in all. Two sisters; one with husband. Two older children and a baby girl. There is another man; *ototema* [his friend], I think."

"You mean you don't know, *Maskosis*. This is a first." There was a mocking tone in the woman's voice.

The young boy ignored the jibe. "I must be going," he announced, "to ensure they stay safe in this storm."

"Wait!" Morning Star exclaimed as the boy backed into the shadows. "When will I see you again?"

The wind lifted the latch on the door. It flew open, and just as abruptly slammed closed.

The specter had gone, leaving the elderly woman to return to her cabin and wait for the downpour to pass. Then she would take her truck and make the short journey around the headland of the lake, and ready the house for its new owners.

Before leaving, however, *Wâpanacahkos* walked to the table. In the thick layer of dust, with her finger, she wrote:

ᐃᐧᐸᓇᒫᐢᑯᐣ ᑎᐣᒌᐦᐃᑲᐤ ᒪᐣᑯᕒᐣ

CHAPTER NINE

TORRENTS OF RAIN REDUCED VISIBILITY TO ALMOST NOTHING. DEE slammed her foot hard on the brake pedal to avoid hitting the rear of the stationary Land Rover. The jolt of the Winnebago stopping caused Ophelia to start crying. Julia responded by leaving the front of the vehicle and moving to an empty dining table seat. Oliver, taking advantage of the situation, moved to occupy the passenger front seat.

"Don't get too comfortable, sunshine," Dee cautioned. "Your mother is sure to want her seat back."

The infant continued crying.

"Not yet, though," Oliver responded. "Why aren't we moving?"

"It isn't safe to drive in this downpour."

Dee tried her cell phone, needing to speak to Federico, but the call went straight to voice mail. *No big deal*, she decided. *We can sit here and wait until the rain eases.*

Oliver, for his part, watched rivulets of water run down the windscreen. The gravel, soon became an ankle-deep pond that spilled off the road in a mini waterfall. With no other distraction, except listening to the stucco sound hammering the vehicle's aluminum roof, it was not long before the boy announced, "This is boring."

"If you like, we can play a game," Dee suggested. "How about I-Spy?"

"That's for young kids," Oliver objected.

"*Spelling Bee*, then?" his aunt proposed.

"Ugh." Oliver was not a fan of spelling games. "I-Spy will be fine. Can I go first?"

"Sure."

"I spy with my little eye something beginning with 'B'."

"Backpack?" Dee suggested.

"Nope," Oliver replied in a gloating tone of voice.

There was a moment while his aunt considered another answer. Forked lightning momentarily illuminated the area outside the RV. Shadow, who had been lolling underneath the dining table, responding to the accompanying clap of thunder, shot like a jackrabbit to the rear of the RV. The dog jumped on the bed and buried himself under a blanket.

Spencer, who now stood behind the front row seats, bellowed, "*B* as in *Bang*! How's that for an answer, Olly?"

Before Oliver could tell his cousin she was wrong, another flash of lightning highlighted the rock formation on their left as well as the flooded road ahead.

"*Boy!*" he screeched. "Over there, on your side, Aunt Dee." Oliver pointed. "There's a boy. Don't you see him?"

"I don't see anybody," Dee replied.

"Me neither," Spencer concurred.

"I'm talking about the boy outside by the cliff face. It's Running Bear."

This time, a flash of longer-lasting luminous white lightning turned their entire surroundings into a floodlit arena.

Dee said in response, "I'm sorry, Olly, but I still can't spot anyone. Perhaps it a trick of the light?"

"No," Oliver protested. "Despite the rain, I can still see him. He is speaking to me."

His aunt stared through the window. All she saw was the rock face, blanketed in cascading water.

"What are you two bickering about?" Julia asked, her attention diverted from Ophelia by the raised voices.

"Running Bear is outside, but Aunt Dee says she can't see him. Neither can Spencer. He's there, I tell you. He's frantically waving. Now he is pointing to the top of the cliff, and shouting, *Klose nanitsh. Tumstones*. What does that mean Aunty?"

"*Klose nanitsh. Tumstones* translates to *Lookout! Falling Rocks*."

At the very mention of the phrase, a shower of small stones came tumbling down the rock face, falling into the puddles of water like pebbles being tossed into a pond.

Dee was quick to put the Winnebago into gear. Hitting the horn as she floored the accelerator, rather than the vehicle bounding forward, all she achieved was producing rear-wheels spin as they sunk into the soft ground.

"Not good," she announced, as she switched to Plan B. However, throwing the gearshift into reverse, and being equally lead-footed, achieved the same result.

Dee hit the horn a second time, hoping someone from the Land Rover would come and ask what the commotion was about.

Julia's phone went to voicemail. Checking, she read the message. "It's from Federico. Roger wants to know what all the ruckus is about."

"Ruckus." Dee spat the word out. "Doesn't he realize, any minute we could have half a mountain slide on top of us? Oliver, go tell your father we need to get out of here urgently, and the RV has its back wheels stuck in the mud."

"But it's raining," Oliver protested.

"Raining rocks," Dee reminded him. "Don't just sit there. Move!"

"I'll get wet," the boy stubbornly objected.

"Leave it to me," Spencer piped up. Easing herself past Julia, she hopped down the vehicle's steps and launched herself into the tempest.

The remaining occupants of the RV observed both front doors of the Land Rover fly open. The two men jumped out. Harper rushed to the rear compartment and retrieved a towrope. The Brazilian, using the attached ladder, climbed high enough to pull down two aluminum sand boards, four feet long.

While Harper attached the rope to the Rover's trailer hitch and then to the Winnebago's tow points, Federico worked on getting the boards under the RV's rear wheels. The unrelenting rain did not make the task any easier. Meanwhile, Dee looked anxiously at the cliff face, taking the opportunity to monitor the size of falling stones with each lightning flash. Eventually, Harper headed back to the Land Rover. The Brazilian opened the RV's side-passenger door and climbed inside, grateful to be out of the rain.

"You're soaked," Dee observed.

"More like a drowned rat," was the reply.

Julia strapped Ophelia into her child seat, went to the kitchen area, found a towel, and offered it to the *drowned rat* to dry off.

"Where's Spencer?" Oliver asked.

"She was told to wait in the Rover. When the rear lights of the vehicle flash twice that will be Harper's signal that he's ready. Oliver, would you mind if I sit there, so I can direct operations."

The boy left the front seat and stood behind the driver. Federico sat down.

"Put the RV into second gear, and a light foot on the gas pedal works best," he instructed. "Now flash your headlights to let Harper know you are ready too."

"Where did you learn to do that, Federico?" Dee asked.

"Afghanistan, when I was a newspaper reporter embedded with the Taliban. But that's a story for another time. Let's get going, shall we?"

There was a jerk as the towrope tightened. Dee dabbed at the accelerator. Thankfully, with minimal wheel spin, the motor home inched forward.

Slowly picking up speed, they began to pull away. Oliver tried looking out of Dee's side window but could see nothing other than the cliff face. Deciding to change position, he moved along the aisle, passing the kitchen area, and knelt on the bed, to peer through the rear window. With the next flash of lightning, he hoped he might see the young brave, but all he saw were tire tracks. Tire tracks partly covered by a ruck of rocks. Rocks, and more rocks. Rocks the size of boulders. Boulders larger than the vehicle he was traveling in.

The dog, deciding it was time to surface, crawled from under the covers and licked Oliver's hand. "Nobody upfront believes I saw Running Bear. What do you think, Shadow?"

The response was a forlorn whimper.

"Not you, too?" Tickling the dog behind the ears encouraged the pooch to nuzzle into the lad's side and wag its tail. "Changed your mind huh?" This time the animal yawned. Oliver smiled. "I'll take that as *a yes*."

CHAPTER TEN

ALTHOUGH IT HAD STOPPED RAINING, OVERCAST CONDITIONS persisted as the Land Rover's navigation system announced they had arrived at their destination. The anticipated picture-perfect panorama was lost to wisps of fog that drifted across the lake, obscuring its western shoreline.

Julia, carrying Ophelia, was the first to exit the RV. Oliver, then Federico, followed. Shadow rushed down the steps, a prelude to searching for its mistress, while Dee brought up the rear in a more dignified manner. Joined by Harper and Spencer, they clustered as a group on the leeward side of the larger vehicle.

"Mr. Davis said the keys to the property are with the caretaker. Any ideas as to where they might live?" Julia asked everyone in general.

Glancing around, it was hard to imagine that Port Douglas once served as the major steamboat port during the Cariboo gold rush. Rickety wooden planking was all that remained of the wharf. The original structures, now piles of rubble, had been demolished long ago, either by design or through the ravages of winter storms. However, as the mist swirled, lines of sight temporarily opened, revealing a cluster of half a dozen cedar cabins. Together with a rusting log loader and a flatbed trailer, they were the legacy from the logging operations that ceased in 1970.

A dilapidated red Ford pickup truck was parked next to the nearest cabin. From the latter resinous white smoke rose from the stone chimney. A door opened and an older woman stepped onto the porch. Wearing a felt boho hat, pushed back on her head to reveal weathered angular features, she walked towards the newcomers. An almost toothless smile was offered by way of greeting.

Shadow, straightway, went into attack mode. The dog rushed forward, frantically barking, running in circles around the perceived interloper. The older woman placed her hands on her hips and stood her ground. Despite Spencer's pleas to the dog to be quiet and come to heal, the barking persisted. Eventually exhausted, the dog stood still, bared its teeth, and menaced a deep guttural growl.

Unfazed, the woman advanced a few steps and then stopped. After slowly raising her arms until her fingers pointed directly at the canine's eyes, from her lips came a high-pitched whistle. Immediately Shadow lay down, assuming a position similar to that of the Great Sphinx of Giza, front paws outstretched. The growling ceased. "Come here, boy, and say hello," she commanded in a firm but gentle voice. The animal warily inched forward, sat down, and allowed his head to be rubbed. "Enough of that snarling nonsense. There is no reason you and I cannot be friends."

The dog rolled onto its back, paws in the air.

"How is that possible?" Oliver asked.

"Some sort of dog whisperer," Spencer responded.

The woman smiled. "Dog whisperer, huh? Never been called that before, but I've always had a way with critters. I do remember the time I came across a grizzly looking for lunch. My little trick proved useful then." Stepping toward the group, she continued, "You must be the new owners. Delighted to meet you all. My name is Morning Star. You have chosen a bad day to travel, but I'm pleased you arrived safely despite the landslide."

"The landslide has already made the news headlines?" Harper responded. "I am surprised."

"Maybe it did. Maybe it didn't. Don't have a television, nor radio either. I enjoy a peaceful life, with no outside interference. Present company excepted."

"Then how do you know?" was Harper's follow-up question.

"A little bird told me, or should I say *bear*." Morning Star grinned, the gaps in her teeth doing nothing to add credibility to her implausible statement.

"Bear?"

"Leave it, Roger," Julia whispered. "We're here to collect the keys, remember."

"Of course you are." Morning Star had the ears of a bat. Reaching into her apron pocket, she produced a bunch of keys, held together with an iron hoop. "The important ones are all tagged. The others ... Well, I'm sure you will figure it out."

Julia stepped forward and took the bunch. "Thank you."

"On the kitchen table, you will find instructions on how to start the generator. I've made sure the fuel tank is topped up." The caretaker smiled once more. "We'll talk again tomorrow. For now, I'll allow you folks to settle in." She turned toward her cabin, then paused. As an afterthought Morning Star added, "I suggest you leave that motor home where it is for the moment. To get to the house, drive around the head of the lake. There is a beam bridge you will have to cross. Don't worry. It's sturdier than you may think. After all the rain, best keep the Land Rover in four-wheel drive."

"Thanks for the advice," Dee responded. "Everyone into the Rover. I'm driving."

"But I was driving earlier," Harper remonstrated. Further protests, however, were stifled by a withering look from his wife, her insisting he start removing some of the provisions from the RV, and loading them into the back of the smaller vehicle.

"Don't just stand there, Federico. Have you lost the use of your arms and legs? You can help too."

"Yes, ma'am," he replied.

Dee smiled to herself. She liked a man who was able to take orders.

"Did you see that necklace around the old woman's neck?" Spencer asked Oliver as the Land Rover headed west.

Julia, who was sitting next to Dee, turned her head to face the second row. "Not so much of the *old woman*, Spencer. I'll be her age one day."

"Sorry," the girl apologized. "But the necklace, was it made up of sharks' teeth?"

Oliver laughed. "Better be careful swimming in the lake, Spence. A friend of Jaws may be lurking there."

"Now you're being ridiculous, Olly," his father retorted. "There are no sharks in Harrison Lake."

"So where did the teeth come from?" Spencer questioned. "They are not human, are they? That would be gross."

"I'm thinking the necklace was made using elk teeth," Dee informed them. "It looked very old. Probably passed down from one First Nations generation to the next."

"Do you think the caretaker speaks that weird language, like Running Bear, Aunt Dee?" Oliver inquired.

"When you see her again you can ask. Now let me concentrate. We are about to cross the bridge."

The jolting of the vehicle's suspension as they the wooden planking caused Ophelia to fuss. Apart from Julia's shushing reassurances, no one else spoke.

Oliver gazed out of his side window, trying to spot a tell-tail shark's fin in the water, to prove everyone wrong. Spencer too looked out, camera-ready, hoping for movement in the trees and a sighting of the mythical creature called Sasquatch. With the mist still impeding their view, neither one saw anything of interest.

Frustrated by his lack of initiative, not using his mind-reading ability to probe Morning Star's brain, Harper was musing on her strange reference to *Little Bird or Bear*.

A couple of minutes later Federico, who was wedged between the older children, broke the silence. "Over there, nestled in the trees." He pointed. "Wow, Julia and Dee. I cannot believe that is what you have inherited. It doesn't look like a house. It's more of a mansion."

CHAPTER ELEVEN

IT TOOK ONLY A MOMENT TO FIND THE KEY TO THE FRONT DOOR and gain access to the gloomy interior. Flashlights in hand, the first priority was to find the kitchen.

"In here," Dee called out. Once the other adults joined her, she picked up the caretaker's instructions and waved the sheet of paper at the two men. "You boys can get the generator going. There's a propane stove behind me. Once the supplies have been brought in, we can have a cooked evening meal. Meanwhile, I will make a pot of tea."

"And I'll go find the kids," Julia volunteered. "I wonder what mischief they are getting into?"

———

Not mischief per se, but exploring the ground floor was game enough.

Oliver had slipped inside the nearest room, and quietly closed the door before crouching down behind a couch. He waited, wondering how long it would take Spencer to realize he was missing.

Not long, apparently. "Olly, where are you?" she cried.

The boy suppressed a giggle as his cousin moved down the hallway, her flashlight showing under the door.

"Oliver?" Her voice was fainter. "This is not funny."

The beam moved back and passed the room once more.

Not hearing Shadow scratching at the door, Oliver decided a better hiding place was under the desk. He moved just before Spencer pressed down on the door handle.

"Ouch!" he complained, banging his head on the underside of the desk.

The girl shone her light around the room. Upon spotting the soles of Oliver's shoes, she declared, "I suppose you think this is hilarious. And for your next trick?"

The dog, enjoying the game, dove under the desk and began licking Oliver's face.

"Get off me, Shadow. I don't like doggie kisses."

"Shush," Spencer snapped. "Someone else is coming. Budge over, so I can hide as well."

"Olly? Spencer? I don't want the pair of you wandering the house until the lights come on."

"It's your mom," Spencer whispered. "Perhaps we should go back to the kitchen."

Footsteps receded back along the hall.

"Let's explore the room, first," Oliver suggested, as he rose to his full height.

Spencer shone her flashlight onto the desktop, highlighting a brass banker's lamp, an ink blotter, a Baccarat crystal inkwell complete with a hinged vintage gold-plated lid, and a quill pen made from a crow's feather. To one side was a sterling silver letter opener fashioned in the shape of an eagle's head, the handle made from a piece of deer antler.

Before she could comment, Oliver spoke. "Wow. Look at all these bookcases." Moving closer, he shone his flashlight's beam along the book spines. "The *Untold History of British Columbia. Gold Mines Of The Frazer Valley. First Nations Customs and Traditions.* Lots and lots of books."

As the faint whine of a generator reached their ears, the lights came on.

"Not just books," Spencer corrected him. She was staring at the walls without bookshelves. "More than a dozen oil paintings and framed sepia photographs."

She approached one and eyed it closely. "Oliver, come look. What do you make of this painting?"

The boy walked over and stood next to her. He stared for a moment. "An oil painting. "So what?"

Spencer, without explanation, raised a hand and pointed at the reflections in the water.

"So what?" her cousin repeated, at the same time matter-of-factly shrugging his shoulders. "There is no artist's signature if that's what you're getting at."

Vexed, the girl testily announced, "Oliver Harper, you are such a dingbat. Do you know that?"

CHAPTER TWELVE

JULIA MADE A POINT OF THANKING THE CARETAKER FOR MAKING UP their beds the previous day. Standing outside her home she asked about the cluster of other cabins. "Are they occupied?"

"A wraith or two from the past, maybe. Otherwise, no."

Julia felt a shudder go down her spine, wondering if the caretaker meant *wraith* as in *ghost*? Or was it just a turn of phrase?

Notwithstanding, Morning Star continued, "There are remnants of the old town here and there, if you know where to look. Follow me, and I'll show you?"

Taken on a short tour, Julia discovered her guide had a wealth of knowledge exemplifying the abandoned community. The woman pointed out the remains of the courthouse. Sadly all that was left was a knee-high stonewall. Next to the ruins was a large and ancient-looking tree that was the site of the first legal hanging in the colony.

"I believe the victim was found innocent after the hanging," Morning Star added, matter-of-factly, as if Julia should be interested.

"Where did everyone go?" Julia asked, suddenly realizing the emptiness that surrounded them.

"The First Nations people? There are only a dozen or so who currently frequent the place. Their lodges are fifteen minutes walk from here, if you follow the valley north. However, they prefer their privacy, and don't take kindly to lookie-loo tourists. As for the settlers, the town was virtually abandoned around 1861. The construction of the Cariboo Waggon Road provided an overland alternative. The nail in its coffin came in 1890 when the regular steamer service to and from Port Douglas ended."

"Very interesting. You certainly know your local history, Morning Star." Julia corrected herself, "Actually, I was referring to my family."

Again, the caretaker offered her near-toothless grin. "Didn't you notice? The older kids sneaked off when we began talking. I expect the three adults followed to make sure they stay out of trouble. In all likelihood, they'll come across the stump of an old totem. Erected in 1876 to commemorate the Indian Act. The *mistikohkân,* for many years, protected all the bands for miles around. Sadly, not anymore."

"You say *not anymore.* Tell me, what happened?"

"Some sixty years ago a sacred stone relic, embedded within the carved raven at the very top of the pole, was stolen," Morning Star replied.

"Wasn't that asking for trouble?"

Morning Star laughed. "Not exactly. Unless you were privy to the secret, you would think the bird's head was simply a part of the decoration."

"Where did this relic come from? "

"Handed down for generations; nobody's sure. Carved from pieces of ..." There was an unusually long pause. Julia could not fathom why. "... from pieces of polished jade, they held a special magic."

"I see. So who knew about the jade's hiding place?"

"Just the tribe's elders."

"But someone found out?" was Julia's next question.

"That's right. And that someone was believed to be Lawrence Hayes, a former owner of the house you currently occupy. Never could prove it, mind you. Otherwise, there might have been another lynching. Died the following winter after being mauled by a grisly he'd shot and wounded. If there is such thing as poetic justice, that might have been it. Except, the bastard left a wife and a six-month old baby. Poor woman, had to eke out a living manufacturing snake oil liniment."

Morning Star noticed Julia's look of astonishment.

"I know. I know. Sounds absurd, especially when you consider this was the 1960s. Nevertheless, over time she built up quite a business, making regular shipments to Vancouver and Victoria. Apparently, some people believed the concoction cures rheumatism. Others used it on warts, for sun burn, and skin lesions."

"Fascinating," Julia responded. "What happened to her baby?"

"That would be William Hayes. Like his father; another rotten apple. In his formative years the boy was always getting into fights with the tribal children. As a teenager he would dig deep pits as animal traps. No hunter's license, but that did not stop him. In my opinion, he harbored a cruel streak and liked to cause critters pain. To everyone's relief, at eighteen he left the valley. Only returned after his mother died, and then for just a few weeks at a time. He was far more interested in pursuing shameless women and gambling in Vancouver casinos. Then one day he stopped returning. Never worried myself as to the reason."

"So how did my father come by the property," was Julia's next question.

"Ah, now that I do know. One evening after Chance Norton had had too much to drink, I was told he won the property in a game of cards along with a heap of cash. That's how the house is in such good condition. Chance moved in, nurtured his affinity for the region, and decided to stay. Frequently he took trips to the bookstore in Hartzell. Was one of their best customers, I imagine. Read one or two of them myself, having the run of the house, on account I cleaned it once a week."

"We stopped in Hartzell and had lunch. Afterward, I spoke to the bookstore owner. She seems a nice lady."

"Somewhat smitten with your dad's personable manner, by all accounts. But Chance was only interested in the books. They are mostly about local history or the First Nations."

"Why is that?" Julia inquired.

"As I said, he had an affinity for the area. A kind man, Chance. Spent some of his time helping the local First Nations community, especially when they fell on hard times. They let him stay in one of the reserve's lodges while the Book House was being renovated. I liked your father. I am sorry that he is gone. I expect you are too."

"I never knew him," Julia admitted. "He left my mother shortly after I was born. Similar thing happened to Dee; the other woman in our party. She is my half-sister, who I never knew existed until two weeks ago. Strange to hear he finally settled down."

"Just goes to show, I didn't know your father as well as I thought," the caretaker remarked as they arrived back at her cabin. "Still, never speak ill of the dead is what I say."

The sound of laughter could be heard, as Spencer approached. She was flying a kite of sorts, on a short length of string. Oliver was running after her, demanding he be allowed a turn.

Catching her breath, the girl stopped in front of Julia.

"What do you think, Mom?" Oliver asked as he caught up. "We found this piece of cloth tied to a tree. When we get home, can we make some proper kites?"

"Give me that," Morning Star demanded, snatching the object away before anyone could protest. "You have not been here a day and you are already upsetting the order of things. Is nothing sacred?"

By the time the other three adults arrived, the caretaker had reached her cabin door, which she slammed shut once inside.

"What was that all about?" Harper asked.

"I don't know," his wife replied. "She was angry at the children for removing a piece of linen from a tree."

"Was there anything written or drawn on the cloth?" Dee inquired.

"A foxes head, an arrow, and two animal paw prints. Look over there on the side of that large boulder," Spencer pointed, "and you'll see the same shapes scratched on the flat surface. Do they mean something?"

Dee walked over to get a closer look and then returned. "The wolf and wolf tracks represent both protection and destruction. The arrow symbolizes defense. I believe what you removed from the tree was a prayer flag to keep away evil spirits. The markings on the rock serve a similar purpose."

"Evil spirits. You don't believe that sort of stuff do you, Dee?"

"It's not what I believe, Federico. It's what the First Nations people believe that matters. We must respect their traditions and culture. I think the best thing I can do is have a word with Morning Star and apologize for what the children did. Why don't the rest of you make your way back to the house? I will be along shortly."

————

Two hours passed before Dee returned. She found Julia in the kitchen preparing lunch. "It's very quiet," she observed. "Where is everyone?"

"Roger and Federico are out the back, chopping wood. They came up with the idea of a log fire in the parlor. I've just finished feeding Ophelia. For the moment, she is in her playpen. Olly and Spence are in the library reading some of the books." Julia began removing chinaware from a wall cupboard and giving them a wipe with a dish towel, as a prelude to laying the table. "You were a long time with the caretaker. I was starting to worry."

Her sister scoffed. "Whatever for? It's not as though I was going to come to any harm." Dee sat down.

"Did you make peace with the caretaker?"

"Of course. Morning Star was the first to admit she had overreacted. I was partly right about the cloth being a prayer flag. Not to keep away evil spirits, however, but to attract a good one."

"How do you mean?" Julia asked, switching her attention to a freshly brewed pot of tea.

Teacups filled, Dee began to explain. "It seems there was more to the story regarding the artifact. A First Nations boy caught the thief in the act of removing the relic from the totem. The lad tried to stop him but was pushed to the ground. He banged his head on a rock and later died of his injury."

"That's very sad." Julia's voice took on a subdued tone. "Was anyone arrested and charged with murder?"

"The Authorities didn't take the death of a native boy seriously, putting it down to an accident. And remember, this was years ago. Hopefully, things have improved since then."

Julia could see her sister was upset at the injustice. Even so, as Dee sipped her tea, she continued, "Call it coincidence, or just plain bad luck, but shortly after the theft things turned for the worst. The potato crop got blight and had to be burned. Hunting was poor, and three of the tribe died that winter from influenza. The elders were convinced all this was caused because the relic had gone. They went as far as chopping down the pole."

"When we were talking earlier, Morning Star told me the stump is all that remains. You mentioned a good spirit, sis. How does that tie in with the story?"

"I'm coming to that. A year or two later things began to pick up. At the same time younger members of the tribe, Morning Star amongst them, reported seeing the ghost of the dead boy. He appeared whenever something detrimental was about to happen. Gave a warning so to speak. The natives began thinking of him as a good spirit. The prayer flag is their way of ensuring he sticks around."

Julia bit her lower lip.

"What are you thinking, Jules?"

"More tea?"

"Come on, out with it."

"You'll laugh?"

"No I won't," Dee replied. "Trust me when I say, I have come across more than a few strange things in my line of research."

"Well." Julia paused, again nibbling at her lip. "Olly said he saw a young boy at the gas station. Spoke to him even. And again he professes to have seen and heard the boy during the thunderstorm. No one else did."

"Right before the landslide, Oliver receives a warning. Is that what you are saying? Interesting." It was Dee's turn to bite her lip.

"*Interesting*. Is that what scientists say when they make an amazing discovery?"

"All right. *Very* interesting." Dee smiled, enjoying the tease. "Especially when you consider the young boy in this First Nations story is named *Running Bear*."

CHAPTER THIRTEEN

LUNCH OVER, WHILE JULIA AND DEE WERE CLEANING THE KITCHEN, Oliver and Spencer went outdoors. With strict instructions not to stray far from the house, the twosome began assembling the drone the boy had received as a birthday present from his parents.

"Have you ever flown a drone before?" Spencer inquired.

"No, but I've practiced using a *quadcopter* simulator three or four times. It shouldn't be too difficult to fly the real thing."

"I admire your confidence, Olly. Can you swim?"

"Of course, I can swim," the boy replied. "Why do you ask?"

"Because if the drone strays over the lake, it might end up in the drink. We should find a better place, rather than here, to launch. How about we follow the track back to Port Douglas? I noticed, on the day of our arrival, an open area just after crossing the bridge. If there are any mishaps, at least they will be over dry land."

"Good idea," Oliver agreed, gathering up the assembled drone and control box. "Lead the way."

Shadow, anticipating the route, forged ahead, stopping now and again to allow the children to catch up.

The boy slowed and looked over his shoulder. "I can no longer see the house. Mom said we shouldn't wander too far."

Spencer laughed. "Define *too far*, Olly. Stop being a wuss. It's only a few hundred yards to the clearing. If necessary we can run back home and be there in less than five minutes. Talking of running, I'll race yah."

She and the dog were off. Oliver struggled to keep up.

"Ha, ha, I won," the girl declared as her cousin arrived out of breath.

"You didn't have to carry the drone and controller," he reminded her.

"I had my backpack. Which reminds me, I have another present for you. I purchased it at the airport in Savannah. There was this super-duper gadget shop that only sells high-tech stuff." Spencer pulled out a gift bag and handed it to the lad.

"Cool," Oliver announced, holding up a box containing a *Marco Polo Recovery System*. It took ten minutes to read up on the device's operation and attach it to the drone's landing gear. On-board camera activated, by using the throttle control rod, the lad increased the speed. "We have liftoff."

Majestically the drone rose into the air. However, having climbed less than twenty feet, the boy tried to fly in a circular pattern. Repeatedly pushing or pulling the controls in the wrong direction, the drone started to spiral toward the ground. It was only when Spencer leaned across and pushed the homing button, did the autogyro kick in, permitting a safe landing.

"How did you know how to do that?"

"Some people take the time to read the instructions," was the answer. "You should do the same. Now, hand the controller over to me." The girl held out her hand, and Oliver acquiesced, silently hoping that Spencer would make an even worse hash of things.

———

"Now look what you've done," Oliver goaded. "Not only have we lost sight of the drone, but it also doesn't respond to the return command."

"That's not my fault, Oliver," she responded frostily. "The battery in the controller is almost dead. When did you charge it last?"

"On my birthday," he replied.

"That's days ago. You should have recharged everything last night. I'm not surprised the drone did not return to base."

Oliver looked glumly at Spencer.

"Cheer up, Olly. All is not lost. Remember, we installed the *Marco Polo* tracker. Let me get its display unit out of the box. It shouldn't take long to find your precious toy."

"It's not a toy," the boy protested, but Spencer was not listing. Carefully monitoring the screen she set off up the valley, following the arrow as best she could, given the density of the trees.

———

Fifteen minutes later, after meandering back and forth, Oliver suggested, "Let's go back to the house and search again tomorrow. Mom will start to worry, we've been away for so long."

"Give it a few minutes longer," Spencer insisted. "The signal is very strong now. The drone can't be far away."

Sure enough, pushing their way through a thicket of long grass, they approached a clearing. The lad raced forward, and then excitedly fist-punched the air before picking up the drone. "I knew we'd find it."

"*We?* Shadow got here first; didn't you boy?" Spencer bent down and handed the dog a treat, while Oliver inspected the rotors. "Is anything broken?"

"Doesn't look like it. Let me check the camera." Instantly, the screen illuminated. "Seems okay. Give me a second and I'll scroll to the start of the video."

"Not now. Didn't you say a short time ago that your mom will worry? Come on. Best be off. You can review the footage later."

"Okay," the lad agreed. "We'll be in enough trouble for being out so long. Promise not to let on we went into the forest."

"What forest?" said Spencer with a grin, as they made their way toward the lake. "Didn't we stay by the water most of the time?"

"*Most* of the time? I don't know about that," Oliver countered, apprehensively.

"Some of the time, then?"

"Hmm. I'm not sure. Mom has a strange knack of knowing whether or not I'm telling the whole truth. When I'm not, she can get real mad at me." Oliver pulled a face at the prospect.

"In that case, let me do all the talking," Spencer suggested.

CHAPTER FOURTEEN

"Aunt Julia, you'll never guess what we have been doing," Spencer blurted out, as she and Oliver burst into the kitchen. "Flying Oliver's drone, and gathering amazing video of the surrounding area."

"And you lost track of the time, I suppose. Good job that clock called a stomach finally brought you both home."

"Don't you want to see the video?" Spencer continued.

"After dinner, dear." Julia spotted the dog. "Look at the floor. How did Shadow's paws get so muddy?"

"Dunno," the pair replied in unison.

"Is that right? Spencer, take your furry friend outside and clean him up. I'll mop the floor. Olly, you can go find Federico and your dad. They are in the outbuilding. Why I'm not sure. Tell them, it's almost time to eat. Once that's done, the both of you need to go upstairs and wash up. One final thing; when you come back downstairs, bring Ophelia from her cot. Like the rest of the troops, she'll want feeding as well."

Once everyone had eaten, with the help of his father, Oliver succeeded in hooking up the camera to a television. There was laughter from the adults as they watched the drone's maiden flight. Making fun at excuses of a strong crosswind and the sun in his eyes, everyone except the boy agreed it was pilot error.

"Not fair," the lad protested. "You all think I can't fly that thing."

Spencer's footage proved more interesting, showing the second flight, which followed the valley, heading north. Soaring above the treetops, the drone turned west. Following a broad vista of conifers marching up the gentle slope, it continued toward a steep rock face devoid of vegetation.

"Awesome, Spencer. It didn't take you long to master the controls," Dee announced. "Well done, girl."

"I've had enough of watching a video taken by someone who thinks they're so smart," Oliver vented. "Beginner's luck is all it is. I'm going to another room." After making the definitive announcement, he stomped out of the parlor.

"Olly, come back," his mother called, with no effect.

A door down the hallway slammed shut.

"I should go after him," Harper suggested.

"No. Let him cool his heels. He needs to learn throwing a temper tantrum is not the way a twelve-year-old should behave," Julia asserted. "Watch the video, Roger. Is that a goat or a sheep scrambling along the rock ledge, about halfway up?"

"Definitely a goat," Federico told them. "One time I managed to get real close to a herd of them when following the trail built by the Incas up the side of Huayna Picchu."

"What makes you so sure?" Julia asked.

"Afterwards, I read up on the difference between mountain sheep and goats. For a start, mountain sheep are bigger, heavier, and have thick, large horns. However, the horns of mountain goats are slender. They also have more prominent beards. Definitely a goat."

"Look, there's another, on a lower ledge, if you can call it a ledge. I'm surprised the animal doesn't fall off."

The goat expert chimed in again, "That is because of their split hooves and rubber-like soles. Some species can climb a near-vertical rock face."

"You learn something new, every day," Harper commented in an off-hand manner, leaving Federico unsure whether the remark was genuine or flippant. Not possessing his friend's mind-reading ability, he would never know the answer.

"Enough with the platitude, Roger. Look the second goat has disappeared."

"Don't tell me it fell off the ledge, Jules." Harper laughed. For a moment he had turned towards the door, having heard a knocking sound coming from another room.

"No silly. It has gone into a cave. I wish the drone had gone nearer."

"I think the drone's batteries were slowly dying, Aunt Julia," Spencer remarked. "It's started to turn back toward base."

"Pity. I wonder what else might be in the cave."

"Maybe it's not a natural cave," Harper suggested. "Perhaps it's a gold mine. If it is on our property, we could be rich."

"Now you are truly being silly, Roger. Besides you are already rich. All the money you won in that poker tournament."

"The same tournament you told me about the other day?" Dee asked her sister.

"The very same," Julia replied "Suffice to say, Roger is no card player, but Mitchell is. They were using some sort of sign language to communicate. Do you want to elaborate, Roger?"

"Not really," Harper responded, not wishing to reveal his hidden talents. "You can read all about it when I publish my book, *How to Cheat At Cards*." He chuckled to himself as if the comment was amusing.

"Oh no!" Federico exclaimed. " The drone is losing height. It's going to crash into that fir tree."

Miraculously, the device only clipped a branch, maintained its auto-rotate feature, and landed safely in a clearing.

"You managed to recover the drone okay?" It was Dee who asked the question.

"That was easy," Spencer professed. "It has a tracker fitted. One that does not rely on a cell phone signal."

"Wait a minute." Julia's mind was turning. "The drone crashed in a clearing in the forest, and you went to find it?"

"Ah. Yes. I was perfectly safe. Olly came with me. Shadow, as well."

"You, Olly, and the dog left the lakeshore and went into the forest?"

Harper interrupted before Julia could pursue her questioning further. "Tell you what. Tomorrow morning, let's go check out the cave we saw on the video."

Full of optimism, Federico corrected him. "You mean the gold mine."

"There are no gold mines around here," Dee categorically announced. "I, for one, am going to bed. *You, amigo*, can dream on. Check things out if you must. I can't wait to say, *I told you so*."

CHAPTER FIFTEEN

FOLLOWING DEE'S EXAMPLE, SPENCER WAS TOLD IT WAS TIME FOR bed. While Julia tidied up, Harper began his search for Oliver. With no success in the kitchen or dining room, upon opening the door to the room they had come to call the library, he found the lad was sitting at the desk, his back to the window.

"There you are. What are you doing, son?"

Looking up from the disassembled banker's lamp, Oliver replied, "Trying to get this cockeyed thing to work. The light is so dim, it doesn't shine like a proper lamp."

"Careful you don't electrocute yourself," Harper cautioned, as he pulled up a chair and sat opposite.

"I'm not stupid, Dad. It's unplugged from the wall socket," he added, holding up the end of the cable.

"Have you figured out the problem?"

"I think it needs a new bulb."

"Let me see," requested his father. Taking the bulb, he held it up to the ceiling light. "The filament is in one piece. It *should* work."

"It does, Dad, but as I said, it's very dim."

After looking more closely, Harper smiled. " There's a simple answer. It's not an ordinary bulb. On the metal base is stamped the capital letter 'U'."

"What does the 'U' stand for?" Before his father could answer, he interjected, "Wait a second. The same letter is engraved on the lid of this inkwell, together with some wording. See for yourself." Picking up the object, he handed it across the desk.

Harper read aloud,

"U shine the light to see more clearly."

"That's kinda weird. What does the phrase mean?"

Harper pondered for a second. Then he said, "Why don't we start by you screwing the bulb back? Good. Now turn the lamp on again, and shine its light over the blotter."

"Wow. It's invisible ink," Oliver declared in amazement. He read the reveal, written in a small, though legible, cursive style:

"Explore the untold history of British Columbia,
    starting from where you are standing.

That's the title of one of the books in the bookcase," Oliver announced, excitedly. "Although I don't know what *where you are standing* refers to."

"That's for another day, son. Spencer is already getting ready for bed."

"Okay," the lad agreed. "Before I go upstairs, though, I have something else to show you." He picked up the letter opener. "Engraved on the blade is another message."

Open with the *I* of an eagle.

"*The 'L' of the eagle?* That doesn't make any sense. Perhaps 'L' is really and 'I'. *The eye of an eagle* sounds better. Is that another clue?"

"If you're right, and it really is a clue, Olly, I wonder who left it?"

"Maybe the answer is in the book on British Columbia."

"Maybe, son. But what did I tell you a moment ago?"

"Bedtime," the boy repeated, with stoic resignation. "Will you help me find out, tomorrow?"

"Of course," Harper replied. "Spencer might like to help as well."

"Spencer? Can't it just be you and me?"

"Whatever for? I thought you and she were best buds. Since she came to stay with us, you've undertaken almost everything together."

"But she always does things better than me. Earlier, you all laughed when you saw how badly I flew the drone."

"We shouldn't have done that, Olly, and I apologize. With practice, you will improve. As for Spencer being better than you, more often than not you beat her at video games, don't you?"

"I suppose so," Oliver reluctantly agreed.

"So she can join us tomorrow?"

"I suppose so," the boy repeated. "Everyone can. That way we'll solve the clues more quickly."

"Great suggestion." Harper switched off the banker's lamp and rose from his chair. "Brush your teeth and then B-E-D. Off you go now. *Vamos.*"

CHAPTER SIXTEEN

THE BEST-LAID PLANS OFTEN CHANGE. HAVING BEEN TOLD ABOUT the video's content, Oliver was happy to put searching for clues in the library on the back burner. The first order of the day was helping his father load the back of the Land Rover with half a dozen flashlights, a coil of rope, a couple of plaid picnic blankets, and a box containing packed lunches. Job done, he sat with Spencer in the second row of seats, waiting for the adults to join them.

The Brazilian reopened the rear door and tossed in an assortment of helmets.

Turning, Spencer asked, "Where did you find those, Rico?"

"In an outbuilding, behind the house," he replied, "along with two kayaks."

"That's cool," Spencer commented. "Have you ever kayaked, Olly?" The boy shook his head. "Another day, when we get the chance, I'll teach you."

Is there anything Spence has not done before? the lad thought. However, before he could dwell on the subject, the door next to him opened.

"Here. You might need these as well," said his father handing over two anoraks and pairs of wellington boots to the duo. Julia, carrying the baby, walked down the porch steps and sat next to the two cousins.

Dee squeezed in beside Federico who had joined Harper in the front. Without further ado, the group set off, taking the track toward the remnants of Port Douglas.

"You've passed the turn we took to recover the drone," Spencer cried. "On the left just behind us."

"I'm going to see if Morning Star is home, first," Harper explained, "to find out if she knows anything about the cave. Is that okay?"

Why should Spencer object? She was grateful Aunt Julia had not told them off for going into the forest on their own. In silence she looked out of the side window, noticing as they crossed the bridge, that the creek had returned to a late summer trickle. Minutes later, the vehicle pulled up beside the caretaker's cabin. Dee got out and rapped on the door.

No answer.

She tried the latch. Finding it unlocked, she pushed the door ajar and called out, "Anybody home?"

Receiving no reply, she quietly closed the door, walked to the former tribal meeting room, and went inside. Like the cabin, nobody was there. However, a sunbeam shone through the far window, illuminating the ping-pong table. Noticing strange shapes scrawled in the dust, Dee pulled her smartphone from her pouch and took a photograph. *Something to send to a colleague*, she decided, curious as to the message's meaning.

"Everything all right?" Julia asked as Dee returned to her seat and fastened the seatbelt. "You took your time."

"Just making sure Morning Star wasn't in one of the other buildings, that's all. It seems we'll have to find out about the cave ourselves, without any local knowledge. Ready when you are, Harper. *Vamos.*"

After restarting the vehicle. Harper selected first gear, completed a slow turn, and headed back the way they had come.

Oliver chuckled to himself. "*Vamos.* That's the same word Dad said to me last night as he hustled me upstairs. What does it mean?"

"*Vamos* is Spanish for *let's go,*" Federico explained, "and Spanish is the main language spoken in Cuba."

"You can speak Spanish, Dad. I didn't know that. Let's hear some phrases."

"I've forgotten most of them," Harper answered, trying to avoid the request, but Spencer joined in the pleading.

"Okay. Let me think." After a couple of seconds, Harper continued, "*¿Dónde está la parada de autobús?*"

"Where is the bus stop?" the Brazilian conveniently translated.

"None around here," Julia informed them. Everyone thought her reply was funny.

"Another," Oliver demanded.

There was a brief pause in the conversation as Harper negotiated the rickety bridge. Then he complied. "How about *¿Dónde está el baño?*"

"I know that one," Dee blurted out before the Brazilian could speak. "Where is the bathroom?"

"None around here," Julia repeated, to the troops' amusement.

A minute later, the vehicle came to a gap in the tree line. Turning north, they proceeded along the route the older children had taken the day before.

Again Spencer cried, "Stop. We need to get out here and walk the rest of the way. Ahead, the trees are too close together to take the Rover."

Equipment and packed lunches unloaded, Harper asked, "What's this?" picking up a small package he found on the floor of the rear compartment.

Dee, who had been standing nearby, responded. "A present for you and Julia. Think of it as a thank you for allowing me to tag along."

As Harper began tearing off the wrapping paper, Julia was drawn into the conversation. "You shouldn't have, Dee. Such a gesture is entirely unnecessary."

"I don't know about that," her sister replied. "Cell phones don't work around here."

Paper off, Harper opened the first of two boxes, handing the second to his wife. "Satellite phones. That's great. I remember how useful one was summoning help when we were trapped on the converted oil rig prison, all those years ago. Do you remember, Jules?"

"I'd rather not, Roger. That is one experience I wish to forget."

"You met *me*. That's got to be a plus," Harper responded.

"I'll give you that. You'll have no excuse for not calling me if you ever become ensconced in the back of beyond. I look forward to hearing you whisper sweet nothings, over these new phones."

Dee chuckled as she began picking up a blanket and large book.

"What's so funny?" Harper asked.

"'You two lovebirds."

"Gross," Spencer, whispered to her cousin, who responded by rolling his eyes.

"Time for sweet nothings later. We'd best get going," Dee pressed.

They set off, Spencer, Oliver, and Shadow in the lead, weaving their way through the clusters of coniferous trees.

At his cousin's side, Oliver whispered, "How do you remember the way?"

"I'll let you into a little secret. I don't. But we are bound to hit the cliff wall in a few minutes."

"And when we do," the boy responded, "do we turn left or right?"

"Good question," Spencer answered. "I'll worry about that when we get there."

———

"We are here," Spencer proclaimed.

"This is where the drone landed?" Federico inquired.

"Not exactly. It landed in the forest. But this is the cliff shown in the video."

"I don't see any cave," the Brazilian said, looking up. "Are you sure we're at the right spot, Spencer?"

Oliver grinned. *Get yourself out of this fine mess, Miss Know-It-All.*

However, Harper came to the rescue, producing the drone from the backpack he had been carrying. "I thought we might need this, to pinpoint the exact spot. As you were such a good test pilot, Spencer, you can take it up again today. Let's start by heading north."

The boy was about to object but decided that if his cousin didn't find the cave, it would damage her credibility. *That would be one point to team Olly.*

In less than a minute the drone's camera picked out the cave.

Score

Team Spencer :   1

Team Oliver :   Nil

Trekking along the foot of the cliff, at the same time looking up, in no time the cave entrance was spotted. Everyone placed their gear on the ground.

Julia took an opportunity to unstrap Ophelia from her sling and sit her down. She then looked at her husband. "Don't think you're dragging me up there, Roger. The climb is impossible in these shoes."

"Me neither," Dee chimed in. "I don't have a head for heights."

"You're no fun," Harper teased.

"You are not taking the kids up there, either," Julia insisted.

Federico began a snorting laugh. "That's a good one, Julia. Kids, as in goats. Get it?"

"I suppose, you are going to be first to climb, then?" she responded. "Take off your boots and show me ... What did you call goats' feet? Cloven hoofs? That's right. Go ahead. Show me your cloven feet."

"I can see a ledge," Spencer interjected. "It shouldn't be too difficult to climb onto. I can easily get up there."

"Didn't you hear me tell Roger *no* to children climbing? It would be bad enough if Federico fell and hit his head. What would I tell your mother, in Bolivia, if you hurt yourself?"

"We've brought helmets," Oliver informed his mother. "And a rope."

"No, no, no. We are miles from the nearest hospital. Send the drone up there for a closer look if you like, but no one is climbing that cliff face. Is that clear?" Julia concluded, adamantly.

Oliver spoke again, "Maybe we don't have to. Look over by the trees. There are more goats."

"They are the same ones on the video", Spencer countered. "I expect they climbed down from the ledges."

Oliver disagreed. "Or not. I watched them appear from the shadows at the base of the cliff."

Harper decided to check it out. After a quick inspection, he turned and walked back. "It's another cave. And I would be surprised if it isn't connected to the one higher up. Well spotted, son."

That's got to be worth two points, Oliver told himself, mentally adjusting the board accordingly.

<u>Score</u>
Team Spencer : ɪ
Team Oliver : 2

CHAPTER SEVENTEEN

HAVING EXHAUSTED HERSELF CRAWLING AROUND A STRETCHED-OUT blanket, Ophelia was sound asleep in the now empty cardboard box used as an improvised crib. With the toddler no longer requiring her mother's constant attention, Julia busied herself sketching the heads of the three goats that had ventured nearer, seemingly unafraid of the visitors.

Sitting on a boulder not six feet away, Dee called out, "How's it going, sis?"

At the sound of a human voice, the goats scattered in alarm.

"It *was* going fine until you scared off my prime subjects."

"Sorry," Dee apologized. "My bad."

"No harm done," Julia responded in a good-humored way. "Before Spencer left with Oliver and the men to explore the cave, she took some photographs. If push comes to shove, I can use them to fill in the details. So what are you reading, that has you so engrossed, Dee?"

"One of the books from our father's library called *The Untold History of British Columbia*. It's fascinating reading, full of tidbits of information I never knew."

The herd, now used to Dee's voice, slunk back and started grazing again, which allowed Julia to resume sketching, at the same time listening to her sister's narrative.

"For example, Whistler, was originally named London Mountain due to the frequent fog at lower elevations. The natives called it ..."

There was a pause as Dee hurriedly leafed back to the section referencing native place names.

"... *Skwikw,* in the Squamish language. That's it!" she exclaimed, raising her fist and touching her forehead. "I should have realized."

"Realized what?" Julia asked, somewhat bewildered.

"The writing on the table in the Community Hall behind Morning Star's cabin is in her native language. Reading the name Squamish, I now recognize the orthographic symbols, although I cannot translate the words."

"Orthographic symbols? In English please, professor."

"Orthography is a set of conventions for writing a language," Dee explained. "You and I use the symbols: H E L L O, to write the word *hello*. We think of them as letters, but essentially they're a standardized set of written symbols. The same word using a different alphabet would patently look different. Let me borrow your iPad for a second and I'll show you. Best open up a new page. I don't want to mess up your drawing."

Julia complied. Dee using the iPad's pencil wrote:

Greek: η ε λ λ o
Russian: ч е л л о
Chinese: 竹 中 中 人
Latin: h e l l o

"I've not translated the word, just used letters from different alphabets."

"I'm impressed," Julia admitted, taking the iPad back and scrutinizing the list closely.

Dee confessed, "Don't be. I only know a few symbols of the Russian and Chinese alphabets. These examples I use as part of a lecture on cultural variations, given to my second-year students."

"Enough tutoring for one day. Do you think our intrepid explores have found anything intriguing in the cave?" Julia asked, changing the subject.

"I doubt it," her sister replied. "Not unless you consider goats' droppings intriguing."

Julia laughed. "In the book then? Any more nuggets of wisdom there?"

Dee leafed back until she found a section covering the Canadian Pacific Railway. "How about this?" She began reading. "*Over the course of constructing the B.C. segment, 9,000 workers were employed . Of these 6,500 were Chinese; many being brought by ship from both California and China.*"

"And 160 years later little has changed. We still rely on Chinese labor for the manufacture of many goods, from plastic toys in Christmas crackers to smart cell phones."

Not wishing to start a discussion on global economics, Dee suggested, "Let's see what this book has to say about Port Douglas."

She turned to the index and found four references. Two concerned the town's importance as a waypoint along a mixed land and water route to the Fraser Canyon goldfields. Another referred to the settlement's logging era. The fourth, however, which peeked Dee's interest, rendered an account of residential and commercial structures since 1858.

After skip-reading the first two pages, she turned the sheet and muttered "Philistine. I hate finding books marred by people dropping food on the paper while reading."

"What do you mean?" Julia asked.

Dee held out the open hardback for her sister to see.

"Looks like a juice stain from an ice pop. It's in the margin though. No big deal, surely?"

"No to you maybe, but to me, being an academic, it's unconscionable."

"I'll try to remember not to allow the kids to suck popsicles while reading if that makes you happy. Apart from the stain, anything else you want to share?"

Dee returned to reading the text aloud. "There's a reference a well-to-do gentleman, who lived in a grandiose dwelling on the western shore of the smaller lake. Judge Lambert Harrison-Hayes held a reputation of being a no-nonsense upholder of the law, earning him the nickname 'Hanging' Judge Harrison. Such was his status in the community, the two lakes were named after him."

Full of excitement, Julia announced, "The grandiose dwelling must be the property we inherited."

"You're right," Dee agreed. "Compared with the other buildings, it was considered overly pretentious. I bet the courthouse was constructed upon the same lines." She quickly read the next couple of paragraphs. "Sure enough, it describes the courthouse with walnut-paneled interior walls and a raised dais for the judge's bench."

"I don't think wall paneling is my thing." Julia mused. "I'm glad there's none inside the *Book House* now."

Dee, only half listening, read on. "There's mention of successive owners, all Judge Harrison's relatives, up to 1999. Nothing on when it came into dad's possession."

"When was the book published?" Julia asked.

"Let me see." Her sister hurriedly turned to the copyright page. "2006. That explains it. Our father acquired the house in 2015."

"Really," Julia responded. "How do know that, sis?"

"The date was stated in the title search; part of the documents in the conveyancing package."

"You surely are a quick reader, Dee. I simply applied my autograph. Could have been signing my life way for all I knew. Any mention of previous selling prices in the book?"

"No."

"Is that unusual?"

"I'm not sure," Dee replied. "We should ask the lawyer."

"Ask a lawyer what?" Harper asked as he came into earshot.

"How long I have to wait before I can declare you legally dead," his wife answered. "You've been gone so long we were starting to worry."

Before Harper could explain, Oliver and Spencer came scampering over. "You'll never guess what we saw in the cave," Oliver exclaimed.

Spencer added, "And I've taken lots of photographs."

Shadow, sensing the enthusiasm, added his two cents worth by barking.

"A pot of gold," Dee surmised.

Federico, who had finally caught up with the others, proclaimed, "Not a *pot* of gold, but a *bag* of gold," He held up a small canvas sack to prove his point.

CHAPTER EIGHTEEN

"FETCH THE PACKED LUNCHES, ROGER. " IT WAS JULIA WHO SPOKE. "I don't know about everyone else, but I'm ready to eat."

"What about our find?" Federico asked. "Don't you want to hear more?"

"Sure we do," Dee replied. "After we've eaten."

There was a mad dash to grab a sandwich by Oliver and Spencer. "Hold up, kids," Julia interceded. "Not so fast. Go wash up in the stream first. Both of you look as though you've crawled through a tunnel backward."

"We did," the pair chorused and then burst into fits of laughter.

"Roger, what have you been up to?"

"Nothing, Jules," he replied, "except explore an occasional passageway or two."

"How come you and Federico are not all covered in dust and mud?"

Harper slowly ran his fingers through his hair, something he often did when carefully formulating an answer. He bit into a sandwich. "This tastes real good. Did you make it, honeybee, or was it you, Dee?"

Meal over, the Brazilian started opening the bag.

Dee spoke up, causing him to hesitate. "Children first, Federico. Your turn will come. Let's begin with the photos Spencer took"

The girl jumped up from the blanket, camera in hand. "Who wants to start," she asked, after switching on the liquid crystal display.

"Julia and I can look at the same time," Dee suggested.

"Wow! Is that a cave painting?" Julia asked. "This is an amazing find. How far in is it?"

"Not far," Oliver told his mother. "There's more than one painting. You and Aunt Dee can easily get to them without going on your hands and knees."

"I don't like heights, and more so, I don't like confined spaces," Dee confessed. "I'm happy to stay right here, thank you very much. On to the next photo, sis."

For five minutes, Dee and Julia examined the series of snapshots Spencer had taken. Julia did most of the talking, identifying scenes of men with spears hunting elk, salmon leaping up rapids, and beavers building a dam. The last one focused on a lake. In the middle was, what looked to be, a whale spouting a tall geyser of water.

"Native art, am I right, Dee?"

"Could be."

"Thousands of years old, perhaps?" Julia decided. "That might account for the whale if the lake was a coastal inlet at the time."

"I'm not sure you have the dating correct, sis. Anything else of note?"

"Next to the whale, is that a paddle steamer?" Julia asked.

Dee nodded and smiled. "Like I said, not that old."

CHAPTER NINETEEN

FEDERICO HAD BEEN WAITING PATIENTLY. NOW IT WAS HIS TURN. With due ceremony, as if he were a magician pulling a rabbit from a hat, the Brazilian produced a piece of rock the size of an unshelled walnut.

"I told you *there's gold in them thar hills*," Federico reaffirmed. As an aside he informed the group he was a Mark Twain fan, the phrase coming from the 1892 novel *The American Claimant*.

That's something Spencer would do, Oliver thought to himself. *She's always quoting snippets from various authors. Part of her 'how clever I am' repertoire.*

The Brazilian passed a sample to Julia, a second to Dee, and continued, "Do you see the veins of gold in these pieces of quartz? I found a dozen or so in this bag."

"That's what took you so long. You were mining nuggets?" Julia asked.

"Did I say mining?" Federico replied. "For starters, I didn't take a hammer with me. No, they were already in the bag. And my thanks go to Spencer and Oliver, who retrieved them for me."

"That explains why the kids got so dirty," Dee deduced. "Was the cave full of narrow passages?"

"Not really," the Brazilian replied. "Much of the cave system consisted of wide tunnels, with ceilings well above our heads. Only in the last stretch, just before the find, did the passage become smaller. Although I could see the sack of gold over the top of a boulder that was blocking the passage, I couldn't squeeze passed. However, there was a gap below, and the children crawled through with no trouble. Neat, don't you think?"

"No, I don't think." Julia sounded cross. She turned to her husband and took her angst out on him. "And you Roger Harper, stood by, allowing Olly and Spencer to be used as child labor?"

"It wasn't like that, Jules. You sound as if we forced them to work down a mine. They got a little dusty that's all."

"And if the tunnel had collapsed?"

"Calm down, sis," said Dee, acting as a self-elected referee. "Nobody got hurt. And while you two have been arguing, I took a closer look at the quartz. Oliver, did you bring your compass with you today?"

"I sure did." The boy reached into his fanny pack. "Here. Are you lost, or something?"

"Not exactly," his aunt replied. Holding the compass to the rock, she continued, "Ah. I thought so. Gather around everyone. See how the needle is dawn to the rock and no longer points north."

"What does that mean?" the Brazilian asked, sounding apprehensive.

"It means, Federico, my friend, what we have here is iron pyrite," Dee informed him. "Commonly known by its other name as fool's gold."

Stifling a laugh, "Fool's gold," Harper repeated. "That's a good one." He slapped his friend on the back. "*There's no fool like an old fool.* John Heywood first cited the phrase I just quoted in his glossary of proverbs back in 1538. You're not the only one well read around here. When in the army, I spent much of my spare time with my head in a book."

CHAPTER TWENTY

EARLY THE FOLLOWING MORNING FEDERICO WAS SITTING ON THE front porch, gazing across the lake at nothing in particular. A deep-throated 'kur-ruk' sound, coming from a bird perched close by, caused him to turn his head. Black in color, approximately the size of a hawk, between calls it was pruning its feathers. The Brazilian was fascinated each time the gurgling sound was repeated, responding to another in the distance.

At one point he could have sworn the birds were mimicking human speech. Far off, one asked, "Whatya doing?"

"Hanging around. Wastin' time," was the nearby reply.

Dee, who came onto the stoop carrying two cups of steaming coffee, sat down in the chair next to Federico and offered him the drink. She followed her companion's line of sight. "Ah. I see you've made a friend in *Corvus corax*. Anything thought provoking in Mr. Raven's conversation?"

"It said, like me, it was wasting time. At least that's what it sounded like."

"Maybe the bird is right. A recent scientific study suggests ravens are as intelligent as great apes. The big question is *are you wasting your time*, Federico?"

"Maybe I am. I thought joining the Harpers on vacation was a good idea. Now I'm not so sure."

"Why do you say that?" Dee asked, with concern. "Nothing serious, I hope."

"I think I've upset Julia. Yesterday evening, over dinner, she hardly said a word, and this morning at breakfast I felt totally ignored. In hindsight, I should never have let the children go scrambling after the gold."

"Fool's gold, you mean."

"Not you as well. Harper has not stopped ribbing me."

"By the end of the day, he'll have found something else to amuse himself. As for Julia, she's not upset over the children; she's upset because you took the bag out of the cave."

"Why does it matter? The contents are worthless."

"That's not the point, Federico. Take that raven in the tree. It holds an important place in the oral tradition of the First Nations people living in British Columbia. Depicted as both a creator and a trickster, the raven's exploits are told in hundreds of stories. One, in particular, comes to mind. It goes something like this:

> "*After a very long journey, guided along by the thin column of smoke, Raven reached the land of the people who owned Fire. The people were not people of earth. Some say they were the Fish people, but no man knows for sure.*
>
> "*Raven noticed that these people sat around in a large circle with Fire in their midst, for it was autumn and the days and nights were chill. Observing Fire was in many places, Raven picked out a spot where there were few people, darted in quickly, and picked up Fire in his beak.*
>
> "*His plan was to return to the earth people and seek a reward for bringing them Fire. However, Fire became so hot that the bird dropped it. Falling to the ground, Fire happened on a place overrun by Wood. Wood became so enamored by the glowing ember that he shared his find with Forest.*
>
> "*Fire and Forest became great friends, Fire dancing with the branches, jumping from tree to tree.*

*"Raven, on the other hand, was so exhausted from flying that he
had to rest. However, the only place he could find was at the
top of a tall tree. Perched on the upmost branch, he watched
as Forest became so engulfed with Fire, the smoke so thick
that it turned Raven's feathers black."*

Dee paused and pointed. "And that is why our friend over there on the branch keeps repeatedly preening himself. It is trying to remove the soot from its feathers and restore them to the original color white."

"A cute story, Dee, but what does it have to do with retuning the quartz to the cave?"

"Everything, Federico. One shouldn't take something that does not belong to you. Or, like Raven, there may be dour consequences."

"Such as my hair falling out." The Brazilian chuckled.

"You are not taking me seriously. The bag and its contents are not yours to remove, and certainly not to keep. Julia wants you to return them to the cave."

"Then why doesn't she say?"

"She did, at the dinner table. Twice."

"I didn't hear her," the Brazilian confessed.

"That is because you were moping over Harper calling you a fool. If it's any conciliation, she's infuriated with Roger as well. Return the booty, and be done. It's the right thing to do. Now drink your coffee and tell me about this book you're writing."

"You know about my blockbuster?"

"The subject matter hardly lends itself to becoming a blockbuster. Harper said you were writing a biography of the Cuban dictator, Fulgencio Batista."

"He obviously didn't tell you. I have abandoned the project. Cuba brings back unhappy memories, and it's too hard to bear."

"So, Federico, if you're not writing an account of the former President, are you planning to return to journalism?"

"No. Again, bad memories. I was thinking of writing a novel. Fiction of some sort, but I cannot decide on a genre, let alone outline a plot."

After taking a sip of coffee, Dee smiled. "Personally, I find it's easier when one writes about what one knows. How about something based on your experiences in Brazil?"

"Again, no. Same reason; bad memories. In 1981, hardliner members of the Brazilian military dictatorship targeted a May Day music concert. Both my parent were killed in the bombing. I was six years old at the time."

"You poor thing. So much tragedy in your life," Dee touched his arm, a gesture of sympathy. "Then write about what is happening right now. Our journey to Port Douglas, the landslide of rocks, the cave paintings you discovered."

Sounding unconvinced, Federico replied,"I could do that, I guess."

"Guess what?" It was Harper's voice. "Are you two playing twenty questions?"

"*Amigo*, I'm noticing you are developing an annoying habit of eavesdropping on people's conversations."

"It's not intentional, I assure you. Just happened to hear the last couple of words. Jules sent me to find you. I'm tasked with persuading you to return the fool's gold." He noticeably lowered his voice as he said the word *fool's* as if that would diminish the embarrassment.

"Dee has already broached the subject."

"Did she give you an earful about our setting a poor example to Olly and Spencer? Jules went on and on about honesty being the best policy."

"For the record, Harper, I'm not in the habit of giving people earfuls," Dee responded huffily. "The pair of you should stop feeling sorry for yourselves. I've already told Federico that taking the swag back is the right thing to do. Besides, someone may come looking for the bag and wonder who took it."

"Unlikely," Harper responded. "There is hardly anyone living around here these days."

The screen door opened and Julia stepped out. "Is this where you're hiding, Roger? You and Federico are supposed to be halfway to the cave by now."

"My fault," Dee confessed. "I was quizzing Federico on the novel he is writing. The men are about to leave."

"We are," Harper confirmed, seizing the opportunity of a get-out-of-jail card. "Come on, Federico, let's get going."

The pair got up and walked down the porch steps. Upon reaching the Land Rover, they removed their jackets from the front seats.

"It's a nice morning, we should walk," Harper told the Brazilian. As they departed, he then turned his head, calling to the women, "See you both later."

"Federico," Dee shouted. "Aren't you forgetting something?"

"What?"

"The fool's gold." Once more the emphasis was on *fool*.

CHAPTER TWENTY-ONE

OLIVER AND SPENCER HAD BEEN PLEADING WITH JULIA OVER breakfast to allow them to go exploring on their own. However, after Harper and Federico had left, she remained adamant that such an enterprise was too dangerous. The children's latest attempt had been overheard by Dee, who point-blank asked her sister what they should be afraid of.

"Lions, tigers, and bears," she replied, without thinking.

Dee laughed. "There are no lions or tigers in B.C. Black bears, yes, and fewer grizzlies, In general, they like to avoid conflict with people. Unless you get too close, trying to take a photograph, for example, they will leave you alone."

"Trying to take a photograph," Julia repeated. "Did you hear that Spencer? That's just the sort of thing you would do."

"I won't, Aunt Julia, I promise. Cross my heart."

"I have some bear repellent in my luggage," Dee volunteered. "The children can take it with them if it makes you feel better, Julia."

"What about other critters? Cougars, raccoons, coyotes, and wolves. I've done my homework. It's not safe out there."

"Have you seen any of these animals from the house?" Dee inquired.

"Well no, but they're out there, waiting," Julia answered defensively. "I just know it."

"Raccoons are just mischievous. They won't attack us humans. Neither will coyotes, although it would be wise to leave Shadow in the house. Cougars? Unlikely. They prefer to roam in areas where they won't be seen. Much of what I am saying comes from personal experience while hiking forest trails." Dee paused, fearing she had overstepped the mark. "But I defer to your decision, sis. You're the parent."

Julia relented. She looked at the wall clock. "Okay, you can go exploring, but I want you both back here by three o'clock."

"Thanks, Aunt Julia," Spencer responded, giving an uncharacteristic hug.

"Can we take a packed lunch, Mom?" was Oliver's less endearing reaction.

"Sure. While I get it ready, why don't the pair of you collect your things?"

No encouragement needed, Oliver and Spencer bounded up the stairs, two steps at a time. Shouts could be heard in the kitchen as each in their own room reminded the other to bring compass, camera, and telescope.

———

With the sun high in the sky and a gentle breeze goading the leaves of the coniferous trees, it took the two intrepid explores ten minutes to skirt the head of Little Harrison Lake and reach Port Douglas Road. Turning north, they walked another fifteen minutes. During that time Spencer repeatedly asking about the elongated backpack her cousin was carrying.

Oliver, enjoying the tease, told her, "You have to guess."

"A bow and arrows?"

"Nope. Try again."

"Golf clubs, then."

"Like there's a golf course around here. Keep guessing."

Fraught with frustration, the girl stopping in her tracks, demanded that unless Oliver was more forthcoming she was going to do an about-turn and return to the Book House forthwith.

"I'll go on my own then," Oliver chided. What do you say to that?"

Spencer laughed. "It's not what *I* say, that counts. Remaining out here by yourself. What will your mom and dad say about that?"

"Point taken." Relenting, the boy removed the pack from his shoulders and laid it on the ground. "I was going to wait until we stopped for lunch, but open it if you must."

The girl inspected the bag. Made of canvas, just over four feet tall but narrow, it had a zipper running its full length.

"Oliver, this is amazing," Spencer declared as she pulled a *Peter Powell* stunt kite from the interior. Still in the original cellophane wrapper, there was a card pinned to the transparent wrapping.

Happy 14th Birthday, Billie
Love Mom

"Last night I found the bag at the back of the wardrobe in my bedroom, tucked behind a stack of empty shoeboxes." Oliver volunteered without being asked. "When the struts are inserted, the stretched fabric shows the image of a kestrel. There's a long tail too, if you want to attach it. The assembly instructions are included. "

"Come on," Spencer urged, unable to contain her enthusiasm. "Let's get going. The sooner were get to higher ground the sooner we can try the kite out."

"Good idea." Oliver rezipped the bag and slung it over his shoulder. "This way."

"Hold up, Olly. We shouldn't push through the cedars. It's too easy to get lost."

"Nonsense, Spence. I have my compass."

"Best stick to the path. Look, a few yards on, there's a track branching off to the left. It leads to the top of the ridge, for sure."

"Okay," Oliver agreed, "if it keeps you happy. I don't want to give you another reason to tattletale to mom that I was reckless." They set off, heading west. "The card inside. Do you think the kite was a present to William Hayes?"

"Got to be," Spencer concluded. "He never used it though. Just goes to show how ungrateful some people are."

Oliver was about to agree but stopped abruptly at the sound of barking coming from behind.

"Shadow, you're supposed to be in the house," Spencer scolded as the dog reached her.

"Managed to get out of jail, did you, mutt?" was Oliver's summation. "Good for you."

"Olly, your mom will be furious when she finds out."

"Not our fault if the grownups don't know how to keep a door closed. And no, we are not turning back. Come on. Shadow you can take the lead."

Soon both children were breathing heavily as their ascent grew steeper. Notwithstanding, the dog, full of energy, bounded back and forth. A small lake appeared on their right as the route began to slowly arc around on itself. At the two-mile point, the track opened into a wide clearing. One of the flat-topped mounds in the center was a good place to sit and eat lunch, they decided.

———

Between bites of a sandwich, Oliver attempted to assemble the kite.

Spencer, amused that it was taking so long, concentrated on feeding her face. At the same time, camera slung around her neck, she studied the surrounding landscape. "Don't move," she whispered.

"Why?" the boy asked, a little too loudly.

"Over there, at the tree-line, there's a deer. I'm going to take a photo."

It was not the click of the camera that spooked the animal, but Shadow. Deciding chase was a good choice, the dog raced towards its quarry. The deer, much faster, dove into the trees and was gone. A short time later, the pooch returned, sat on its haunches, tongue out, trying to cool down.

"Never try to outrun a greyhound, Shadow. You'd lose by a mile."

"Stop being mean to my dog, Olly. He was only wanting to make friends." As the girl spoke her cousin, with outstretched arms, pointed his index fingers at the canine.

The dog's response was to cock its head to one side.

"Whatever are you doing, Olly?"

"Practicing being a dog whisperer, like Morning Star."

Spencer scoffed. "Shadow isn't barking; he's sitting quietly."

"Goes to show how good I am. Maybe, I should train him to do something useful."

"Like what?"

"A security guard or a guide dog." Spencer looked at Oliver skeptically, shaking her head. "A mountain rescue dog then, like they have in the Swiss Alps. Shadow could even have a flask of brandy around his neck."

"Don't listen to Olly's nonsense, my little fuzzball. Come here, there's a good boy." The dog immediately obeyed, receiving a hug as a reward. "You'll always be my companion, and that's all I'll ever ask."

"Are you two done?" Oliver asked. "I need some help with these two lines."

"All right. Let me take over," his cousin insisted. "Finish your lunch while you watch and learn."

It took Spencer a minute to attach the tail and the two kite lines. Once complete she held up the pair of kite spools. "Now pay attention, Olly. What I'm about to tell you is important. You see the spools are different colors. Red you hold in your right hand; blue in your left. Don't mix them up or you won't be able to control the kite properly."

"How do you know that? You didn't read the manual?"

"I've flown kites before, with my dad, lots of times."

"And I suppose you are about to give me a demonstration?" Oliver asked, doing his best to conceal his frustration.

"Of course."

———

Except for the kite, the pair had packed away their gear. With Oliver's help, Spencer launched the kite, which rose majestically into the air. Skillfully she demonstrated how to create lift, drag, and thrust with various walking patterns, arm movements, even spinning around like a dancer. The painted kestrel swooped and climbed just like a real bird. Oliver had to admit he was impressed.

Following the dictates of the easterly wind, the children had left the clearing and were now following the track that led to the brow of the hill. The kite bobbed and weaved more intensely, as it gained more altitude.

"It's time I had a turn," Oliver begged. "Do you have to land the kite first?"

"Not at all, Olly. Put down your newfangled backpack and then stand in front of me. I'll put the kite spools in your hands and then grab your wrists. This way I can teach you how to move your arms to make the hawk soar."

And soar it did. Gaining confidence, Oliver slowly let the lines unspool until they were at maximum length.

"This is fun," the boy declared, quickening his pace as the wind pulled him forward. Soon he was walking so fast he was almost running. He reached the crest of the hill and started on the downward slope, now moving as fast as an athlete in a fifty-yard dash.

"Let go!" Spencer shouted.

"And risk loosing the kite?" Oliver responded. "No way. We may never get it back."

"It's not important. Let go, before you get pulled over the edge."

CHAPTER TWENTY-TWO

OLIVER SCREAMED FIRST; SPENCER A MOMENT LATER. THE GIRL rushed forward in time to see her cousin sliding down the scree slope on his back.

Helplessly she watched until Oliver eventually stopped, head cocked to one side, unmoving.

"Olly," Spencer shouted. "I'm coming."

Not choosing the same route as the boy, she took a more cautious approach. Backtracking, she found a zigzagging animal track to the side of the accumulation of small loose stones. Less dramatic but decidedly safer, it took five minutes to reach Oliver. Shadow was already there, giving the boy face-licks, trying to revive him.

"What now?" the girl asked herself.

The canine came over and rested its head in her lap. "Should I stay here or get help?"

After volunteering a yelp in response to his mistress's question, Shadow darted down the hillside as fast as his short legs would carry him.

"No, Shadow, no. Come back!" she pointlessly pleaded; the animal was too far away to hear. Abandoned, Spencer fist-smudged the tears welling up in her eyes, stoically fighting back a feeling of helplessness.

She covered her cousin with her anorak, regularly checked his condition, and waited.

Minutes turned into hours. Although remaining semi-conscious, Spencer took comfort from Oliver's regular breathing and the color returning to his face.

The girl dozed off, only to be awakened by a dog barking. Shadow in the lead, she saw four of the local First Nations band carefully descending the slope. Between them they carried a makeshift gurney of lashed poles.

"How did you know to bring a stretcher?" Spencer asked as the men gently lifted the boy off the ground.

"Your dog went to Morning Star's cabin, and she came and found us. The healer told us we needed a litter," *Myeengun*, older than his companions, replied.

"I've seen her talk to dogs before," a second man volunteered. "I think that's how she knew."

The third man tittered, adding, "Or that spirit-friend whispered in her ear." Again he chuckled.

"Don't make fun of Running Bear," Oliver protested, who was now fully conscious and party to the conversation. "I have seen the him twice. One time he warned me about falling rocks."

"Olly, you're awake. Thank God." Spencer sounded relieved.

"No one should be disrespectful of Morning Star," *Myeengun* counseled the other stretcher-bearers. "*Onâtawihowiw miyaskam mâwacîs.*" [She is a shaman, after all.]

"The boy needs to be taken to the healer," the fourth suggested. "She will know what to do next. Walk behind us, little one. Stay close. We don't want you having an accident as well."

"Okay," Spencer replied. Following the four stretcher-bearers, she remembered Dee telling her the caretaker was the go-to person for successfully treating numerous ailments, including injuries.

Having climbed back to the top of the hill, the group resolutely pushed east, following the route the children had taken that morning.

"Hold up," Spencer pleaded. "I need to catch my breath."

"We all do, little one," the older man agreed. "But only for a few minutes. The quicker we get you friend to the healer the better."

"Why didn't we descend into the valley?" Spencer asked. "That was the way Shadow, thats' my dog, went."

"It my not seem so, but that way is longer. The river flows into the larger lake. To reach Morning Star's cabin we would have to get to the east side of the canal." The man chucked. "From the looks of you dog's matted coat, he must have swam across."

"I see," the girl acknowledged, only then realizing how disheveled Shadow appeared. She reached forward and patted the animal on the head.

"No time for petting the mutt. Come, little one; on your feet. Best be moving."

It was another thirty minutes before the party reached Morning Star's cabin. Spencer was exhausted.

Once inside, the *onâtawihowêw* took her time carefully examining Oliver. After running her hands over his limbs and body, probing with her fingers, she pronounced the boy had nothing more than severe scrapes and bruising. "No broken bones or concussion," she declared. "Nothing so serious that a poultice of pine pitch and wild ginger cannot cure."

Checkup over, Oliver was taken outside, loaded into the bed of Morning Star's truck, and then driven to the Book House.

"I think Aunt Julia will be mad at us," the uninjured Spencer told Morning Star as they crossed the bridge, halfway to their destination.

"It was an accident, sunflower," she was told in a sympathetic voice. "I'll speak with Oliver's mom, and reassure her he's all right."

———

All right he might be in the eyes of the healer woman. Not so much, as far as Julia was concerned.

Federico and Harper had returned well before the older children arrived. Her husband bore the blunt force of her tongue-lashing when he agreed the applied poultice was probably sufficient.

"Probably sufficient, Roger? How can Morning Star tell there are no fractures? Does she have an X-ray machine stored in that other building? No. And I'm supposed to take her word Olly has suffered nothing to be concerned about. There might be internal bleeding for all we know."

Dee joined the discussion. "Oliver is resting on a couch in the library. After he went to the bathroom. I asked if he had blood in his urine, and he replied *no*. There is no deep-seated pain in his head, chest, abdomen, arms, or legs. His blood pressure is good. Heart rate is normal. All in all, he is in high spirits. My suggestion would be, between the four of us, we keep an eye on the lad day and night, for the next few days. If his condition worsens we can arrange for Oliver to be medevacked to a hospital."

"Dee's suggestion seems like a sensible way forward, don't you agree, Jules?" said Harper, trying to mollify the situation.

There was a commotion outside the room as Spencer raced down the hallway. Stopping at the doorway, out of breath, she asked, "Has anyone seen a pack of spare batteries. Oliver is complaining his video game controller is not working."

"If that isn't an indication that Olly is making a rapid recovery, I don't know what is," Harper added. "Now stop worrying, Jules. Everything will be fine."

"I hope you're right. If anything happens, I will never forgive myself."

CHAPTER TWENTY-THREE

OLIVER WAS ENJOYING THE WAITRESS SERVICE FOR HIS EVENING meal, and afterward the constant attention as the adults looked in on him at regular intervals. Around 8:30 PM everyone congregated in the library. As they gathered around the patient, his father was smiling.

"Do you remember, son, the other evening, we discovered the banker's lamp on the desk behind me had a special bulb?"

"Sure, Dad. You told me it was ultraviolet and that allowed us to read the secret writing hidden on the ink blotter."

"Well. While eating dinner, Dee was bringing Federico and me up to speed, telling us about the book she had been reading while we were exploring the cave. She happened to mention there was a stain in the margin of one of the pages. A juice stain, your mother thought. Which got me thinking. Often an ingredient for making invisible ink includes juice; lemon juice."

"You think there is secret writing in that book?" Oliver asked.

"Let's find out, shall we. Dee, why don't you go fetch it?"

A short time later, Dee returned. Indicating the relevant page, she asked Harper to do the honors. "Place it under the lamp, and tell us what, if anything, you find."

Penned in the smallest of script Harper read:

"The quick brown fox jumps over the lazy dog."

Julia wondered, "What's that all about?"

"I remember the phrase is commonly used for touch-typing practice, because it contains all the letters of the alphabet," Dee responded. "Why Chance would hide such a note it in the margin beats me."

"Specifically, the notation is written opposite the entry about this house being transferred to William Chester Hayes. There has to be a reason," Harper concluded.

"We've found secret writing in one book, but there are dozens in the library," Oliver reminded the group. "Maybe the answer is in another."

"How about this moth-eaten paperback?" Spencer suggested, having pulled it from the bookshelf. "There are scuff marks on the cover, the spine is falling apart, and some pages have their top corner turned in."

"Ugh. Another of my pet hates," Dee huffed. "In my opinion, bookmarking a page that way is bordering on sacrilege. What's the title?"

"*Poker Tells* by Matthew Lewkowich."

"Bring it over here, Spencer," Harper requested. "Let's pick out a tagged page and see what we've got."

The chapter was titled *Big -v- Small Hands*. The text listed possible tells an opponent might display depending on the strength of their hand. In the right margin, next to the phrase '*more relaxed players often make eye contact*' were hidden the words

WH frequently avoided eye contact when holding a strong hand.

Further down, again only showing under ultraviolet light, was written

Exactly what WH did. A sure giveaway.

Presumably referring to the main body of text suggesting *leaving the stack of chips untouched signified that a player was holding a weak hand.*

"Is *WH* signifying William Hayes?" Federico inquired.

"I can't imagine it would be anyone else," was Julia's conclusion. "Assuming our father special-ordered this book from the Hartzel bookstore, reading it was a way to improve his poker play."

"And the target was William Chester Hayes. Why would Dad set his sights on that man in particular?" Dee pondered. "And why would be want to bring him down at the poker table?"

"I recall Morning Star telling me, she believed Willam Hayes' father was responsible for Running Bear's death," Julia informed the group. "However, how foxes, dogs and playing cards come together is a mystery."

"Quite so," Dee agreed, "and a good example of cryptic clues that warrant inclusion in your forthcoming novel, Federico. I hope you're taking mental notes."

CHAPTER TWENTY-FOUR

"WHAT ARE YOU DOING?" SPENCER ASKED WHEN SHE SAW AUNT DEE busy typing on her laptop computer.

It was the following day. Although Oliver was desperate to start moving around again, on strict instruction from his mother he was to spend another day resting. Spencer had become tired of playing video games and sort an alternative distraction.

"I'm composing a quick email to a colleague of mine at Vancouver University. He's a linguist who has worked alongside some of the native speakers, collecting Squamish legends. Having published several books on the subject, I'm hoping he can translate some text for me. If he can't then I'm sure he knows someone who can."

"How are you going to send your email, Aunt Dee? There's no cable here. We are too remote."

"Cable no, but dish yes. This morning Harper found a bill in your late great-uncle's desk. He used his satellite phone to contact the company and was able to quickly reactivate the account. Now, we have not only Internet but television too."

"Cool," Spencer commented. "I have photos of strange writing, that I took behind the gas station, on our way here. The symbols were carved into the base of a totem pole lying on its side. Maybe your college friend can translate those as well?" I'll go get my camera.

———

The email had been sent. Not only did it include the text found by Dee in the dust of the redundant Community Hall behind Morning Star's cabin, and Spencer's totem photographs, but also pictures of the cave drawings. All they had to do was wait for a reply.

———

To Dee's astonishment, the response arrived in less than two hours. Before opening the email, she found Spencer conveniently sitting with the patient. Of equal surprise was the fact that the missive did not start with the Squamish text. Rather it was a categorical proclamation that the cave art was a sham.

Not of any anthropological interest. Probably drawn by a child.

Dee was already dubious about the dating but *drawn by a child*, added a fresh dimension to the mystery.

Below the critical comment was an attachment. Opening it revealed a digital copy of a sepia photograph. An upright totem, the sender's comment read:

Notation of back records location and date - Port Douglas c 1919

Is there a totem still standing at Port Douglas? If there is, then the picture you sent, be it on the ground, is its twin. If no longer there, congratulations. You have discovered where it ended up. Either way, the carved inscription is the same.

Remember, that which is held within your heart will never leave you.

Dee repeated the phrase out loud. Shaking her head, she tried to recall when and where she had heard the words before, but nothing came to mind.

Last but not least, the Community Hall symbols were addressed.

ᐊᐸᓄᗋᐦᑯᐣ ᔿᐣᑦᐦᐊᖁᐤ ᒪᐣᑯᕒᐣ

Morning Star misses her Bear Cub.

In this instance, there was no comment from Dee's linguist college, just the straight translation.

"Well that's a disappointment," Dee concluded. "We are no closer to finding out what all this means."

"What do we do now?" the girl asked.

"Go find some answers. "

"How?"

"By speaking to Morning Star. It's a nice day for a stroll. Are you coming with me, Spencer?"

CHAPTER TWENTY-FIVE

Morning Star had the hood of her truck raised. Spanner in hand, she was tightening the battery terminals. As Dee and Spencer approached, she looked up.

"Anything I can do to help?" Dee asked.

"Turn the ignition key and see if this piece of shite will start," was the unladylike reply.

Sliding into the driver's seat, Dee did as requested. The dashboard lights illuminated briefly and then went out.

"Damn you, Henry. Now is not the time to act up." The elderly woman kicked a front tire, emphasizing her frustration.

"Henry?" Spencer inquired, as her aunt rejoined them. "You call your truck Henry?"

"After my ex. It's about as reliable too. And before you ask, he was a lumberjack. Left as soon as he learned I was pregnant. Haven't seen hide nor hair of that pathetic dipstick since. I don't see no wedding ring on your finger, Miss Dee. Wise woman. I wish I had your common sense."

"I was once," Dee confessed. "Married when I was an undergraduate at university. Didn't last though. My then-husband could never settle into a job, wanted to play student for the rest of his life."

"His name wasn't Henry by any chance?" Morning Star was grinning.

"Nope, but it sounds as though they could have been brothers by different mothers."

Both women laughed.

Spencer, feeling left out, asked, "What's so important about using the truck today, Morning Star?"

"To fetch supplies from Tipello. There's an airstrip southwest of here, One has to take the forest road northwest, cross the Lillooet River where there is a bridge, and come back down again on the other side. A total of some forty-eight kilometers."

"We don't use kilometers in the United States. How far is that in miles?" Spencer asked of her aunt.

"About thirty, sweetie. Quite a drive considering the settlement is just over the hill, a few miles away."

"Tell me about it, Morning Star," responded. "But I don't have a choice."

"I can get Harper to bring over the Land Rover and give you a jump start," Dee offered on behalf of her brother-in-law.

"I'll take you up on that," Morning Star replied. "But you didn't come here on the off-chance I needed roadside assistance."

"You're right. I have some questions for you, that I hope you might answer".

"Then come inside, the two of you. I have no electricity in the cabin, but the wood-burning stove is always lit. I'll make us a nice pot of tea."

———

Spencer was not a tea person, but she was too polite to ask for coffee. As Dee and Morning Star made small talk, she concentrated on a large tapestry that hung on a windowless wall, depicting a hunting scene.

Tuning out the adult's conversation, the girl studied the textile's embroidery in more detail. Spear carrying warriors stalking elk where patently evident. As was the steamboat and whale, be they in slightly different positions on the lake. In addition, however, she spotted the crude portrayal of a jet-plane, half-hidden within the weave of white fluffy clouds. She wondered why something similar had not been drawn on the cave wall.

"Can you tell me anything about the drawings inside a cave, not far from here?"

At Dee's mention of drawings and cave, Spencer was jolted out of her introspection and began listening to the discussion.

"That piece of nonsense." Morning Star laughed. "You didn't think there were ancient aboriginal drawings, did you?"

"No," Dee answered. "The steamboat put the kibosh on that."

"Bear Cub's idea. He was always a one for practical jokes. As kids, nine years old, we had this crazy notion to offer summer visitors a tour of the cavern. Charge them admission to see the wall paintings. For those who were more adventurous, we planned to take them further into the cave. Show them the gold mine. Even selling them a small piece of rock with yellow veins embedded in the quartz."

"The fool's gold you mean." Spencer could not contain herself. "Aunt Dee spotted that right away. A smart cookie is my aunt."

"Yes, fool's gold," Morning Star confirmed. Sadness crept into her voice as she continued, "But alas, our little scheme was short-lived. My Bear Cub was always nimble on his feet. He would never fall without being pushed by the man who stole the relic from inside the raven's head."

"I recall Julia telling me a young boy was killed at the time of the theft, but I didn't realize you were referring to your childhood friend. I am so sorry." Dee deliberated as to whether or not she should continue with her questioning, or quietly depart. Not wishing to leave Morning Star in such a depressed frame of mind, she chose the former.

"What happened, to the totem pole once it was chopped down?"

"The elders decided to throw it into the lake and let it float away. I think some lumberjacks guided it through the channel connecting Little Harrison to the larger lake. From there, who knows? It wasn't taken by the logging company that's for sure. They had heard the story of bad luck and left it alone."

"It drifted with the current, presumably?"

"I guess so," Morning Star responded.

"Do you think it could have reached Harrison Hot Springs at the southern end of the main lake?"

"Possibly. Why do you ask?"

Not answering the question Dee countered, "Do you want it back?"

"Not especially. Not unless the stone is recovered." The older woman thought for a moment. "Even then, the pole would be too short."

Spencer, having seen jade pendants in the Hartzell gift shop, wondered, "What is so special about a stolen stone? Can't you replace it with another?"

"The relic was unique in its spiritual properties and consequently irreplaceable. Chance Norton, however, was doing research trying to track down its whereabouts. That is why he purchased all those books. He kept notes in a diary, which is probably somewhere in the house."

"We haven't found it," Spencer informed the caretaker. "We did discover messages written in the margin of some books, though, using invisible ink."

"Invisible ink," the older woman repeated. "Typical Chance. He always kept his findings close to his chest." Morning Star allowed herself a deep sigh. "There came a point in time when Chance apparently stopped looking. He never shared the reason why, and that has always puzzled me. Now that he has passed on, we will never know."

————

Heading back to the Book House, Spencer remarked, "You never asked about the writing carved near the base of the totem pole I found at the gas station. Why not, Aunt Dee?"

"Because I sensed Morning Star was upset enough talking about the death of her friend. There will be another opportunity to do so, I'm sure."

"What about the words you found written in the dust of the ping-pong table?"

"For the same reason, sweetie. Bear Cub and Running Bear are one and the same. She spoke about the boy being surefooted. That's something children would know about each other if they played together."

Spencer thought for a moment, and then continued, "*Morning Star misses her Bear Cub* was a message left for Running Bear, then?"

"I believe so?" Dee replied.

"So Oliver is not the only one who can see him?"

"See him, hear him; one way or another I think they communicate."

"Morning Star is an old woman. Running Bear is still a boy. Do you think he is a ghost?"

"A ghost or a spirit, yes. How that is possible I don't know." Dee looked up at the sky. "Come on, pick up the pace. Do you see those ominous dark clouds? Let's get back home before the rain starts. Remind me to tell Harper and Federico to take the Land Rover to Morning Star's place and jump-start her truck."

"What will you be doing, Aunt Dee?"

"Helping Julia, I expect. Do you and Oliver have anything planned?"

"Stay indoors and play *Go Fish,* or some other card game, I expect. Do you have another suggestion?"

"I do." Her aunt smiled. "How about a treasure hunt?"

"For real gold, this time?" Spencer asked, excited at the prospect.

"No, not gold. Morning Star said Chance Norton kept a diary. She thinks it is somewhere in the house. You and Oliver can try to find it."

CHAPTER TWENTY-SIX

"Aunt Dee, Aunt Julia, we have it," Spencer cried as she ran down the hallway to the kitchen. Oliver, apparently fully recovered, was hard on her heels.

"They are not here," the boy announced, stating the obvious.

"Dee told me she was going to help my mother. They can't be outside. It is still raining."

The sound of someone talking drifted from two rooms away. The children set off at a lick. The two sisters were watching television.

"A cooking show, I might have guessed," said Oliver. "Does that mean we'll have something new for dinner, Mom?"

"Not unless you've found a side of venison in the freezer," Julia replied.

"Not venison, but granddad's diary. It was in the library."

"Figures," Dee remarked. "Was it easy to find?"

"No," Spencer answered. "Olly was searching in the desk drawers, at the same time telling me about the engraved messages on the lid of the inkwell and blade of the letter opener. I was looking in a bookcase. He gave me this long explanation of how he had worked out that the letter 'I' was not to be taken literally, but stood for the word eye, E - Y

- E. The phrase actually meant: *An eye of the eagle*. Anyway, at that very moment, I spotted a book with a one word title on the spine: *Eagle*. Removing it from the shelf, an eagle's head was embossed on the cover, with its eye made from a tiny flat round bead made of pearl."

"That's not all," Oliver interjected. "It was not a book at all, but a leather-bound box."

"Was it locked?" Julia asked, intrigued.

"Yes, but there was a slot in the side, so I used the blade of the letter opener."

"It only took a second and we were inside. *Et voilà!*" Spencer exclaimed. With pride, she held up Chance's diary.

––––––

The television having been turned off, the four of them took turns reading extracts from the journal.

There was a detailed description of Chance Norton arriving in Port Douglas for the first time, as part of a one-off lake cruise starting at the Harrison Hot Springs. While the rest of the visitors toured the abandoned town, Chance wandered the top end of the smaller lake and spotted a lone house on the west shore. Walking nearer he was confronted with a large sign announcing:

PRIVATE PROPERTY
TRESPASSERS WILL BE SHOT.

Ignoring the warning, he stepped onto the front porch and looked through a window. Much of the furniture was covered with dust sheets. Finding nobody at home he returned to the east side of the lake. There he met Morning Star, who informed him the owner had abandoned the dwelling years ago, although she knew not why.

"Is it for sale?" Chance had asked.

"That's anyone's guess," he was told.

"Do you know his name?"

"William Hayes. Where he is now, I don't know."

"Then I shall have to find him," Chance declared.

"Good luck with that," Morning Star responded, not taking the visitor's resolve seriously.

However the caretaker was wrong. Overhearing some gossip during a trip to Tipello airport to pick up supplies, Chance learned that William Hayes was a compulsive gambler. Consequently, he set about improving his poker play, studying books on game theory, probability, and reading one's opponents for telltale signs. Months later he returned to the card tables. Not only did he win the pot, leaving Hayes penniless, but Chance also cashed in the IOU, with the lake house as collateral, written by his hapless opponent.

One entry, Dee read, described starting the restoration of the house.

Then she hit the all-important account of when her father, unable to rectify the injustice of the death of Running Bear, doubled down on his commitment to recover the relic. Consequently, Chance Norton returned to the casino, hoping to question Hayes further. However, to his dismay, he learned the gambler had been killed in a brawl over a woman.

The narration abruptly ceased, save for a short note saying Chance was returning to the Book House for the winter.

"That's that then," Dee declared.

Julia silently continued turning blank pages. "Hold on. There's more stuff toward the back. Nothing of much interest, I'm afraid. Just a list of the books acquired during his visits to Hartzell." She turned another page. "Wait a second. There's one last entry. Chance picks up on his narrative about the artifact."

Spring is finally here, and I'm able to return to my quest. Will start again with the casino."

The entry prompted Dee to wonder why their father decided there was mileage in returning to the casino?"

"If we can pinpoint which casino, maybe we'll find out," Julia replied.

"Hmm," Dee pondered, "Sounds like a task for Harper and Federico."

"My ears are burning. Have we missed something?" Federico asked as the two men retuned from Port Douglas.

CHAPTER TWENTY-SEVEN

JULIA ENQUIRED ABOUT THE MEN'S SOAKING WET CLOTHES. THEY explained that despite numerous attempts, they were unable to get the truck to start. In the end, Harper suggested Morning Star borrow the Land Rover for her trip to Tipello, and while she was there to purchase a new battery. Consequently, not risking the Winnebago to the rickety bridge, they walked back to the house.

"Why don't the pair of you change into some dry gear? Then the children can tell you what they've discovered while you were away. Meanwhile, I need to check on Ophelia."

"And I'll start preparing the evening meal," Dee volunteered.

———

Oliver told Federico and his father about how they had found Chance's journal concealed inside a leather-bound box in the library. Next, Spencer enlightened them on how, after reading some of the entries, Chance wrote about winning the deeds to the house in a poker game.

"From William Hayes." Oliver blurted out.

"Hmm. I wonder if he is the one who disposed of the relic?" Harper wondered.

"Possibly," Spencer agreed. "On the same page, Chance wrote about his decision to try and recover the stone."

"Obviously, Norton was not successful otherwise the stone would again be in the possession of the local tribe," was Federico's contribution. "Does the diary tell us anything else?"

"Maybe not in plain text, but there might be some secret writing in the margins," Oliver suggested. "I'll go fetch it and you can see for yourself."

"Bring the ultraviolet lamp, at the same time," Spencer advised.

A couple of minutes later, having returned, the lad quickly opened the journal to the correct page.

"There, I suspect." Harper pointed. "Where the paper is slightly discolored."

Lamp plugged into the nearest wall socket, the open diary was placed under the light.

"Oh, no. I don't believe it." Federico, who had been looking over Harper's shoulder, announced. "There is a note but it's so faint, you cannot read anything."

Undaunted, Harper asked his niece if he could borrow her spectacles. Using one of the lenses as a magnifier, he informed the others, "It's very faint, but I can make out the word:

Shaughness.

I wonder where that is?"

The lounge door opened and Dee walked into the room. "Cold cuts this evening, guys. We eat in twenty minutes, okay? Everyone go wash up."

While the children and Federico left their seats, Harper remained on the couch, still holding the diary.

"No exceptions. That includes you, Harper."

"Yes, siree," he replied. "Quick question, though. Have you heard of a place called *Shaughness*?"

"If you mean *Shaughnessy*, it's a neighborhood in central Vancouver. Started in the early 1900s, the undertaking was meant as an alternative to the West End, which was the traditional home for the city's budding elite."

After setting the book on the table next to the banker's lamp, Harper stood up. "I wonder why your father would make reference to that in his journal?"

"Shaughnessy is very upmarket, Harper. I recall reading a newspaper article on a 16,000 square foot mansion, built around 1915, on sale for twenty-seven million. If I were to make an informed guess, that could well be a district where a well-heeled collector of antiquities might reside."

"Something prompted Chance to visit the area?" Harper surmised. "How large is this neighborhood?"

"Too large for you to go from door to door, if that's what you're proposing," Dee informed him.

"Then we need another approach. Over dinner, I'll ask if anyone has a bright idea as to how we might proceed."

CHAPTER TWENTY-EIGHT

As the group sat around the table eating sliced roast beef, honey ham, and salami, together with fresh tomatoes and new potatoes, the discussion centered on art galleries to be found in Vancouver. Breaking the house rule about using laptops or tablets during mealtimes, Julia did a quick search. "There are thirty-three listed on the Internet."

"It could take days visiting each one," Federico decided.

Harper agreed. "And there's no guarantee we'll find the buyer. They may well be a private collector who does not own a retail outlet."

"Perhaps we are going about this the wrong way," Dee asked rhetorically. "Chance Norton spent a lot of time improving his card-playing in order to beat William Hayes at poker. Maybe we can find out which casino William Hayes visited most often?"

"How are we going to do that?" Spencer asked. "There must be dozens."

"Let's find out, shall we?" Julia proposed. Another quick search on the Internet and she began reading for the list pinpointed on Google Maps. "River Rock Resort. Yukon Gold. Lazy Fox. Parq Casino ..."

"Stop!" Oliver exclaimed. "It's the Lazy Fox."

"What makes you think that, son?" Harper inquired.

"Because granddad liked to leave cryptic clues. One was *the quick brown fox jumps over the lazy dog.*"

"Clever lad, Olly," Dee declared. "You could be right. I'll make a phone call and we can find out. Julia, what's their phone number?"

———

"Lazy Fox Casino. This is Lindsay. How can I help today?"

Dee began by introducing herself as an associate professor at the University of Vancouver's Anthropology Department. She explained that she was trying to track down a native artifact, and had reason to believe at one time it came into the possession of a William Hayes.

"Look lady," Lindsey responded, frostily, "this is a casino; not a museum. Unless you want to make a reservation for dinner, stop taking up my time."

Unfazed, Dee spoke in a soft voice, "There's a substantial reward for anyone able to assist with its recovery."

"Yeah, yeah. Pull the other one."

"Twenty thousand dollars."

There was a long pause as Lindsay processed the amount. "You're serious?"

"I am. Twenty thousand dollars if you can provide me with pertinent information."

"What's the guy's name again?"

"William Hayes. I'm told he used to frequent your casino some seven or eight years ago."

"Before my time. I've only been a croupier here for three years. Sorry."

Instead of hanging up, Dee persisted, "You might still share the reward. Even a snippet of information could qualify."

"Really. Like if I ask Jean-Paul to speak with you? He's been a barman at the Lazy Fox ever since it opened."

"Sounds promising. Is he available right now?"

The casino's phone was placed on the counter. Dee waited for almost five minutes. About to give up, a man with a strong French-

Canadian accent spoke. "Lindsey tells me you are asking about William 'ayes."

"That's right. Do you recall Hayes frequenting your establishment years ago?"

"'ow could I forget, 'e was one of our best customers. Compulsive gambler; 'e would win some, but more times lose. Though 'e did have one big winning streak. Amassed over two 'undred thousand dollars. Claimed the seed money, which came from selling an India relic, was the source of 'is good fortune." Jean-Paul chuckled. "Lost it soon after, 'owever. To some 'ick who wore a buckskin jacket and 'igh leather boots, as I recall. Took all of 'ayes' money; 'is 'ouse as well."

"I see. That's very helpful, Dee confirmed. "Do who know to whom Hayes sold this relic?" The University wishes to restore it to the First Nations people."

"'ayes never said. What's this relic made off?"

"Jade, I've been told," Dee replied.

Another chuckle, this time more forceful. "If that is the case, the person who bought I must have been *fous*. 'ow you say? Crazy. Jade is easily quarried in the Frazer Valley. Great big boulders of the stuff just lying around. One can obtain uncut jade for as little as $400 a kilogram. I know because my wife uses the gemstone crafting necklaces, broaches, and earrings. Regardless, 'ayes received $3,000; all $20 bills. I know because I saw them with my own eyes."

"Good information, Jean-Paul. Do you happen to know the whereabouts of William Hayes now?"

"I sure do."

"Do you have an address?"

"One Cemetery Row." Another boisterous laugh. "Died after a bar fight, I 'eard. Typical 'ayes. 'e always was the first to start a brawl."

"Hayes is dead, then?"

"Pushing up daises. Hold on *une seconde*."

Despite covering the mouthpiece, Dee could hear someone urging Jean-Paul to return to work.

"We need to make this quick, *la demoiselle*. Any other questions?"

"Just one. Did this Chance fellow ever revisit your casino?"

"Just the once. Spent the evening plying *le meilleur ami de* 'ayes with drinks. I don't know where this best friend is now, though. You might try tracking down Chance. Maybe 'e can give you answers?"

"Sadly, Chance is dead," Dee replied, trying to not sound like a grieving relative.

"*Deux morts*, 'a. Still, you can't win 'em all. Got to go or the manager will have my guts. Don't forget the reward," were the barman's closing remarks before he hung up.

"I don't think Jean-Paul was taking you seriously, sis," Julia commented.

"Maybe not the reward, but I believe he was truthful about the artifact being sold to a private collector."

Harper sighed. "This is so frustrating. Without an address, we are no further forward."

"Maybe there's another clue to be found in the house," Spencer suggested.

"Again, no guarantee we will find anything," Federico repeated.

"Agreed." Julia sounded equally despondent. "Any other ideas, anyone?"

Everyone looked at Dee as if she was an authority on such matters. "Let me think." She smiled. "Okay, I have it. If you sold something to someone, what do you expect in return?"

"Money," Oliver cried. "You sell something and get paid."

"And ... ?" There was silence as Dee tried to coax another answer. Choosing her brother-in-law, she offered an example. "Harper, imagine you own a car that you wish to sell. Let's assume you start by placing an advert in the local paper. I come along, we agree on a price and I pay you cash. Apart from my taking possession of the vehicle, and you handing over the title, is there anything else I might receive from you?"

Harper, not into the second-hand car business, was lost for a reply.

Julia, however, was not. "A receipt. I would give you a receipt to prove you had paid me."

"That's right. A receipt that would show *my* name and address, possibly *your* name and address, brief details of what the item was, and the amount paid."

"A receipt, which is given to the purchaser." Harper clarified. "Exactly how does that help us find the buyer, may I ask?"

"Because, if *I* was the seller, I would keep a duplicate for my records, just in case there was any comeback."

Federico, still the naysayer, was not won over. "That's a long shot, Dee. Given a copy existed, when Chance moved in he probably threw Hayes' stuff away."

"You could be right, Federico. But, let's say it was not Chance who cleared out Hayes' possessions. Let's suppose it was Morning Star. As caretaker, not sure what Chance might want to keep, she'd store the former owner's belongings in the ... Any guesses?"

"The attic!" Spencer exclaimed, so excited she nearly knocked over her glass of water.

"Precisely." Dee covered her mouth, suppressing a yawn. "You know it's hard work teasing answers out of you lot. I'm glad you're not my students, Spencer excepted."

"We should go look now," Oliver proposed, "and I think there should be a prize given to whoever finds it."

"We should finish dinner first, Olly," his mother objected. "Eat up your veggies."

Harper looked at the wall clock. "The children usually go to bed around nine o'clock. I suggest we stop searching the attic then. Tomorrow is another day. There are other places to look. The outbuilding, for example. Talking of outbuilding, may I remind everyone about the kayaks stored there? Any takers?"

"Me," Oliver was quick to announce. "I get first dibs. And Dad can accompany me."

"That's not fair," Spencer protested. "Why can't Aunt Julia and I be first?"

It was Federico who broke the potential impasse. "May I suggest, whoever finds the receipt gets *first dibs*, whatever that is?"

The Brazilian's last remark made the older children laugh.

"Oliver, Spencer, stop it. Can either of you speak Portuguese or Spanish?"

They shook their heads.

"Then be nice to Federico."

There was the sound of a horn tooting, as a vehicle arrived at the front of the house.

Harper left his chair. "I expect that is Morning Star, back from Tipello. I'm going to drive her back to the cabin. While I'm away, why don't you kids be polite enough to explain to Federico the meaning of your little catchphrase?"

———

It took Harper only a few minutes to drop Morning Star off at Port Douglas. About to return to the Book House his satellite phone rang. It was Julia telling him Ophelia was almost out of pull-ups. He needed to bring some stored in the Winnebago motor home.

"Look in the cupboards under the kitchen sink," he had been told. "And bring any canned food you happen to find."

Five minutes later, Harper was once more in the Land Rover. With three packs of training underwear, a box of tinned fruit, for good measure a six-pack of beer had been added to the mix. Looking forward to settling down to something more refreshing than iced tea, he gunned the Land Rover a little too enthusiastically crossing the bridge. The vehicle bucked in annoyance as it came off the planking onto the packed earth track. The phone, which had been placed on the empty front seat, bounced off the cushioning before skidding across the floor. Harper continued driving, not too concerned, as the device was designed to be waterproof and shock-resistant.

He soon reached the house, turned off the ignition and headlights, before groping on the floor for the phone. His fingers touched a bunch of keys. It was only after turning on the interior light, he saw the phone had slid into the far corner of the footwell. Loaded with provisions, keys, and phone, he went inside. With little thought, he placed the smaller items on the hall stand, before taking the rest into the kitchen.

"Hello," he cried, not seeing any lights as he walked past the dining room. Nobody was in the kitchen either.

"I'm back," Harper shouted, as he stood at the foot of the stairs. "Where is everyone?"

"Up here," Julia replied, sounding far away.

He proceeded to climb the first flight of stairs but no one was on the landing. "Where's here?"

Nobody answered.

"Come on, Jules. I'm not in the mood for hide-and-seek."

He heard someone giggling.

"The attic. I should have known." Harper, who had never been to this part of the house before, climbed the final staircase that led to the roof space. He opened the door.

"Boo!" Wearing a Halloween mask of a ghoul, Oliver sprang from behind a dressing table that had seen better days.

Portrayed as a fanged demon, a second figure appeared next to the boy. "Did we scare you?"

"Ever so, Spencer. I'm quaking in my shoes."

"There you are, Roger. I thought you got lost." Julia came over, hair, face, and clothes covered in dust. "Isn't this place amazing? Look around you. There's stuff here that dates back decades."

Dee joined them. "Want a flat iron?" she asked, holding the object in her left hand. "Or a bed warmer?" held in the other.

"Not at the moment, thanks. I usually send my suits to the dry cleaners, and I have my wife to keep me warm at night," Harper replied jocularly. "I see you wasted no time rummaging around up here. Has anyone found the receipt?"

"A few old newspapers and magazines, that's all," Dee answered placing her finds down on the dressing table. "So far, no personal papers."

"Well, I don't know about everyone else, but I'm all for calling it a day. I found half a dozen cans of beer in the RV, Federico. Do want to join me for a drink downstairs, before bed?"

The Brazilian came to the doorway. "Thanks, I will. But before you go, come take a look at what we have found at the far end of the room."

The others led the way. Harper followed.

Amongst a century's worth of bric-a-brac was a steamer trunk. The edges of both the truck itself and the lid were reinforced with angle iron painted black. Deep gouges supplemented its appearance, possibly from being in the holds of ships, loaded onto wagon flatbeds, and consigned to railway boxcars.

"I have only seen those in old movies, but none with a substantial padlock such as this," Harper observed. "Those initials branded on the lid lends to its character."

L H H.

Dee remembered the entry in the book on British Columbia she had been reading while sitting outside the cave containing the wall paintings. "Lambert Harrison-Hayes. Presumably, his trunk at one time. Locked, I'm afraid, Roger. It would be a shame to damage the latch trying to get it open."

"I've seen one of these initials recently?" Harper said to himself, as he stroked his chin. "I know. Downstairs, on the hall stand."

"You're talking in riddles, Harper," said Federico. "How many beers are left in that six-pack?"

CHAPTER TWENTY-NINE

PLANS TO RELAX WITH A BEER BEFORE GOING TO BED WERE abandoned, as Harper raced down the flights of stairs to the hallway. Returning with the bunch of keys he had found, he explained how he had spotted them after his satellite phone had slid onto the floor of the Land Rover. Concluding they must belong to Morning Star, he had planned to return them the next day.

"Won't she need them tonight?" Julia asked, concerned she might be locked out of her cabin.

"She'll be fine," Harper replied. "I saw her go inside. Much of the time, I don't think she bothers to lock the door."

"I thought she had given us all the keys to the house on the afternoon of our arrival," Federico reminded everybody.

"Obviously not," Dee decided. "Perhaps one slipped her mind."

"Perhaps she doesn't want us going through Hayes' things. Maybe it was intentional." Julia was having doubts."

"Regardless, unless we open the trunk we will never know who owned the contents. I vote we open it." Harper raised his hand.

Federico, Oliver, and Spencer did the same. Julia voted to wait and ask Morning Star first. Dee abstained.

With four votes in favor, Harper selected one key in particular, which had the initial H in the bow.

With a reluctant turn, the shackle released. He lifted the lid.

Welcome to a hotchpotch receipt nightmare, if you are an accountant that is. Invoices for lumber. Sales tickets for roofing shingles. A quote for the supply and installation of an electrical generator. An estimate for the whole house to be rewired. The cost of paint. A charge for re-glazing six windows. Income tax demands. Property taxes. Final income tax demands. Papers. More, more, and still more papers. All thrown into the trunk as if it were the definitive wastepaper bin. A quick review showed the majority concerned Chance's improvement projects. The tax demands belonged to William. Other documents went back much further. Included in the medley were old newspaper cuttings. If you were invested in a Stanley Steam Car - Model 7 Roadster, the November 1st 1910 edition of the *Vancouver Daily World* carried an advertisement of interest to you. A year later another clip recorded a diamond heist. Harper decided thievery was a trait that knew no temporal constraints.

"This is a disaster, Roger," Julia declared. "Somewhere in this mess, you're hoping to find a receipt for a piece of jade? I think not."

"We won't know unless we search," Dee said encouragingly. "Let's divide everything into three piles. Julia and Harper can sift through one. Oliver and Spencer, the second. Federico and I will sort the third.

We can check each other's work, making sure nothing gets overlooked."

"All right," Julia agreed. "I'll give it another hour, then I'm off to take a shower and bed. This dust is worse than summer allergies."

———

"*É isso aí!*" shouted the Brazilian. "I can hardly believe we've finally found the bill of sale."

"And Federico and I get first dibs on using the kayaks," Dee reminded everyone.

"Kayaks? Who cares about the kayaks? Now we are back on track to recovering the stolen jade. Show me the receipt, please, Federico."

Harper took the crumpled piece of paper. A carbon copy, pulled out of a genuine receipt book, the heading read:

Collector Of Fine Art, Antiques & Period Jewelry

Below the description and the price, the signature was that of a William Hodges. The seller's address showed Victoria; the province's capital city. By giving a false surname and abode, Harper suspected Hayes wanted to maintain his anonymity. At the very top of the letter-head was an address.

Selkirk Street, Vancouver

No name or house number, but even so. Harper was not averse to knocking on a few doors. In his euphoria, he missed the reference to there being not one but *four* relics.

CHAPTER THIRTY

ROGER HARPER REMAINED INSIDE THE BOOK HOUSE, PLANNING HIS trip to Vancouver and strategizing ways of obtaining the jade stone. Dee and Federico, on the other hand, were soaking up the sunshine, enjoying the start of a kayaking expedition.

The Brazilian confessed he was a complete novice. Consequently, after showing him how to hold the paddle, Dee spent some time teaching him the basic strokes of forward, back, draw, and sweep.

"You're a natural," she told him with a smile. "Are you sure you've never done this before?"

"The nearest I've ever come to being on a lake was as a very young child. With my parents, I visited a Rio de Janeiro Amusement Park. While my father pulled on the oars of a small rowboat, my mother and I sat back and took in the scenery."

"No lolling around today, partner. You set off. I'll follow."

Proceeding slowly to the center of Little Harrison Lake, all the time Federico's proficiency improved. So much so, that Dee suggested they be more adventuresome, and head for the larger body of water; Harrison Lake itself.

An hour passed. Federico rested his paddle across the cockpit's coaming and wiped his brow. Despite wearing a Havana hat, he was feeling the heat from the sun as it rose in the sky. The long sleeve T-shirt, which he wore under his floatation device, was soaked with sweat.

"I need to take a break," he informed Dee, who readily agreed they should paddle to the east shore and pull the kayaks onto the beach. Once there, she produced bottles of water and packs of corned beef sandwiches.

"We make quite a team," Dee remarked between bites.

"How do you mean?" the Brazilian inquired.

"You and me, the way we worked together, quickly sorting through the piles of papers yesterday evening. And just now, when we were on the lake, we were paddling in perfect unison, as though we'd been kayaking together numerous times before."

"I must admit, I am enjoying being with you, Dee. Your jovial manner has done wonders keeping me away from moods of melancholy. The novel I'm working on is starting to come together. I've already written the first draft of a dozen chapters."

"You must let me read them, sometime."

"It's early days," Federico professed, hesitancy in his voice.

"Surely you're not afraid of a little constructive criticism? As a journalist, I'm sure you've experienced the fury of the copy editor's red pen?"

"Not often. I like to think I was a very good reporter."

There was a long silence, Dee deciding not to push the point. Federico finished his last sandwich, took a long swig from his water bottle, and then lay back on the pebble beach. Resting his head on cupped hands, he stared at the occasional cloud drifting across his line of vision, thinking how peaceful it was.

Dee moved closer. The Brazilian turned to look at her momentarily and smiled. *Peaceful indeed.* His gaze returned skyward. After a few minutes, he sighed and closed his eyes.

He felt the tips of Dee's fingers drawing small circles on his left temple, a gentle motion that seemed to clear his head of troubling memories.

Federico opened his eyes once more. Again he smiled. A strong smile accentuated the dimples in his cheeks. "You have a soft touch," he told her. "I like that."

After shifting position, Dee asked, "Do you like this as well?" and then immediately kissed him on the lips.

Federico moved his arms and locked them around Dee's shoulders, pulling her closer. He felt an inner warmth that he had not experienced for over two years. The Brazilian wished this juncture in time would last forever.

Not so. Coming from the forested area away from the shore, a mournful cry interrupted that moment of reflection. Whether it was animal or human, it was hard to tell. The sound came again.

Dee and Federico rose quickly to their feet and began running. At the tree line, they stopped. Save for a bird screeching a warning to stay away, they heard nothing.

"False alarm," the Brazilian commented, catching his breath.

"No. Listen."

"Mama!"

"Someone is calling for their mother," Federico decided. "Possibly a child who is lost?"

The word was repeated. "Mama." followed by another, barely audible. "*Klahowya.*"

"What does that mean?"

"I'm not sure," Dee replied. "Let's get nearer. Maybe we'll hear the youngster more clearly."

Diagonally to their right, they slowly proceeded inland, weaving in and out of the cedar trees. With the dense overhead canopy, it felt like stepping into a darkened room.

"*Klahowyum,* Mama. *Klahowyum!*"

"It's Chinook Wawa. *Klahowyum* means, *I'm hungry, please help me.*"

The plea came again, and again. With each iteration, the cries grew louder.

The trees thinned, revealing a clearing thick with sedge and patches of clubmoss as ground cover. Except in the center, which exposed a steeped side depression. The sides were slick with clay, kept moist by the water runoff from a nearby spring. However, what focused their attention was a dirty-faced young girl, hair and clothes caked in mud, arms wrapped around her knees, huddled at the bottom of the pit.

"*Nika tseepie wayhut, Mama. Sick tumtum.*"

Dee translated as best she could. "The girl is saying she is sorry for taking the wrong path." Thinking for a second, she asked her name, "*Iktah nem?*"

"*Kwîhkwîsiw,*" was the plaintive reply.

"Don't worry. We'll get you out of there," Federico reassured her.

"How?" Dee queried. "We don't have any rope."

"Don't worry, I'll lift her out."

Dee watched as the Brazilian, laying on his stomach, angled his arms over the edge of the pit.

"I can't quite reach. Sit on my legs Dee, then I can lean further over."

Try as he might, Federico could not connect with the girl's outstretched hands. He told Dee to get up. The Brazilian did the same, and then to his companion's surprise, he jumped into the hole.

In no time, he had *Kwîhkwîsiw* in his arms. Dee was able to reach down and pull her up and out of the pit.

"Good job, Federico. You've rescued the girl. However, we still have one slight problem. How am I to get *you* out?"

"No worries. Just pull me up."

After three attempts, they gave up.

"I wish we had brought one of the satellite phones, then I could call the house," Dee speculated.

"Hindsight is 20/20 vision," Federico reminded her.

"I know. Perhaps I should go fetch Harper. What do you think?"

"That will take ages, Dee. Go back to the beach, and bring the paddles. The life preservers as well. I have a plan."

While Dee was gone, Federico kept up a one-sided conversation with the girl. He thought nothing of the fact there was no reply, as she probably did not understand a word he was saying.

He waited patiently; telling himself Dee would not be much longer.

"Where has *Kwîhkwîsiw* gone?" were her first words, as she approached the pit once more.

"What do you mean?"

"She's no longer here," Dee replied, sounding worried. "But getting you out of there is our first priority."

"You're right. Pass me one of those paddles."

Using one end as a shovel Federico began digging. Throwing the sticky soil toward one side, Dee stood, watching. Offering encouragement, she said, "You're doing great, but I'm guessing it will take a while."

"And there's nothing you can do to speed things along. In the meantime, why don't you see if you can find *Kwîhkwîsiw*? I'll holler if I need you."

CHAPTER THIRTY-ONE

AN HOUR LATER THEY WERE BACK ON THE WATER, HEADING towards the canal that linked the two lakes. Dee was in the lead, making strong, powerful strokes as she paddled against the current. Federico doubled his efforts to keep up.

"What's your rush in getting back to the house," he asked, breathless.

"We're not heading directly home," Dee informed him. "We are going to visit Morning Star and see if she is aware of a missing child."

Concentrating on paddling, trying to maintain pace, there was no time for a casual two-way conversation. Notwithstanding, Federico did steal the occasional glance at the shoreline. Respite came when they entered the canal, Dee reducing speed. Back on Little Harrison Lake, heading diagonally toward the caretaker's cabin, the couple was once more able to paddle side by side.

Dee spoke first. "I should congratulate you. Not only did you construct a ramp to shorten the distance you needed to climb out of the hole, but using those life preservers was pure genius. I wouldn't have thought of tying them together, dropping over the edge, and then using the loops like rugs of a ladder."

"Thank you, too. Fastening the top straps around that boulder was a great idea," Federico reminded her.

"Another example of teamwork," Dee replied. "It's a pity the girl wandered off, though."

"Are you blaming me for not keeping an eye on her?"

"Of course not. How could you? Stuck at the bottom of the eight-foot-deep pit, you could hardly be held responsible for *Kwihkwisiw* behavior. The fact I didn't find her was bad luck, that's all."

Billowing like ship's sails, a clothesline of bed linen could be seen as they grew nearer to the cabin.

"There's something I need to tell you, Dee. I know this may sound silly, but just before we went ashore for lunch, and also on our way back here, I think someone was stalking us."

"A stalker; how exciting."

"You aren't taking me seriously," Federico protested. "Someone in a canoe on the far side of the lake was following us."

"Is he following us now?" she asked, pausing in her stroke and swiveling around.

"No. He left as we entered the canal."

"Federico, it's not unusual for people to canoe on Harrison Lake. Close to Harrison Hot Springs you'd see dozens of them."

"We are a long way from the hot springs," the Brazilian reminded her.

"True. You know, partner, you worry too much. Although the idea of a stalker would add some spice to your novel. Why don't you weave that into the plot?"

Federico did not answer the question. Instead, he repeated to himself, *Partner. That's the second time today Dee has used that word.*

"We're almost there," his companion informed him as they approached the wharf.

Train of thought disrupted, the Brazilian switched to another question that had been troubling him. "Dee, do you think that pit was natural or man-made?"

"I'm guessing a bit of both. Probably a depression, which was deepened by some locals."

"But why?"

"To trap animals of course. Wild pig or deer, I expect. At one time, branches and brush would have covered it. There might even have been pointed stakes in the bottom."

"Good job there were no sharpened stakes in there today. If there were, *Kwîhkwîsiw* could have been seriously injured, or worse; killed."

Dee nodded her head in agreement, at the same time grimacing at the thought of someone being impaled.

Having looped her kayak's bowline over a mooring post, Dee deftly climbed onto the decking. The Brazilian tried to imitate her actions, but as he stood up the kayak began to wobble. He lost his balance. There was a resounding splash, which caused Dee to burst into fits of laughter.

"It's not funny," Federico protested, offering his hand in the hope she would help him climb out.

"Oh no you don't," he was told. "First, you need to wash off the mud from your clothes, face, arms, and legs. At the moment you look like a wallowing warthog."

Five minutes later, a cleaner version of the novice kayaker stood on the dock. After ringing the excess water from his T-shirt, he turned the left-hand pocket inside out and squeezed it hard. About to do the same to the right-hand pocket, he realized it contained an object. "Oh my gosh. I completely forgot. When digging, I found this bracelet in the bottom of the pit."

Dee took the ornamental hoop, and with her fingers rubbed the metal clean of mud. "There's a name engraved here. Not English though, and I'm unable to translate."

Federico looked for himself.

ρ·ⁿρ·ᒉo

"It must belong to the young girl. If we ever find her, we can give it back."

"I believe your prayers have just been answered, Federico. Listen carefully. That's the sound of children's voices coming from behind Morning Star's cabin."

As they walked around the side, the Brazilian asked, "Where is

Morning Star, by the way. I'm surprised she hasn't come out to greet us."

"That's because she's not here. Have you not noticed, her pickup truck has gone?"

They continued walking and found the open space between the cabin and the next building was empty. A door slammed, blown by the wind.

"The Community Hall?"

The couple hurried to the entry porch. Federico caught the handle before the door could slam again. He waited for Dee to enter first, and quickly followed.

Once their eyes adjusted to the dim light, she announced, "Things look different from my last visit."

"In what way?"

"The ping-pong table. It's now level. Before it had a slight tilt on the far right-hand side. There is no longer writing on the top, because now it is shiny clean. Furthermore, it looks as though someone has been playing ping-pong recently. There are a couple of paddles left out, and a ball is trapped in the net."

"The children we heard, I suspect," Federico concluded, "But they are not here now. We should try the caretaker's cabin?"

"Okay," Dee agreed. "It won't hurt to peek inside."

Like a puppy dog, the Brazilian closely followed, surprised when Dee stopped suddenly at the doorway. "You're not coming inside and dripping water all over the floor. Stay here. I'll only be a minute or two." With the door ajar, Dee paused and turned. "While you're waiting take off those shorts and ring them out properly. Otherwise Julia will say I didn't take enough care of you."

"Yes ma'am."

———

Inside, the cabin was just as she remembered from her last visit, without the owner of course. No found child, either. *Sadly, a wild goose chase,* Dee decided, no nearer to finding the girl.

About to leave, the light for the window reflected in the glass of a picture frame perched on the mantel above the fireplace. Curiosity aroused, she walked over for a closer look.

In the foreground, a woman, in her late twenties or early thirties, had an arm around a young girl. Both were smiling, the latter missing two front teeth. They were standing on the deck of a pleasure boat. The background showed off the clear-blue waters of a lake, and in the distance a range of snow-topped mountain peaks.

A feeling of unease crept through Dee's body. The phrase psychic chills sprung to mind, as she wondered if this was a clean-faced variant of the girl they had found in the pit. Before returning the photograph to its rightful place on the shelf, she looked at the back of the frame.

Momma and Blue Jay.
Trip to Hot Springs, 1979

Better times, Dee concluded. Before leaving she draped the bracelet over a top corner of the frame.

"You look half presentable," she told Federico who was patiently waiting on the porch.

"Thanks. No one home, I presume."

Dee nodded.

"Perhaps we should leave a message?"

"Saying what? That we found and then lost a little girl."

"Does make us sound rather foolish, I agree. Looking on the bright side, she probably comes from around here. I expect she safely home with her family by now."

"Let's hope so, partner."

The couple headed for the dock. The Brazilian settled himself into the kayak without capsizing. Dee did the same.

"Come on, Federico. Last one to the Book House puts both kayaks inside the storage shed."

Before she could shoot off, Federico managed to grab the rope at the stern of his companion's boat. "Oh, no you don't. No racing. My shoulders are sore from trying to keep up with you earlier."

"All right, no racing."

"Promise?"

"Cross my heart, I promise." Dee blew him a kiss.

About to set off, Federico cried, "Wait. I've just remembered something. As I was holding *Kwîhkwîsiw* by the waist, so you could lift her out, for a second I looked down to make sure I had a sound footing, That's when I noticed the girl had a tattoo on the inside of her left leg, just above the ankle."

"What color was it?" Dee inquired.

"Blue. The tattoo was done using bright blue ink."

"In the shape of a bird?"

"Yes. How did you know that, Dee?"

"A jay?"

Federico could not hide his surprise. "I'm no ornithologist, but yes, a blue jay. How do you know?"

Without answering, Dee began quickening the speed of her strokes.

"Hey," the Brazilian protested. "You promised, no racing, remember?"

"So I did."

Dee slowed, allowing her companion to draw alongside. "I can't stop worrying about the young girl," Federico confessed.

Kwîhkwîsiw will come to no further harm."

"Really?" Federico looked, bewildered.

"Yes, really." Dee grinned. "I know my winsome friend, because the girl we rescued from the pit is a ghost."

CHAPTER THIRTY-TWO

TAKING THE FOREST TRACK, THAT PARALLELED THE WEST SIDE OF Harrison Lake, the drive from Port Douglas left the three occupants of the Land Rover weary and sore. The constant change in gradient, the bouncing up and down, as the wheels lurched from one slab of rock to another, left Harper wondering if there was a better way to complete the first two-thirds of their journey to Vancouver. Eventually, they reached Harrison Hot Springs. From there it was further ninety miles to Dee's home, via Highway BC-1 West.

Choosing to retire early, Harper told Federico to be ready to leave for Selkirk Street at 9:00 AM sharp, at which time they would begin their search for the home of the person they had come to refer to as *The Collector*.

———

The weather favored their outing, with bright sunshine playing tag with scattered cumulus clouds.

Selkirk Street ran north to south, starting at Mathews Avenue and terminating at a fifty-five-acre oasis known as Van Dusen Botanic Gardens. Harper chose to start the search approximately halfway along the 1,500-yard thoroughfare, at the junction with King George Avenue. He spent a few minutes explaining to Federico that he would work the houses on both sides, heading south. If he had no success, he would retrace his steps and make his way north. Meanwhile, the Brazilian was to take a taxi to the nearest public library. There he was to inspect the electoral register for the inhabitants of Selkirk, and only Selkirk, seeing if he could find a cross match with anyone owning a registered business dealing in fine art. They would meet at the north end of the street at noon and compare notes.

Harper watched as Federico's taxi drove away, muttering to himself, "Now I've got you out of my hair, *amigo*, I can get down to business." His strategy was to saunter past each residence, applying his unique skill of entering people's minds, seeking anyone whose head was filled with thoughts of paintings, sculptures, jewelry, or ceramics.

Thirty minutes later, Harper, having had no success, decided the locale's parochial style of construction proffered limited appeal to a sophisticated art collector. Thus, he headed north, crossed the dual carriageway that was King Edward Avenue, and once more started his probing.

He came across a philatelist, a hoarder of gold bullion, and a collector of 1930s memorabilia. Further along, a housemaid was complaining to herself about the pile of dirty dishes left in the sink by her employer. At another home, a pool boy was wondering if it was the right time to ask the owner for a raise. None of the above got Harper any nearer to finding *The Collector*.

A UPS truck stopped on the opposite side of the road, the driver quickly exiting the van to deliver a package. Upon the woman's return, Harper asked if any homes in the area had regular deliveries requiring a signature from the recipient. He was met with a blunt, "Afraid I can't tell you, mister. That's confidential information."

A mind-meld realized nothing of interest. Why should it? Someone who purchased expensive items at auction would invariably use a specialist courier service.

Wiping the sweat off his brow as the morning grew warmer; he wished he had brought with him a bottle of water. Deciding it was too much effort to return to the vehicle he plodded on.

Harpers stopped outside a grandiose house where, on the circular driveway, a carmine red Porsche Cayenne was parked. The front door must have just closed, for he sensed two people in conversation; a maid and a visitor. The latter carrying a package, Harper surmised, for caller asked where it should be left. "In the parlor." he was told. "Ms. Norell will join you shortly."

Heart thumping, Harper slipped through the open gate. Choosing to hide behind the low-hanging foliage of a sycamore maple, he continued to eavesdrop.

"Robert, how good to see you. You've brought me something of interest, I hope."

"A Yuan Dynasty porcelain vase featuring artwork of phoenix, qilin, ducks, and fish."

There was a lull in the conversation. Harper assumed the item was being unboxed.

"Cobalt blue is not my favorite color. I thought you knew that, Robert."

"I do. However, my aunt is a little strapped for cash. I'm wondering if you might find her a buyer. Your usual commission, of course."

"Mmm. Good condition. No chips or cracks. Might fetch $80,000. A little more if we are lucky."

"Wonderful, Cameron. Simply wonderful. I'll leave it in your capable hands."

"Bullseye!" Harper exclaimed. About to leave his hiding place, he tarried a while longer. Making another incursion into *The Collector's* mind, he sought essential information required for his forthcoming nocturnal escapade. As soon as he had finished, Harper made a mental note of the house number, before quickly exiting the grounds and heading back to the vehicle.

By the time Federico arrived, he was already orchestrating a plan to retrieve the jade. However, not wishing to divulge to the Brazilian how he had located *The Collector's* home, he asked if his friend had any luck at the library.

"Nope," was the curt reply. "Lots of names and addresses, but nothing matched art dealers or collectors. You?"

"I think we have a winner." Harper smiled. "I happened to be passing one house when someone was removing a large antique vase from the trunk of a Porsche. I'd bet money that is the place."

"So what's next?" the Brazilian asked.

"Lunch. Then back to Dee's place to recharge our batteries before our next adventure."

"What do you have planned now, Harper?"

"*Amigo*, do you remember how, undetected, I snuck into Fulgencio Batista's office inside the former Presidential Palace, Cuba. Tonight, you and I are going to repeat the exercise, be it a different venue, and if we are caught we won't be facing a firing squad."

Federico shook his head. "Harper, I cannot believe you are proposing we break into someone's home to steal the jade."

"We're only liberating something that was illegally acquired in the first place, so believe it, pal. Prepare yourself to make mental notes during the coming night's events. You can use them to thicken the plot of the novel you are planning to publish."

CHAPTER THIRTY-THREE

Roger Harper and his friend, Federico, crept through the ornamental wrought iron gate, heading for the front entrance of the Norell residence. By Harper's wristwatch, it had just gone midnight, a time when all inside were judged to be asleep. The moon threw long sticklike shadows onto the driveway, reminiscent of the craggy, emaciated figures sculptured by Alberto Giacometti, the famous 20th-century Swiss artist. Unknown to the two aspiring cat burglars, a portrait painted by the same artist, that of his brother, hung on the wall of the study; their objective.

Reaching the porte cochère without detection, Harper placed his hand on the front door lock.

"What are you doing?" Federico whispered.

"Shush. I'm listening, checking if anyone is still awake."

Unknown to the Brazilian, Harper was busy focusing his telekinetic power on the lock. Feeling the deadbolt mechanism move, he pressed down on the handle, opened the door, and stepped inside. Federico followed.

In the darkness, the security alarm was responding to the opened front door by emitting a series of soft bleeps. Without hesitation,

Harper strolled over and entered a four-digit code into the panel. The sound stopped.

The Brazilian's next query was, "You knew the combination?"

Without explaining, Harper hissed. "Be quiet, Federico. Someone may hear you. The safe is this way?"

"How do you know that?"

Harper was losing his temper. "For the last time, Federico; no talking."

As they crept across the vestibule, unbothered by the intruders, a grandfather clock quietly ticked away the seconds. Four minutes had passed since passing through the front gate.

"This one is the study," Harper declared, in a low voice. "Don't ask," he added before his friend could speak.

He eased the door open, but as they entered the floorboards creaked.

Should have anticipated that, Harper reflected, pausing for a few seconds, making sure no sound came from the second floor to indicate someone had left their bed.

The Brazilian, once inside the study, gently closed the door, allowing Harper to turn on his flashlight. Wainscoting wall panels and a beamed ceiling evoked an ambiance of both style and wealth. In the bay window, he espied an antique desk and padded chair. A large fireplace, in working order, occupied much of the wall adjacent to the door, a mix of polished walnut framing and elegant Italian glazed brick tiles.

If I were a wall safe, where would I be hiding? Harper asked himself as he slowly did a 360-degree pirouette. *Not above the fireplace; too high to reach. In back of the tapestry, to my left? Worth a look.*

He gently lifted the drape away from the wall.

Not there. Behind the framed drawing on the remaining wall, perhaps?

While Federico remained near the door, Harper walked over to the portrait. He noted the signature, Alberto Giacometti, but the artist meant nothing to him. He squinted between the frame and the wall paneling. Using the flashlight, he could see the shadows of concealed hinges.

This has to be the place.

Reaching up, he touched the opposite edge of the frame. As he was about to pull it open, the satellite phone, tucked into the belt of his trousers, vibrated. Straightaway, he grabbed the device. His instinct was to silence it immediately, but seeing the caller ID was Julia, and given the time of night, he answered.

"What's up, honeybee?" he whispered.

"Speak up, Roger. I can hardly hear you," Julia replied.

"What's the emergency?" Harper asked, pressing the mouthpiece closer to his jaw.

Federico pleaded, "Are you nuts? You'll have the whole ménage awake if you are not careful."

Ignoring the Brazilian's concern, Harper continued his conversation. "Is something wrong?"

"Why are you taking so quietly, Roger?" Julia persisted. "You're not in *The Collector*'s house, are you?"

The question took her husband off guard. "How do you know where I am?"

"That's not important, right now. It's vital that you hear what Oliver has to say before you do anything rash. Hold on, I'll hand him the phone."

"Dad, is that you?"

"Yes, Olly. What is so urgent?"

"A short while ago, Running Bear came to me in a dream. After I woke up, I went to Aunt Dee and asked her to translate what he had said. Then I got Mom to call you."

"Go on."

"Running Bear told me that the return of the artifact must be voluntary. If the magic is to remain, stealing it back is not an acceptable way."

"I am not planning to steal anything, Olly. *Retrieving* would be a better word."

"Running Bear knows you are in *The Collector*'s home and are about to take the relic without permission, Dad. You have to persuade the lady to *huyhuy*."

"*Huyhuy*? What's that?"

"It's the word Running Bear used. It means to *barter* or *exchange*."

"I'm not sure I understand, Olly."

Having cracked the door, Federico urged Harper, to hang up. "I can hear someone moving on the landing. We need to leave now."

"Okay. Okay," was the response. "Keep your pantyhose on."

Taking his time, Harper said goodbye to his son, returned the phone to his belt, checked that the tapestry showed no sign of being disturbed, and nonchalantly walked through the doorway.

He boldly crossed the vestibule, unconcerned that Cameron Norell stood at the top of the stairs, a Glock 19 pistol in her right hand, a cell phone held to her left ear.

The Brazilian, who was hard on Harper's heels, was astonished that she did not react to their presence.

Reaching the front door, Harper grabbed Federico's arm, urging him to stop gawking at the woman wearing a dressing gown. As the two men stepped onto the porch, just before Harper pulled the front door closed, the Brazilian heard her say, "It looks like a false alarm, officer. Sorry to have bothered you."

"*False alarm, officer*. Those were her exact words, Harper. How could she have not seen us in the hallway?"

Harper continued walking, seemingly unconcerned, heading for the Land Rover parked a block away. "Beats me, *amigo*. Maybe she wasn't wearing her contact lenses?"

CHAPTER THIRTY-FOUR

DEE WAS EMPTYING THE DISHWASHER WHEN HARPER CAME INTO THE kitchen. Federico was seated at the table spooning breakfast cereal into his mouth, at the same time reading the newspaper.

"Coffee?" Dee asked.

Harper, trying to suppress a yawn, replied. "Yes, please. Black. No sugar."

"What time did you two get in this morning?" was his sister-in-law's next question. "Your friend here was rather vague."

"Around 2:00 AM. Did we wake you?"

"I didn't hear a thing. You must have snuck in like church mice. You didn't go clubbing did you?"

"No," Federico answered. "Nightclubs are not my scene. We were ... "

Harper, now sitting down, cut his coconspirator off with a loud forced cough.

"Not going to say, huh? Then let me guess. You were trying to retrieve the jade stone."

"What makes you assume that?"

"Courtesy of your wife, Harper. She phoned soon after she spoke to you last night. Trying to steal back the relic was a ludicrous thing to attempt." She brought Harper his cup of coffee, placing it on the table with a thud, emphasizing her displeasure. "What were you both thinking? You could have been arrested."

"But we weren't," said Federico, cheerfully. "*Mi amigo* [my friend] chickened out at the last minute."

"You mean after *tu amigo* [your friend] was told not to. There are few secrets between sisters."

The Brazilian picked up the newspaper and folded it at the sports section. On the reverse, a byline about the tourist industry caught Harper's eye.

"Let me borrow the paper for a second, Federico. There's something I'd like to check out."

"What's so important?" Dee asked.

It took a minute for Harper to read the article, and then he answered. "A tourist company is in financial trouble and has suspended operations."

"Let me see." Dee took the newspaper. "That *is* unusual. Harrison Lake and the Harrison River are beehives of activity for boating, fishing, hiking, and water sports. There's also the attraction of the hot springs themselves. You should take Julia there, Harper. She would enjoy the spa."

"You know I might just find the time to check it out," Harper replied. "Would you like to come with me?"

"Believe it or not, before you came down for breakfast, I suggested to Federico we go sightseeing."

"Suits me fine," Harper responded. "I've got to go and see the rental company about the RV. Being unable to return the Winnebago until that landslide on the forest access road is cleared, I need to negotiate a long-term discount."

"That's settled then," Dee concluded with a smile. "You go run your errands, while Federico and I enjoy our leisurely jaunt." Suddenly, realizing Harper had not eaten, she asked, "Are you only drinking coffee for breakfast? Not much in the refrigerator, I'm afraid, but there are some waffles in the freezer."

"Waffles are fine, thank you," Harper answered. "Do you have any maple syrup?"

"Of course. This is Canada, after all."

Dee retrieved a stack of four waffles and put them in the microwave. While she was doing that, Harper whispered to his friend, "Don't forget to take her out to lunch."

"Where?" Federico replied.

Harper pointed to the paper left lying on the table "Look in the ad section. Make sure you choose somewhere fancy. Pretend you are on a date."

"Your waffles will be ready in a minute. More coffee?" his sister-in-law asked; syrup bottle in one hand, coffee pot in the other.

"Yes please, Dee," Harper acknowledged. Then to the Brazilian he whispered, "Remember, *amigo*; date."

"Date? What date?" Dee sounded confused. Even more so when she followed up with, "Is there something wrong, Federico? Your face has turned bright red."

CHAPTER THIRTY-FIVE

HAVING CONCLUDED HIS NEGOTIATIONS WITH THE RENTAL company, Harper was pleased with the outcome. He had purchased the Land Rover outright and had parleyed a sizable saving on long-term leasing of the motor home. His next stop was Harrison Hot Springs. Once there he toured the hotel resort, purchased tickets to their spa, concluding by eating lunch at one of the outside tables.

Wondered how Federico was doing taking Dee on, Harper's words, *a date*, he laughed to himself. *Just like a schoolboy taking a girl to a high school prom for the first time, are you going to steal a kiss as well?*

From the restaurant, he walked the lakeshore. Out of curiosity, he spent some time in conversation with the proprietor of the company experiencing financial problems. *Perhaps a disgruntled employee is skimming off the takings*, he wondered, but that was not his concern. The owner seemed cheerful enough; optimistically hoping business would improve in the future.

Back in the Land Rover, driving away from the town Harper's satellite phone rang. He recognized the area code of 604; Vancouver. Thinking it might be Dee, he answered.

"I hope you enjoyed your lunch, basking in the sun?"

The voice was female, but not his sister-in-law.

"Who's this? How did you know where I've been?"

There was a slight chuckle. "If you must leave the GPS tracking switched on when carrying a satellite phone, what do you expect? I'd have presumed a house burglar would have more gumption than that, Mr. Harper."

"How do you know my name, and where did you get this number?"

"I have my means. Are you still interested in acquiring the artifact?"

"Ms. Norell?"

"Of course. Perhaps I am wrong, and last night's little debacle has nothing to do with acquiring the relic. Rather it was a chance to get the lay of the land, so you could come back another time to steal the *Giacometti* from my study."

"I don't know what you are talking about. Yesterday evening I was with my sister-in-law," Harper lied. "Nonetheless, I am still eager to acquire the stone. Did Chance Norton try to buy it back from you."

"Yes, he did. The poor man was so desperate, he offered twice what my father paid. At the time I declined his offer. However, circumstances change. If you genuinely want it, I have a proposition for you. If successful, I shall be happy to give the stones to you, gratis." Harper could hear the clicking of a keyboard coming from the other end of the transmission. "I see, on my monitor, you are roughly an hour's drive from my place. See you shortly." There was a pause before Cameron spoke again. "One more thing, Mr. Harper. A word from the wise. Turn off that GPS, for I'm sure the police can track your movements as easily as I can."

"But I don't know how?" Harper confessed, talking to thin air. *The Collector* had already broken the connection.

CHAPTER THIRTY-SIX

CAMERON NORELL POURED TEA FROM AN ANTIQUE RUSSIAN Samovar into a pair of equally exquisite Imperial Russian silver-gilt and enamel cups. "Please help yourself to milk and sugar. Personally, I take neither. Milk, so I've been told, negates the infusion's health benefits. Furthermore, sugar is called *white death* for a reason."

They sat at a window table, on what Harper considered uncomfortable Eastlake dining chairs. Taking *The Collector's* advice, he drank his tea black. Between sips, he nibbled on a ginger biscuit, gazing around the room, surreptitiously trying to appraise its contents.

"Before we get down to business, Mr. Harper, I want to show you a video recording made in the early hours of this morning." Cameron turned on the tablet computer that had been earlier placed on the table. She swiveled the device so that her guest was not looking at the recording upside down.

"You will recognize the study, no doubt. The view is taken from the mantel over the fireplace. One of the pair of Chinese porcelain cats has a miniature camera concealed behind its left eye. That's you I believe, walking over to stand in front of my latest acquisition, recently purchased at Sotheby's London Auction House. A bona fide art connoisseur would know what the painting is worth. Give me your best estimate."

Waiting for an answer, *The Collector* concentrated intently on her guest's eye movement, looking for any tell that might indicate he was a fraudster or a charlatan.

"How can I, if I was never in the room?" Harper responded, presenting his best poker face. "One cannot see the intruder from the front. It certainly not me."

"Stop playing games, Mr. Harper." She reached over and fast forwarded the recording to the moment his satellite phone vibrated. "As soon as the device became active, a sniffer device, located in my basement was able to discern your phone number, as well as that of the caller, together with your entire call history. Additionally, it ascertained the GPS tracker was active, allowing me to determine your where-abouts this afternoon. But you know that already."

The Collector sideswiped the tablet to bring up a close-up image of the canvas itself.

Harper remembered the artist's signature, that he had read less than thirteen hours before, but nothing else. However, after a quick foray into Cameron's mind, he was able to gather enough information to formulate his reply. "What I am looking at shows all the characteristics of Giacometti's style. Typically, as we see here, he paints his portraits with quick, rough brush marks, using limited colors. In this instance, the grays give the painting an unfinished quality." Harper touched the screen with his fingers. "See how the lines are drawn and redrawn showing the artist is concerned with getting the correct measurements, but they are never quite right. One feels he might continue to do so into infinity."

"I'm impressed, Mr. Harper. I could not have described the work better myself. Anything else you might add?"

Harper touched his chin, pretending he was in deep thought. "I must confess, the framing has a heavier emphasis than the majority of his paintings. You can authenticate its providence, I presume?"

Cameron smiled and politely nodded, deeming such an audacious question did not warrant a verbal response.

"In that case, I congratulate you on acquiring a previously undiscovered masterpiece. Given this rendition is very similar to his 1959 'Diego' I thinking the reserve was in the region of 200,000. You probably paid around 400,000. I'm talking US dollars."

Cameron clapped her hands together in delight. "I paid £285,000. That's equivalent to just over $490,000 Canadian or $382,000 US. For the price, I consider it a steal."

At the mention of the word *steal,* the room filled with a pervasive silence. However *The Collector* quickly regained her composure.

"You clearly know the fine art market, Mr. Harper. Since we've already determined it was you in the study, let's listen carefully to your part of the conversation with the second caller."

Once the video was correctly queued, she touched the play button.

> "*Yes, Olly. What is so urgent?*"
>
> [Incoming conversation inaudible]
>
> "*Go on.*"
>
> [Incoming conversation inaudible]
>
> "*I am not planning to steal anything, Olly. Retrieving would be a better word.*"
>
> [Incoming conversation inaudible]
>
> "*Huyhuy? What's that?*"
>
> [Incoming conversation inaudible]

"Almost immediately after that, you hesitated, deciding not to open the hinged frame of the painting. Evidently, the caller warned you not to do so, since Olly knew about *Hugh Hay.*"

"*Hugh Hay?*" Harper repeated.

"Yes. Hugh Hay, my security consultant. Amongst other things, he is the one who installed the trip switch, behind the picture frame. It's on a separate circuit to the house alarm. If you had tried to access the wall safe, it would have sounded a siren."

"How did your associate know about Mr. Hay?"

"I plead The Fifth," Harper replied, concealing the fact the phone call was unrelated to her security guy.

"No matter, Mr. Harper. Aside from your misstep with the satellite phone, I'm impressed. You seemed to be knowledgeable about fine art.

Also, you have contacts that can gain information on your intended targets, be it in my case received at the very last second."

Harper graciously replied, "I'll take that as a compliment."

"When we first spoke on the phone today, I said I had a proposition for you. Before I explain in detail, allow me to escort you to the dining room. I would appreciate you looking at another oil painting, and giving me your opinion."

The Queen Anne dining table and eight chairs impressed Harper. As did the Louis XVI crystal chandelier, a focal point for the ornate Edwardian plaster ceiling rose and cornice skirting. However, his attention was inescapably drawn to the oil painting, set in a 28-inch wide by 24-inch high frame, on the far wall.

"Well?" Cameron asked, expectantly.

Again relying on his mind probe, Harper began, "*War Canoes, Alert Bay,* painted by Canadian artist Emily Carr in ..." There was a pause as Harper struggled to interpreted the complex thoughts swirling in *The Collector's* mind. "... in 1908. Not to be confused with her 1912 rendering, which has a group of people standing in the immediate background."

"Everything you have told me so far, I could have obtained from Wikipedia. Surely, Mr. Harper, you can do better than that?"

Harper looked more closely. "Strange. If I recall correctly, the original was a watercolor. This is oil."

"Carr has been know to create copies in a different medium," *The Collector* countered. "The 1912 version is a good example."

Harper, not to be deceived by her subterfuge, muttered, "Huh," and then asked, "You wouldn't, by chance, happen to have a magnifying glass handy?"

"Will a jeweler's loupe, do?" Cameron removed a chain from around her neck, from which the lens hung.

"A fake, if I'm not mistaken," he declared. Seeing Cameron's face twitch, Harper added, "Or, if you prefer, a reproduction. I won't bore you with the old witticism about the difference between the two."

"Yes, Mr. Harper, you are correct. A reproduction. Tell me how you reached that conclusion."

"The simple giveaway is the absence of cracking in the canvas. What I'm looking at is nowhere near a hundred years old."

"It was painted to replace the original taken by my prodigal older brother. Before my father died, apart from a small trust fund, he cut Tommy out of his will, leaving everything to me. That presented a predicament for my brother. Having developed an unquenchable thirst for fast cars, fast women, and hard liquor, he soon burned through his endowment. Hence, Tommy resorted to petty theft to refill the empty coffers."

"Having no siblings I've been spared such an ordeal. However, you have my sympathy, Ms. Norell."

Cameron continued, "Taken illegally, and sold to an attorney who lives in the suburbs of Victoria, I tried to buy it back. However, the man was not prepared to sell, not for twice the price."

"A story that sounds familiar," Harper reminded her.

The Collector ignored the remark. "Which brings me to my proposition. If you can recover the authentic Carr painting for me, I will be more than happy to return the relic to you."

Harper decided this was the best deal he was going to get, even if he now had to 'liberate' a painting rather than a piece of jade.

"May I take this painting with me?" he requested, nodding in the direction of the one hanging on the dining room wall.

"If you must, but may I ask why you need it?"

"I am going to swap the two paintings. It's as simple as that. Hopefully, this attorney you speak of knows more about the law than he does about the effects of aging on oil paintings."

"You have a plan?" *The Collector* inquired.

"Working on it," was the brusque reply.

CHAPTER THIRTY-SEVEN

HAVING BOTH BUSINESS AND HOME ADDRESSES OF THE CURRENT owner of the original Emily Carr painting, Harper decided to obtain the measure of the man by taking a trip to Victoria. Noting that Alistair Lockward was an immigration attorney, he decided the perfect approach would be to arrange an appointment for a consultation. In his initial phone call, he told the receptionist that his family had recently inherited property in British Columbia, and were considering applying for Canadian citizenship. Furthermore, he specifically asked to meet with Lockward, as he was highly recommended by a business associate.

So it was, at 10:20 AM, Harper drove the Land Rover into the parking lot of 1110 McKenzie Avenue. After making a mental note that a Tim Hortons fast-food restaurant occupied the ground floor of the premises, he ascended the stairs to the second floor. The bronze plate announced LOCKWARD & ASSOCIATES. IMMIGRATION LAW. On the plate-glass door, etched in finer print were the names of the partners: Alistair Lockward, Tobias Marks, and Nicole Tremblay.

The receptionist smiled sweetly as Harper entered the lobby. Confirming he had a 10:30 appointment, he was shown into a well-appointed conference room, with a highly polished cherry wood table capable of seating sixteen people. In contrast, the view out of the far-end window exposed a scorched grass soccer field, adjacent to an architecturally uninspiring elementary school.

On the walls were six oil paintings. Harper walked over and inspected the signatures. All by Emily Carr, the fourth from the left portrayed the war canoes.

Harper was reminded of a quote by Mark Twain, *Fortune knocks on every man's door once in a life*. Today was that day for Roger Harper.

The ajar door opened wider. Presenting the very antithesis of the stereotyped courtroom lawyer, the gentleman wore a knitted sweater over corduroy trousers. Salt and pepper hair, crow's feet around the eyes, a slight stoop in posture; all supporting the conclusion of someone in their early sixties. Speaking in a kind voice, his handshake sincere, he introduced himself. "Mr. Harper, I'm pleased to make your acquaintance. Alistair Lockward, Esquire, at your service. I apologize for our meeting like this. My office is being redecorated at the moment. As a matter of fact, this very room will be next."

Harper smiled. "Not a problem, Mr. Lockward. You have quite a collection of Carr paintings."

"A hobby of mine, ever since a client approached me wanting to make some quick money. I was captivated and could not refuse. Previously, whenever the opportunity presented itself, I have acquired more. Alas, with today's auction prices, I fear that has almost certainly come to an end."

"If you don't mind me asking, Mr. Lockward, why keep them here. Surely you would prefer to view them in your own home."

The attorney chuckled. "We have a team of full-time security guards on the premises, day and night. Much safer than relying on a house alarm system, I can assure you. Although that is not the foremost reason. In truth, my collection is somewhat of a sore point with my dear wife. She frequently tells me I shouldn't wait until I pass away, that they should be sold and the proceeds placed in trust to further our grandchildren's education."

Harper cleared his throat. "No disrespect to your wife, sir, but I had no trust fund steering me through college. Had to scrimp for every nickel and dime. Nevertheless, I became a successful businessman."

"Quite so, Mr. Harper. Our receptionist gave me a summary of your earlier phone call. You wish to become a Canadian citizen, she informed me. Sit down, tell me more about yourself, and then I shall be better able to apprise you of our services."

———

The meeting lasted for just over an hour, with a brief interlude for coffee and donuts, the latter purchased from the Tim Hortons restaurant. Harper made up a story that he was a venture capitalist, wishing to spend more time with his family. Reiterating his wife had recently inherited property in the province, now seemed like a good time to relocate to British Columbia permanently.

"Where is this property situated?" Lockward asked.

"Port Douglas, at the northern end of Little Lake Harrison."

The attorney reminded Harper that there was little left of the town. "A handful of cabins, as I recall." It was obvious the man was struggling to maintain his composure; falsely assuming the inherited property was of little worth.

"Five or six cabins yes, but tucked away on the opposite shore of the lake is a rather fine abode, originally built for a prominent justice of the peace when Port Douglas was in its heyday. Furthermore, in recent years extensive renovations were carried out by my late father-in-law."

Harper continued to be quizzed, establishing that his wife's half-sister lived in Vancouver. He and his wife had two children, a boy and a girl. In addition, Julia's first cousin's twelve-year-old daughter was temperately staying with them, while her parents were teaching at a missionary school in South America.

The conversation continued, outlining the eligibility requirements to become a Canadian citizen. The attorney seemed delighted when Harper confirmed he had more than CA$300,000 available for investment. The proposal was to start an enterprise providing regular boat tours from Harrison Hot Springs to Port Douglas, with the prospect of offering employment to the local First Nations community.

Lockward became elated. "I cannot make any promises, but your business project is a very laudable thing, and will almost likely gain an endorsement from the powers that be."

He gave Harper several brochures and forms, suggesting he read them thoroughly. After he did so, with his right hand the attorney pulled the left sleeve over his trembling index and middle fingers.

Out of politeness Harper simply smiled, saying nothing other than, "Thank you for your time. If my wife and I decide to proceed, I'll call for another appointment."

Business complete, he had succeeded in establishing the location of the painting. Furthermore, while Lockward was talking, Harper surreptitiously instilled a fresh idea into the man's mind. Namely, before the conference room was redecorated, to ensure the Emily Carr paintings were adequately protected, they should be placed in a climate-controlled storage unit.

After he left, Harper, sitting in the restaurant, phoned Dee. He needed the name and address of the nearest secure storage unit to McKenzie Avenue, Victoria; one that offered climate control. A bowl of soup and a cup of coffee were consumed as he waited.

After Dee returned his call, with information in hand, one final task remained before he drove away. Harper went once more to the second floor of the building. This time not entering the offices, he trolled the minds of its occupants. Once he connected with the receptionist, he augmented the idea of the paintings being placed in storage during the conference room's redecoration, adding the name and address that Dee had provided.

––––––––

It was time to return to Dee's place, but not before Harper made the short detour to the storage company's premises. Once there, he hired a lockup of his own, paying cash for one month's rent in advance.

"By the way, I recommended your facilities to the law firm of *Lock-*

ward, Marks, and Tremblay, while they redecorate their premises. Let me know if they take my advice. Here's my phone number."

On the way out, Harper again recited to himself, *Fortune kicks on everyman's door once. Yes, indeedy. Swapping out the paintings is going to be a walk in the park.*

CHAPTER THIRTY-EIGHT

"WHAT'S WITH THE REQUEST FOR A CLIMATE-CONTROLLED STORAGE unit?" was the first question Harper was asked once he entered Dee's home. "And why are you so late?"

"I need to house the oil painting given to me by *The Collector* in a safe environment," he replied.

"In Victoria? Why not Vancouver?"

"If you must know, I went to see a highly recommended immigration attorney. Purely exploratory, in case Julia and I decide to live in Canada long term. As it happens, he is an avid art lover, with quite a collection of his own. We got to talk off-topic and he highly recommended a storage company near his office. He even got his secretary to write down the address. However, when I got to the Land Rover I couldn't find the sheet of paper she gave me. Not wanting to appear foolish by going back and admitting I had lost it, I telephoned you. My last port of call was inspecting the premises before I came back here."

Unconvinced, Dee responded, "Lawyers and storage units; hmm? Sounds like part of a convoluted scheme to recover the jade." However, before Harper could protest, she held up a hand. "Say no more. The less I know the better. By the way, I need to pop into work tomorrow.

Whatever you're planning, take Federico with you. That way, you can try to keep each other out of trouble."

Harper smiled. Everything was falling into place. Feeling in a generous mood, he suggested he take Dee and Federico out to dinner that evening.

———

The next morning Dee left the house early, forcing the two men to get their own breakfasts. The Brazilian was full of questions, which Harper patiently answered.

"Let me get this straight. You plan to swap out the painting while it is in storage, right?" Harper nodded. "So tell me," Federico persisted, "How are you going to gain access to someone else's lockup wthout a copy of their key?"

"You don't by any chance know how to pick a padlock, do you, Federico?"

"No. What makes you think I would?"

"Just asking, that's all. On our way to the storage units, maybe we'll pass a bookstore."

"And buy a book on lock-picking?" The Brazilian facetiously commented, "I bet we'll be spoiled for choice."

"Good point. Do you think Dee would mind if I use her computer, in order to access the Internet?"

"She let me use it yesterday, while you were on your little jaunt. I can still remember her password."

Federico remained at the kitchen table, sipping orange juice.

"Done just sit there. The sooner you log me in, the sooner I can watch a video on opening a padlock without using a key."

It took Harper only a few minutes to find the pertinent information. Federico, who had been observing over his friend's shoulder, remarked, "Looks easy enough. No fancy set of picks, just a metal clip from a pen cap and a bobby pin, is all one needs."

"Sure does." Harper opened a drawer in the kitchen cabinet and found a cheap ballpoint pen. After clipping it inside the breast pocket of his shirt, he placed his plate and coffee cup in the dishwasher.

The Brazilian watched.

"I suppose you are expecting me to clear your glass from the table as well?"

"That would be nice."

"Okay. I'll do that, while you go upstairs to Dee's bedroom."

"Without her permission, I can't," Federico objected.

"Yes you can. It's a bobby pin I need to borrow; not a lady's dress. Now, move it, *amigo*. I haven't got all day. Tick tock. Tick tock. Time's a-wastin'."

CHAPTER THIRTY-NINE

ONCE AT THE PREMISES OF THE SELF-STORAGE FACILITY, HARPER discovered he needed a padlock to secure his reserved unit. The proprietor conveniently provided one.

It took only a few minutes to place the reproduction painting in the steel-lined cubicle and lock the door. On the way out, he waved at the owner, who was still in his office.

Reaching the Land Rover, they heard a shout. "Mr. Jones, hold up." The man hurried to the vehicle. Out of breath, he added. "I meant to tell you. That law firm you mentioned called first thing today. They are bringing over their artwork tomorrow morning. Thank you for the recommendation."

"My pleasure. Have you assigned them a unit yet?"

"Of course, but I can't possibly tell you. Confidentiality, and all."

"Quite so. Rude of me to ask."

Grinning, Harper drove away

"What's got you in such a good mood, Harper? All the man did was say thank you."

"You're right, Federico. All he said was thank you."

The conversation lapsed into silence, with Harper concentrating on the Land Rover's GPS display. As he exited the city, Federico gazed out of the passenger side window, for lack of anything else to do.

Five minutes went by.

Unexpectedly Harper asked, "Do you still remember Dee's computer password?"

"Of course. Why?"

"Then do me a favor. Remember the number B68."

"Whatever for?"

"It's the unit that will house the attorney's paintings."

Coming up on the office building housing the law firm, Harper swung the vehicle into their parking lot. "Fancy lunch at Tim Hortons?" he asked. "They do a nice bowl of clam chowder. They also have cream of broccoli, if you prefer."

Ignoring the menu, Federico looked at Harper wide-eyed, and asked, "How do you obtain B68?"

"Because it was written on the back of the man's hand." Harper lied.

"Really? I didn't spot that."

"That's why I am driving, and you're not."

CHAPTER FORTY

"A donut for breakfast? You should be ashamed of yourself, Dee."

"At least I didn't scoff half the box last night. That was you and Federico, and not the mice, I'm assuming."

"Okay. I admit it." Harper poured himself coffee. "What are your plans for the day? Anything exciting?"

"I'm going to the university library. I need to review my students' reading lists before the start of the Fall Semester. What about you?"

"I'm going to see the immigration attorney again. Not about Canadian citizenship this time, but to see if he will sell the Emily Carr oil painting that *The Collector* so desperately wants."

"I hope you've got a deep pocket. Her work is in high demand. Are you taking Federico with you?"

"I'll ask him, once he decides to get out of bed. Enjoying a ride to Victoria or sitting in a library? I wonder which he will choose."

Moments later, the Brazilian walked into the kitchen.

"There you are, *amigo*. Dee and I were just talking about you."

"Accessing the attorney's storage unit; are you sure this is wise, Harper? What if we are caught on camera?"

"Stop fussing, Federico. There are no cameras in this part of the building. I checked, on my first visit."

"And you are going to pick the padlock?"

"No. I'm going to use a stick of dynamite. Now, go collect the reproduction from our lockup. Here's the key."

Alone, Harper chose the easier option of telekinetically opening the padlock.

A few minutes later, the Brazilian rapped on the door of B68. Harper sighed with frustration at such mundane behavior. He went to the already ajar door and pushed it wider.

"Come in, before you alert the neighborhood, and help me find the painting. And close the door after you."

Once inside, Federico, making no attempt to lend a hand, stood by the door watching as Harper, for the third time, rifled through the bubble-wrapped canvases.

"*Pare de ser cabeça dura.* [Stop being so hardheaded.] It's not here. Can't you see, the pieces you have gone through are larger than the one I'm holding in my hand."

"Put that painting down and check the cartons at the back of the unit."

"If you say so."

Minutes later, Federico pronounced, apart from a handful of packing labels, that the boxes were empty.

"That's that then," Harper declared. "A total wild goose chase. Let's get out of here."

After picking up the fake painting, Federico hesitated.

"What now?" Harper demanded. "Are you proposing we spend the night here?"

"Shush, Harper. Somebody is coming. I can hear them whistling. Turn off the light."

The whistling stopped outside the unit. There was a metallic scraping noise, followed by a sharp click as something snapped closed. The whistling started up again, fading as the individual walked away.

The light came back on.

Sounding annoyed, Harper asked, "Well?"

"Well, what?"

"When are you going to open the door, Federico?"

The Brazilian rattled the handle. "I can't. It's locked."

"Let me try."

Harper yanked the handle down and pushed. The door latch had retracted, but the door itself, restrained by a hasp latch, would not budge. He pulled and pushed a couple more tines. On each occasion, the closed padlock thumped against the paneling.

"Damn!" Harper exclaimed. "I told myself this was going to be a walk in the park. I spoke too soon."

"How are we going to get out? It's beginning to feel claustrophobic in here."

"Relax, Federico. Didn't I bust us out of Guantanamo Bay Detention Camp? Give me a few minutes, and I'll think of something."

Pressing his hand on the panel next to the lock, his eyes tight shut, Harper concentrated.

"What are you doing, Harper? This is no time for isometric exercises."

"Stop staring at me, *amigo*. You're making me nervous. Do something useful. Straighten up the paintings that the law firm placed in here, and insert our painting in the middle."

While the Brazilian sorted through the wrapped artwork, Harper, closed his eyes and concentrated. After mentally depressing the tumbler pins inside the padlock and rotating the spindle, there was a faint click. The locking plate moved and the shackle's heal was freed. He then attempted lifting the padlock itself in order to release it from the hasp latch. Try as Harper might it would not move, despite the odd curse thrown in for good measure.

Federico shook his head. "I saw you praying, Harper. Were you expecting some sort of Devine deliverance?"

"Leave out the sarcasm," Harper protested. "Do you have any suggestions?"

The Brazilian thought for a moment. "Have you tried talking to the padlock?" The response from his companion resulted in a blank stare. "That should work because communication is the key."

"Ha, ha. Very droll. Is that the best you can do?"

"Afraid so." Federico sighed. "You are supposed to be the brains of this duo. I came along simply to keep you out of trouble, remember."

"And how's that working out, huh?" Exasperated, Harper decided his only option was to call in the cavalry.

————

Two-and-a-half hours later there was another wrap on the door.

"Harper, Federico, are you in there?" a female asked.

The reply was in a whisper "Yes. Are you alone?"

"Of course, I'm alone. Did you expect me to bring the fire brigade? I told the manager I had brought you some items you forgot this morning. When he looked at me suspiciously, I confirmed the number of the storage unit you rented."

"Okay. I didn't ask for your life history. Please, remove the paddock's shackle from the hasp so we can get out of here."

Once in the corridor, Dee's props of empty suitcases in hand, the three of them began walking towards the exit.

"Hey! Just a minute." It was the owner who had shouted. "That's not your unit. You have no business being inside."

The trio stood still. Harper slowly turned towards the man and smiled. "Sorry. A simple mistake, I'm dyslexic, you see. Got the numbers mixed up. When I got here, I found the padlock on the unit was undone, so I went inside to confirm my stuff was okay."

As the owner listened, he frowned. "Must be a faulty padlock. Not three hours ago, I spotted the same thing. I thought I had closed it securely."

"Seemingly not. I'm told certain makes don't always lock properly. One brand, in particular, fails over fifty percent of the time," Harper added as if he was an authority on such matters.

They made to leave.

"Not so fast. Let me check inside. Can't have you stealing valuable paintings now can we?"

"Check away," Harper, replied, unconcerned. "All I saw was half-a-dozen gift-wrapped items. You'll notice the packing tape has not been disturbed."

———

Following Dee's car onto Highway 17, heading for the Swartz Bay ferry terminal, the Brazilian remarked, "Dyslexic, indeed. Since when?"

"I had to say something," Harper explained, "to account for us being in the wrong unit. It worked didn't it?"

"I suppose so," Federico replied, before lapsing into silence. However, he could not quite fathom how their unit, B55, would be confused with B68. Moreover, it was more puzzling that the owner of the storage units had not questioned the discrepancy.

Harper sensed wheels were turning in his friend's head. A fleeting mind-melt confirmed the issue. Just as he had placated the owner, he pushed the conundrum to the very depths of Federico's consciousness, never to be recalled again.

Was the same technique going to work on Dee, was the big question. *Let's hope*, Harper thought to himself, for he did not want any hiccups delaying his next plan of action.

CHAPTER FORTY-ONE

OLIVER AND SPENCER SAT ON THE STOOP OF THE FRONT PORCH, elbows resting on knees, hands supporting chins. Moodily staring at the ground, they did not hear Morning Star approach the Book House as today she was on foot.

"Why the long faces?" she asked. "You look as miserable as a pair of beavers who have lost their tails."

Startled, they both looked up. The boy was the first to speak.

"Last night we heard strange noises as if someone was roaming around outside. I told my mom but she doesn't believe us."

"We even said there was a glow coming from the trees, like a flashlight being waved around, Aunt Julia said it was a trick of the moonlight shining off the lake," Spencer elaborated.

"She could be right," the caretaker agreed. "On occasion, I've heard noises myself, when I've been doing a spot of cleaning. I shouldn't bother your young heads if I were you. Old houses are full of squeaks and groans. It's part of their job description."

"Maybe it was a ghost?" Oliver suggested.

"I'm not sure ghosts need flashlights," Morning Star responded, sharing Julia's skepticism. However, seeing the children's looks of disappointment, she added, "Could have been a person though. To be certain, you would need to find some evidence. A footprint, for example."

"Tried that already," Spencer replied. "Found nothing. Perhaps you could help us look."

"I've got better things to do with my time. My truck is playing up again. I've come to ask if I can borrow some spanners your grandfather kept in the outbuilding."

"Mom is in the kitchen. I'm sure she'll agree. Why don't you go inside?"

"Thanks, I will." Morning Star carefully navigated her way between the children, who remained seated. She opened the screen door, paused, and looked back. "You know, if you want people to believe you, you need to set a trap."

"Like a bear trap?" the boy inquired, wide-eyed.

The caretaker laughed. "Hardly. I recall you telling me you bought a dream catcher, on your way here from Vancouver. Suspend it by the handle from the porch ceiling." She looked up and pointed. "Use one of those hooks. During the summer, your grandfather used to hang baskets of rosemary and basil. Claimed they kept away the mosquitoes."

"A dream catcher is hardly big enough to catch an intruder," Spencer pointed out.

"Hang it up, exactly as I told you, before you go to bed," Morning Star reiterated. "Check again in the morning and let me know what you find."

"Let you know what?" the girl asked, but there was no answer. The screen door slammed shut, leaving the pair alone to speculate.

———

Early the following morning, Julia challenged the two children as they tried to sneak passed the kitchen's open door. "Where do you think the pair of you are going?"

"Outside."

"Not before eating breakfast, you don't. You have the whole day ahead of you. Why the rush?"

There was a quick exchange of glances. Spencer, shaking her head, indicated they should not disclose the reason.

"No rush," Oliver replied. "Any chance we can have waffles?"

"Yes, please. Waffles with *oodles* of maple syrup," Spencer added, full of fake enthusiasm.

"Okay, but I need one of you to volunteer and finish feeding Ophelia."

Oliver, looking for an excuse to opt-out, suggested he fetch the pitcher of orange juice from the refrigerator, leaving Spencer locked into Julia's questioning gaze.

"Okay. I'll do it," the girl responded somewhat begrudgingly. "Next time it's your turn, Oliver. After all, she is your sister."

"That sounds like a good idea," her aunt agreed as she left the table, handed the baby spoon to her niece, and walked over to the stove. "Small amounts at a time, Spencer. We don't want Ophelia to choke."

Oliver returned, filled two glasses full of juice, and sat down. Neither he nor his cousin spoke, wishing their ordeal was over.

"It's unusual for you two to be up so early," Julia observed, ignorant of the pair's ulterior motive.

"We're hungry, that's all," Spencer nonchalantly replied, giving Oliver a friendly kick under the table to stall him from answering first and spilling the beans.

"I suppose you were awake half the night, listening for strange noises."

"Busted!" Spencer exclaimed, happy to let her aunt reach her own, inaccurate, conclusion.

A few minutes later, carrying a plate loaded with waffles, Julia sat down at the kitchen table as well.

"Isn't this cozy? Everyone enjoying breakfast together."

"Hardly. Dad isn't here," Oliver reminded his mother.

"Neither is Rico," Spencer added. "He promised to teach me Spanish."

"Hopefully, they'll be back soon" Julia replied, trying to sound optimistic. "Which reminds me. I haven't heard from Roger in two days. I wonder what chicanery he's getting into."

CHAPTER FORTY-TWO

CHICANERY WAS NOT THE WORD HARPER WOULD HAVE CHOSEN TO describe the following night's exploits, but it was pretty close to the truth.

He looked at his wristwatch. Judging it was time, Harper sneaked along the walkway between a pair of detached houses, their rear gardens backing onto the cove's waterfront. He chose the home he knew to be owned by Alistair Lockward and his wife, Kay.

Given the late hour, the unoccupied terrace allowed him to spend time taking in the moonlit view across the bay to the mountains beyond. Otherwise lost against the blackness of the ocean, Harper observed the running lights of passing ships twinkling at the extremities of the vessels' silhouettes. He was reminded of lines from one of Henry Wadsworth Longfellow's poems:

> Ships that pass in the night, and speak each other in
> passing, only a signal shown, and a distant voice in
> the darkness ....

Harper's soliloquizing was interrupted by the mournful sound of a ship's horn somewhere in the distance. Consequently, he turned his attention towards the house; an ultra-modern expression of luxury and good taste. Deliberately remaining in the shadows, Harper closed his eyes and concentrated. It took no more than a few seconds to locate the two people who occupied the master bedroom. As they had done on countless nights previously, both slept peacefully.

Gently searching the lawyer's memory, without effort the mind reader pulled details of the week's events at work.

There it was. The spur-of-the-moment decision to remove one of the paintings taken off the conference room wall before the remainder went into the climate controlled warehouse. Brought home, it now hung in the library. Harper was relieved he had reached the correct conclusion as to why Carr's *War Canoes* was missing from the storage unit.

After further delving, Harper established the property's internal layout. The room where Alistair and Kay slept. Two more bedrooms, both unoccupied, fed off the landing.

Harper learned of the expansive living room, a showpiece kitchen, and an adjacent eating area. Additionally, he mentally surveyed the all-important library, and the even more important Emily Carr painting.

Now for the tricky part. Harper began to build a series of dream-like events in Alistair's mind, carefully orchestrating the way they played out.

A laptop computer currently occupied a small writing table, located in an overlooked corner of the living room. Plugged into a wall socket to recharge, ready for the next day, the owner thought nothing of the fact that a window drape brushed against the device.

The fan emitted an uncharacteristically loud whining sound, before finally stopping. As the computer's casing became abnormally hot, the desktop's veneer began to blister, producing wisps of acrid smoke.

Alistair groaned, unable to break out of the induced nightmare.

With a whooshing sound, the device burst into flames, that quickly jumped to the drapes. The fire then danced across the ceiling and down another wall. Finding more fuel in the armoire that housed a television, it spread to the floor.

The flames started cavorting, with fervor. The rug in front of the fireplace, the couches, and easy chairs joined the blaze.

It was the smoke alarm that roused the occupants. As they both donned dressing gowns, a metallic voice clamored 'Fire, Fire'. The home's central alarm system announced that emergency services had been called.

The bedroom door was cracked open, only to be hastily closed. Billowing black smoke had reached the landing.

Alistair went to the closet and pulled a heavy outdoor coat off its hanger. Like a shroud, he placed it over his head, and once more made for the landing.

His wife, taking the initiative, pulled her husband by the sleeve. "Oh no you don't, Alistair. You are not risking your life for the sake of a stupid piece of artwork."

Despite her husband's protests, she dragged him into the bathroom, wetted washcloths as makeshift masks, and stretched rolled towels across the closed door's threshold.

For now, all they could do was wait and pray for rescue before it was too late.

The dream switched to the lawn area in front of the house.

"Thank you. Thank you. We cannot thank you enough," the woman kept repeating, as she lay on a gurney.

"You had a lucky escape, ma'am," the paramedic told her. "I'm surprised the fire spread so quickly."

Overhearing the conversation, a fireman advised the other survivor, "You should consider having a sprinkler system installed as part of the rebuild, Mr. Lockward."

Wrapped in a blanket, seated on the rear step of the ambulance, Alistair looked up. "Believe me, I will," he responded. In his next breath however, he asked. "Did you manage to save the painting?"

"Not me personally," was the reply, "but my colleague did. Here he comes now."

"I don't know much about fine art," the second fireman confessed, "but it seems to have survived undamaged, despite being in the room next to the heart of the blaze. There's not a smudge-mark of soot to be seen."

The lawyer smiled as he took the painting. "It's a true miracle."

"No less a miracle, we managed to get out of the house unscathed," Kay told him. "Alistair, we owe these men our lives, and all you can do is worry about an inconsequential piece of art. The day you brought it into the house, I told you it was a bad idea. There are more meaningful things in life than oil paintings. As far as I'm concerned you should give it away and be done."

"You're right my dear, as always. Gentlemen, please accept this painting, as a token of our gratitude."

"How much is it worth?" one fireman asked. The other fireman shook his head, disapproving of such an audacious question.

"If you have to ask, you can't afford it," Alistair told them, with a chuckle.

———

Kay woke up with a start, to find her husband standing at the foot of the bed.

"Alistair, why are you wearing that great big outdoor coat?" Sitting up, she looked at the muddy footprints on the bedroom carpet. "You've been sleepwalking again, in the garden of all places."

Lockward looked at her confused. "Have I? I dreamed the house was on fire. We both got rescued, though, which would explain me being outside."

"Do I look as though I've been outside, you old fool? You forgot to take your medication, this evening, I know it." Kay concluded. Seeing her husband's shamefaced look, she continued to scold. "This is not the first time. Wash up and get back into bed. I'm going to check the rest of the house to make sure you didn't do anything else outlandish."

Ten minutes later, Kay returned. Getting under the bed covers, she turned off the light. Before she could get back to sleep. Alistair announced, "You know, dear, that painting I normally keep in the office, in my dream I gave it away to one of the firemen. He asked me how much it was worth."

"Don't tell me," his wife interjected, "you told him that corny joke of yours."

"As a matter of fact, I did. You know me to a tee, sweetheart. How many years have we been married?"

"Too many." For a while all was quiet. Then, Kay suddenly turned to face her husband. "What do you mean, the painting you normally keep in the office? Isn't it there now?"

"No. I brought it home, a couple of days ago. The conference room is being redecorated. It's hanging in the library."

"Alistair, are you feeling all right? I've just checked the library. There is no office painting in there; only that replica of Renoir's *Dance at Bougival* which I bought because it reminds me of our honeymoon in France. It was on the floor, propped against the wall. Did you move it?"

"I suppose."

"You suppose, huh. Is that all you can say? It's all that stress at work. If you ask me. You need to take more time off."

Her husband timidly agreed, praying the berating would cease.

"After tonight's fiasco, maybe I should give it away."

"I'm sorry, my love. It won't happen again."

"It had better not. Now go to sleep. It will soon be time to get up for breakfast."

———

Harper was on his way back to Vancouver. The original Emily Carr oil painting, protected by layers of bubble wrap, lay in the rear of the Land Rover. He savored how the mind-game had persuaded the sleep-walking Alistair Lockward to remove the oil painting from the library wall and present it to the fireman; the fireman, of course, being himself. The grand finale was when Harper carefully erased the last part from Alistair's memory.

If Julia or Dee quizzes me, he told himself, *hand on heart, I can truly say that I didn't steal the painting. It was a gift.*

Harper recalled the hackneyed joke Lockward came out with. *If you have to ask, you can't afford it.* The lawyer would never know that the mind reader did not have to ask, for he already knew how much the authentic *War Canoes* painting would likely fetch at auction; the repro-duction not quite as much.

CHAPTER FORTY-THREE

HIDDEN BY THE SHRUBBERY, SOMEBODY *WAS WATCHING* THE NORELL residence. They saw Harper park his vehicle in the driveway, walk to the front door, and ring the bell. After a short delay, the maid answered.

"My apologies for the late hour, but I have something the lady of the house will want to see." Harper indicated the bubble-wrapped package he had tucked under his left arm.

"This way, sir. If you will wait in the dining room, I will tell my mistress you are here."

The maid left Harper alone, wondering why this room, rather than the parlor, had been chosen as the reception area. Then he remembered Cameron was able to monitor his whereabouts using the satellite phone's GPS. He never could figure out how to turn the tracker off. Hence, she probably knew he had been to Lockward's law office, the storage unit, and the man's home.

As he waited, once again browsing the contents of the room, he recalled his last visit. Something was different. He tried to decide if the black cat on the mantelpiece was a new addition. Similar to the pair he had seen in the study, its left eye seemed to admit a dull red glow. *Another hidden camera?* he asked himself, as *The Collector* walked into the room.

A quick mind probe gave Harper the answer, which in turn prompted the assertion, "Spying on me, I see."

"You can never be too cautious these days. Only the other night, someone broke into the house." Cameron sounded jocular in her retort. Obviously, she had been informed Harper had brought something of interest.

The Collector walked over to the package, conveniently placed on the dining table. "For me? And it isn't even my birthday," she quipped, as she started to unwrap the item.

"I must confess, Mr. Lockward gave me quite the run-around. When I went to his place of work I discovered the painting, along with five others, was about to be temporarily placed into climate-controlled storage. With some difficulty," Harper exaggerated, "I managed to gain access to the storage facility, only to find it was not there. However, I correctly assumed the old codger had decided to take the *War Canoes* to his place of residence, at the last minute."

"So you went there," Cameron told him. "How resourceful of you. The majority of houses are notoriously insecure. It must have been a cakewalk for a man as resourceful as yourself."

"Not so much," Harper cautioned, as *The Collector* was about to remove the last piece of bubble wrap.

"What do you mean?" Cameron asked, genuinely surprised.

"At the last minute, I couldn't bring myself to steal it."

"Don't tell me you persuaded Lockward to sell you the painting? The old codger, as you call him, is no fool. He knows its market value."

"I don't carry that sort of spending money in my wallet, I'm afraid. So, no, I didn't buy back the painting either."

"Huh."

Harper could not decide as to whether her *huh* was an expression of surprise, disbelief, or disdain at his apparent failure. However, deciding not to respond, he watched as the exposed painting was held under the light of the chandelier.

He patiently waited, as the woman remove the jeweler's loupe from around her neck and examined the artwork closely. Unable to resist the temptation, Harper launched another mind probe, enjoying the moment as an array of emotions raced through *The Collector*'s brain. Confusion, wonder, excitement, joy, came to the fore. Her facial expression changed from a frown to a broad grin.

"You sly dog, Mr. Harper. You've been messing with me. This *is* the original Emily Carr; the one removed from this house and sold by my despicable brother. The cracking in the canvas confirms its age, but more importantly, my father's initials are penciled on the back. Tell me how did you do it?"

"Simple. I knocked on Lockward's front door, invited myself in, and we had a philosophical conversation about ships passing in the night."

"And that persuaded him to hand over the original?"

"With his wife privy to the conversation, yes. When she learned that you were the rightful owner, she told him it was the honest thing to do."

Still skeptical she asked, "And that's truthfully what happened?"

Remaining silent, Harper simply raised his eyebrows.

"I guess I'll never know. Anyway, it's time for me to keep my end of the bargain. Let us go into the study. The artifact is kept in the safe."

Ten minutes later, Harper was back in the Land Rover. With a box containing the relic tucked inside his buttoned-up jacket, he felt a warm sensation against his chest.

Is this an omen predicting a favorable outcome to the inevitable grilling I'll receive from Julia and Dee? Harper wondered. *Perhaps they will be so delighted at the relic's recovery, they won't pressed for details on what really happened? If the latter, without doubt, I shall be in deep doo-doo.*

CHAPTER FORTY-FOUR

"Job well done, old son," Harper said to himself, as he eased the vehicle's selector into *drive* and proceeded toward the gated exit of *The Collector*'s property. An ominous crunching sound came from the nearside front wheel dragging on the graveled driveway.

Leaving the Land Rover, he walked around the front and surveyed the deflated tire. "Darn," Harper vexed, regretting his premature self-congratulations. Notwithstanding, once the vehicle was jacked up, it took but a few minutes to remove the wheel and replace it with the spare. With one, two, three lug nuts in place, he picked up the fourth and began threading it onto one of the two remaining wheel studs.

"Just goes to show life is not all peaches and cream. Here's you, stuck in someone's driveway, needing to leave *tout de suite* [right away]." The words, delivered with a gruff voice, came from a disheveled-looking man in his early sixties. Wearing an open knee-length coat, his grubby white shirt was in keeping with the unkempt red hair. "Some vandal must have stuck the blade of a bowie knife into the rubber and released all that air in one big whoosh."

Harper looked up. "Who on earth are you?" were the first words that came out of his mouth.

"Roadside assistance," was the answer, conveyed in a mocking tone. "Here to lighten your load by relieving you of something of mine."

"You're talking gibberish, man." Harper redirected his attention to tightening the fourth lug nut. "I don't even know you."

"William Hayes. Does the name ring a bell?"

Harper stood up. "Really? I heard Hayes was killed in a fight over a woman."

"Sorry to disappoint you, *friend*. As you can see, I am very much alive. Not so much the other fella. I slit his throat, just before I passed out from being hit on the head. Do you want to see my war wound?" Without waiting for a reply, Hayes bent his head forward and parted his hair along the line of the crown to reveal a crisscross patchwork of scars.

Harper, still confused, asked, "What do you want?"

"The artifact, *mon pote*, given to you by Madam Norell, a few minutes ago."

"How do you know that?" Harper was still baffled.

"You have a hidden microphone attached to the underside of your jacket's left lapel. I put it there during your lunch at the Hot Springs Hotel. You really should take more care of your personal possessions. You are lucky nobody stole it when you went to the bathroom. I've been listening to your conversations for days now."

Snatching at his jacket collar Harper fumbled for a second, before feeling a small round plastic object. With a wrench, he pulled on the Velcro attachment and threw the device to the ground, before smashing it with the heel of his shoe.

"Clever," Harper conceded. "When did you start keeping tabs on me?"

"Soon after your arrived. A buddy, who lives in Tipello, alerted me. Lights on in my house were the giveaway that strangers had taken up residence. So I came to take a look."

"*Your* house. You lost it playing cards with my father-in-law, Chance Norton."

"Bah! I couldn't quite figure out the connection, but now I know. The weasel plied me with whiskey and then talked me into a game of poker. But with the relic back in my possession, my luck will change."

"What makes you think that?" was Harper's next question, asked as he walked back around the vehicle to stand directly opposite Hayes.

"Don't come any closer. I have a gun."

"Oh yeah." Ignoring the warning, Harper took a step forward, only to stop abruptly when his adversary drew his weapon.

"Nobody needs to get hurt. Just hand over the stones, and I will be on my way." Harper noted the man's hand was shaking as he spoke.

"Nervous are we? You don't have it in you to pull the trigger."

"What's in your hand?" Hayes asked, as his opponent lifted his right arm.

"Oh, this?" Harper spread his fingers to reveal the Land Rover's fifth lug nut.

The gunman laughed. "You're going to assault me with that? I don't think so. Drop it on the ground or I'll shoot you right now." Hayes instructed, sounding more confident.

"Nobody is going to shoot anybody," Harper spoke with authority as he let go of the nut, which, upon hitting a compacted section of the driveway, rolled a few inches towards the aggressor.

"Enough of this nonsense. Give me the stones, right now."

"Go ahead, shoot," said Harper, baiting his adversary. "Let's count to three, shall we. One ..."

"What are you? Some kind of nutcase with a death wish?"

"Two ..."

"Wait a second. I've read about the likes of you, claiming to have the ability to control people's minds. If you think you can get inside my head, you're mistaken."

"Let's find out, shall we?" Harper replied softly, trying to probe the man's brain. "Why don't you turn the weapon away from me, and point it at yourself? Not a pretty sight, after a man blows his own head off."

The barrel, still pointing at Harper, wavered as the shakes returned. Hayes, using his left hand, steadied his aim. Nevertheless, the man's Adam's apple bobbed nervously accentuated by a spider tattoo.

"I'm not feeling the need to shoot myself. Quite the opposite in fact. You know, Harper, you're full of baloney."

Despite Harper's best efforts, he was not seeing the gun move at all. Time for Plan B.

"I'll give you the artifact, Hayes, if you'll answer one question for me. Those scars on your scalp how did you get them?"

"You *are* a nutter. At a time like this, what sort of question is that?"

"Humor me, please. I'm a fan of the TV series *Grey's Anatomy*."

"Okay. If you must know, like I said, during that bar fight I hit my head. Rushed to hospital, the doctors told me my skull was as thin as a calcium-deficient hen's egg. I spent eight weeks recuperating, after a surgeon inserted a stainless steel plate, in the shape of my brainpan, under the skin. Thank the Lord for Canada's free health service. In the United States, with no health insurance, I expect you'd kiss goodbye to $300,000 or more. Without going into you my full medical history, does that answer your question?"

"Totally unbelievable. What are the odds?" Harper replied, rhetorically.

"Whatever are you talking about now?"

"Let me give you a hypothetical, Mr. Hayes. Suppose, in normal circumstances, I was capable of getting inside someone's head and thus persuade them to shoot themselves. However, you are the exception. Because of the metal plate protecting your skull, it does not work. What do you think happens next?"

Hayes grinned. " Simple. I win; you lose. Hand over the stones, this instant, or it's checkmate for you."

"I'm afraid, I cannot do that. The relic belongs to the First Nations people who live near Port Douglas. They deserve to have it returned. Especially since Running Bear gave his life trying to stop your father from stealing it."

William Hayes looked puzzled. "Who is Running Bear?"

"The young brave who, like you, hit his head. Unlike you, he was not so fortunate. Although you may not have known his name, doesn't the boy's death rest on your conscience?"

Hayes shrugged his shoulders. "It was the kid's own fault. He shouldn't have gotten in the way."

"No remorse then?"

"None whatsoever. Besides, it was my dad who was responsible; not me. Now give me the stones, or I'll blow your pesky brains out. "

Closing his eyes, Harper focused his telekinetic power. The lug nut at his feet flew towards Hayes, with the force of a bullet.

Falling backward, Harper's assailant hit the floor clutching his left shoulder. "What the heck! You might have killed me."

"Think yourself blessed, Mr. Hayes, that I didn't." Harper reached down and picked up the lug nut. "I'll be leaving now. There's no need to get up on my account."

"Wait. I need medical attention. Can't you see, I'm bleeding to death?"

"I hardly think so. However, if I ever set eyes on your sorry face again, I'm sure I can make an exception."

Without further ado, Harper installed the fifth lug, before climbing into the Land Rover, and left.

CHAPTER FORTY-FIVE

WHEN HARPER CAME DOWNSTAIRS THE NEXT MORNING, AS expected, both Dee and Federico wanted to know why, without prior explanation, he had stayed out much of the night. Dee gave him more of a scolding for not being kept in the loop, especially after the humiliation, her words, of having to rescue the pair from the locked storage unit. However, as soon as he produced a small square-shaped gift box, covered in plush green velvet, Dee blurted out, "That's rather an upmarket case for a piece of jade, if you don't mind me saying."

Harper looked at the pair quizzically, prompting the Brazilian to remark, "Don't tell me *The Collector* persuaded you to accept a diamond necklace instead."

Harper offered a broad smile as he placed the box on the kitchen table. "Dee, why don't you do the honors?"

Lifting the lid, after a moment, his sister-in-law indignantly exclaimed, "Really, Harper? All this trouble over four old bones!"

Federico was unduly scathing. "I can't believe you allowed yourself to be duped, Harper. Whatever happened to the jade stone?"

Harper admitted he was equally surprised. "There was never any jade," he explained. "You're looking at the artifact purchased by *The Collector*'s father. Before either of you say more, she showed me the original bill of sale, which refers to Indian Artifacts. The copy, found in the Book House attic, referred to the same. At the time, I for one assumed they were made of jade because that is what Morning Star told Julia."

"That was rather deceitful on her part if you ask me," Dee commented.

"Let's be charitable," Harper suggested, "and assume Morning Star was being wily because she didn't want the relic to fall into the wrong hands."

The Brazilian huffed in response. "More like, she didn't want us to find it."

Harper posed the question, "Why would she do that? Surely she wants prosperity restored to the reserve."

"Because ..." Dee took a second to formulate her answer. "Because, as a shaman, Morning Star knows full well that with the artifact returned, Running Bear would have no reason to stay in the valley. She lost him once when he was killed. She can't stand losing him for a second time."

"If you are correct in your assertion, Dee, we should not trust Morning Star by consigning these bones into her custody," Federico concluded.

Harper nodded in agreement. "Best we find another way. Entrusting the relics to the tribal elders, for example."

More nodding heads.

Notwithstanding, there remained the mystery of the bones themselves, and why there were four of them. Consequently, Harper began by imparting the information about the artifacts, as told to him by Ms. Norell the previous evening. "Cameron, curious as to why her late father had paid so much, sent the artifacts to the Natural History Museum in Victoria. An expert reported back that all four bones were from male elk; shinbones from forelegs, to be precise."

The Brazilian picked up a matching pair. Both were approximately nine inches long; the knuckles at each end having been neatly sawn off. Peering down one end, he said. "It looks as though the marrow has been removed and replaced by some sort of milky white substance that has fibrous streaks disappearing inside."

"That would be ..." Harper consulted the palm of his hand where he had written one word to jog his memory. "... *ulexite*, in its crystal form. The two bones remaining in the box contain the same mineral."

Dee picked up one of them, and like Federico peered into one end. "The fibers are still showing, but these are a golden color."

"What you are looking at, lady and gentleman, is nature's answer to fiber optics. These crystals supposedly act as a conduit for a beam of light."

"Let's find out shall we," Federico suggested. "Dee, do you have a flashlight?"

"Try the right-hand drawer behind you."

Having retrieved the penlight, the Brazilian shone it into the top of a bone. "It works!" he exclaimed.

"I can see that," Harper responded sharply. "Try the other bone you're holding."

"It's the same. Here, Dee, try it on yours." The Brazilian handed over the small light.

Dee's shinbone still had the top knuckle in place, which had been dexterously carved out to form a cavity. Consequently, she shone the beam through the sawn-off end. "Nada."

Strange," Harper reflected. "Try the bone left in the box."

"Still nothing."

"Might it be something to do with the cavity at the end," Federico advocated.

The two bones were flipped. "Something inside sparkles," Dee informed the two men. "Could be a piece of glass?"

"The museum had the bones X-rayed. All have fiber optic crystals running through them. The cavities contain right-angled prisms."

"Prisms similar to those found in some periscopes, telescopes, and cameras?" the Brazilian queried.

"If the idea is to change the light's direction, yes," Harper answered.

While this dialog was taking place, Dee had reversed the bones she was holding and once more look down at the ulexite from the sawn-off end. "This is fascinating. Take a look, you two." She passed a bone to Harper; the other to Federico. "Notice anything?"

"Yellow is yellow," Harper asserted.

"Not in this instance," Dee contradicted. "Before I exposed the crystals to the flashlight, they were pale greenish-yellow in color. Now they have taken on a darker hue."

"What does that imply? Any ideas?"

"Beats me," Federico answered. "Was anything like this described in the report?"

"No," Harper replied. "Nothing was said by Cameron either. Then again, she wasn't especially enamored with the artifact. Remember, it was her father who originally made the acquisition."

"I'm not an expert in mineralogy," Dee responded, "I could take the bones to the University's Chemistry Department, and ask them to run more tests."

"No time for that," Harper countered. "Jules will be expecting us to return to Port Douglas. Which reminds me, last night the Land Rover picked up a puncture. This morning I need to find a place to get it fixed. How about the two of you; do you have anything special planned?"

"Dee has offered to take me to a botanical garden," the Brazilian volunteered.

"I didn't know you were into horticulture," remarked Harper. "Still, Jules often says I should start a hobby. Let me know how you get on."

"I saw that, Harper," said Dee.

"Saw what?"

"You winked."

"Did I? Must be something in my eye."

"Is that right?" Federico offered a stern stare. "Come on, Dee. Let's leave *Roger* to run his errand. After the Gardens, if you like, I'll take you to a restaurant."

"Can I come?" Harper asked.

In unison, Dee and Federico replied with an emphatic, "No!"

CHAPTER FORTY-SIX

DAY TWO OF CHECKING THE DREAM CATCHER FOR CORROBORATING evidence of an intruder proved more fruitful than the first morning. The exit from their bedrooms was timed to coincide with Julia bathing Ophelia. Soundlessly they tiptoed down the stairs, along the hallway, and quietly opened the front door.

Spencer, reaching up to unhook the handle before Oliver could object, was the first to spot the hollowed-out cocoon-like ball caught in the dream catcher's net.

"Better put it somewhere where Mom won't find it," the boy suggested. "How about under the desk in the library?"

"I'm not sure that's a good idea," was the apprehensive reply. "Whatever that stuff is, it looks similar to a funnel web. I don't like spiders, especially indoors."

"How about the outbuilding where the kayaks are stored?"

"Okay. Then, we can go and see if Morning Star is in her cabin."

"We should tell my mom first," Oliver proposed, "or we'll be in trouble."

"I don't care if you need to speak to Morning Star right away, you are not going out on your own. The first time you wandered into the forest. The second time you, Oliver, fell down a cliff and nearly broke your neck."

"That's an exaggeration, Aunt Julia. Olly suffered a few scrapes and bruises, that's all."

"Neither of you is going to change my mind, so don't try. With Roger, Dee, and Federico away I do not want to risk either of you having an accident. Anyway, what's the urgency?"

Deciding further protests were pointless, Spencer glumly replied, "It's not important."

"Then you'll just have to wait until Morning Star comes to visit. In the meantime, go do something constructive. You're spoiled for choice when it comes to books to read."

———

Reading books did not take precedence over scheming a way to contact the caretaker. Oliver lolling on his bed, gazing at the ceiling, suggested they sneak out the back.

Spencer, who stood in the bedroom doorway, vetoed the idea, deciding if they got caught a total grounding was inevitable. "We need to think of a way of contacting Morning Star from here, without going outside."

"We could use a flashlight and send a signal. Dot, dot, dot, dash, dash, dash," Oliver advocated.

"Like Morning Star knows morse code. Besides with the sun reflecting off the windows, I doubt if she would see our message."

"You have a point," Oliver conceded. "I suppose, Miss Smarty Pants, has a better idea."

"As a matter of fact, I just might," Spencer replied, spotting a plugged-in electrical cable snaking from a wall socket to a battery charger.

CHAPTER FORTY-SEVEN

MORNING STAR TOOTED THE HORN OF HER TRUCK, ALERTING THE occupants of the Book House of her arrival. Oliver and Spencer crashed down the stairs at breakneck speed, and along the hallway. Passing the kitchen, Oliver shouted, "She's here," which prompted his mother to stop kneading dough and make her way to the front door.

The children were nowhere to be seen when Julia stepped onto the porch. "Where did they go?" was her obvious question to Morning Star, who was leaning against the hood of her truck.

"They shot off around the side of the house. I expect they will be back in a minute."

"What a coincidence that you decided to drive over," Julia commented. " Earlier, the kids wanted to go visit your cabin, but they wouldn't say why."

"I know why," the caretaker responded. "They sent me a message."

Julia looked puzzled. "Sorry, I don't understand. A message, you say? How?"

"They used the modern-day equivalent of a carrier pigeon. What do the native children call those things? Buzzbirds? No, that's not it. Droids? Not that either. I have it. *Drones.*"

"I might have guessed. And the reason you came?"

"Ask them yourself. They're back."

Julia turned, expecting a whirlwind running. But no. The pair walked slowly. Spencer cradled the dream catcher, while Oliver, using an empty hessian sack, sheltered the webbing from the breeze that had picked up since daybreak.

"What have you got there, young'uns?" Morning Star asked.

"Not sure," Oliver replied, lowering the sacking.

Julia, who had moved nearer, let out a shriek. "Keep that thing away from me."

"Don't be afraid Missus. It's not what you think."

"Spider webs are spider webs, in my opinion, no matter how you sugarcoat them."

The older children laughed.

"It's not funny. I hate spiders."

"Me, too," Spencer volunteered. "There are no spiders in the dream catcher, I can assure you, Aunt Julia. I had Olly take a close look."

"So what's that fluffy cotton-ball thingie that's trapped in the catcher?"

Oliver and Spencer chuckled again, as did Morning Star.

"Wait a minute. Is this some form of practical joke, and Morning Star is in on it? You're not trying to get back at me because I poo-pooed your claim of someone hanging around the house during the night? And don't tell me you've caught a dream."

Her conclusion caused a further burst of laughter from the children. Julia joined in, assuming she had been truly punked.

Morning Star, however, having adopted a solemn expression, signaled the dream catcher should be brought to her. After a methodical inspection, she again smiled. "You've done a good job, kids. I must confess, I didn't take your message seriously. If I did I would have brought my *wâsenamawinâpisk.*"

"Your what?" Julia asked. "I'm sorry. Can you translate into English?"

"The nearest equivalent would be glass globe or crystal ball."

"You are still pranking me, aren't you? Enough is enough. I'm going back indoors. I need to check up on Ophelia and put my bread in the oven. You can all come inside for a glass of lemonade when you've finished fiddling around out here. Just make sure the dream catcher stays outside, and far away from the house."

The screen door closed, leaving the children wondering if they had overstepped the mark.

"Sometimes people find it hard to accept things they don't understand. Go put the catcher back where you were storing it. This afternoon I have to finish my crafting. Tomorrow I'll be back with my crystal ball."

"We have a crystal ball," Spencer exclaimed. "It may not be the same as yours, but it was made by someone from the First Nations. Federico purchased it from the craft shop in Hartzell."

"I'll go fetch it if you like. I'm sure Rico won't mind you borrowing it." Without waiting for an answer the boy raced indoors. Minutes later he was back, out of breath but proudly holding the Brazilian's globe.

———

Gazing through the sphere, Morning Star took her time examining the trapped web, both held up to the sun. Spencer began to fidget. Oliver looked on; still hoping the caretaker could confirm the presence of an intruder. Eventually, she placed the globe and dream catcher on the hood of her truck.

"Someone was on the porch, that's indisputable," Morning Star announced. "And I don't mean anyone currently living in the house. Last night, around midnight, I estimate. Male."

Sounding disappointed, Oliver asked, "Is that all?"

"I'm not a shaman for nothing, you disrespectful little chipmunk. No, that's not all. I know where they are hiding during the day."

"All that from a few strands of whitish fiber. Amazing," Oliver declared.

"You said male," Spencer confirmed. "You didn't say it was a man though."

"The intruder walked on two legs," the caretaker, confirmed.

Oliver suggested, "A bear, perhaps."

"Unlikely," Spencer countered. Letting out a squeal of delight, she proclaimed, "It's Sasquatch! I just knew they lived around here. And you, Morning Star, are being cagy because you don't want anyone to discover their secret. Oliver, I've decided on our next project. You can help me rig the drone's video camera, so we can monitor the porch for the next couple of nights."

Shaking her head as the children discussed the logistics of their surveillance, the caretaker headed back to her cabin. *Good luck on that one*, she thought. As the truck rattled across the bridge, she said absentmindedly to no one in particular, "Don't worry. Your secret is safe with me." However, she could not help wondering if *no one in particular* was out there watching.

CHAPTER FORTY-EIGHT

THE LAND ROVER'S TIRE REPLACED, HARPER WAS BACK AT DEE'S residence, sitting at the kitchen table. Between munching on a McDonald's burger and popping fries into his mouth, intermittently he glanced at the closed jewelry box that had been placed on the dresser.

Eventually, he reached across and set the box down to the side of his plate. Opening the lid he removed one of the bones and stared long and hard. There was something about the artifact that eluded him.

Eyes closed, holding one piece of the relic in the palm of his left hand, he gently stroked its surface with the index finger of the other. Two, three, four minutes passed. With his mind blank, Harper became aware of minuscule variations on the bone's surface. Opening his eyes again, he saw these scratches as hand-engraved letters. Not from the modern English alphabet, but that of the Squamish language. What was required was a translation.

Harper decided he needed to take pictures and email them to Dee. She could take it from there.

The first task was to find his smartphone, which had not been used for weeks. Going upstairs he discovered the device in a side pocket of his travel bag, together with a charger. Once the phone was charging, he endeavored to record the engraving with its camera. However, with the markings so faint they were illegible.

Harper rummaged in the dresser drawers looking for black boot polish. Unsuccessful, he tried the laundry room. Finding not only polish but brushes as well, he carefully stained the engravings before cleaning up the top surface with the rub of his thumb.

———

"Hello."

"Dee, it's me."

"Harper! I nearly ignored you, thinking this was a robocall. Are you checking up on us?"

"No. I'm sure Federico is behaving like a perfect gentleman. Listen. I've taken another look at the bones given to me by *The Collector* and discovered some lettering etched into their surfaces. Take a look at the attached photos I'm about to send you. See if someone at the University can translate."

"Will do."

"How's the trip to the botanic gardens. Have you picked up any free samples?"

Dee chuckled. "No. We've only just arrived. Earlier, I was showing Federico around the Anthropology Department."

"That must have been exciting. Hope you didn't poke him with an assegai."

"You and your wisecracks, Harper. I don't have any southern African spears decorating the walls of my office. Regardless, I did bump into my boss. I told him that you had found the lost relic and were planning to return it to the First Nations people living near Port Douglas. And guess what? When I said I would miss attending the inauguration ceremony, he suggested I should go. *Take as much time as you need. Just be sure to publish a paper in Anthropologica* [the official journal of the Canadian Anthropology Society], *when you return*, where his exact words." With a titter of excitement, she added, "So, Harper, there will be three of us returning to the Book House, not just you and Federico."

"Jules will be pleased to hear that. I'm sending you the photos, as soon as you give me your email address."

———

The ping from his smartphone startled Harper, who had dozed off shortly after disconnecting his call to Dee. Only fifteen minutes had passed. He opened the reply and was pleased to read the Squamish lettering had been translated.

ᑊᖮ· ᑭᕒᑬᐤ {**mêkwâ-kîsikâw**} while it is daylight
ᐊᐣᑕᒉᐅᐧᕽ {**nastachikowin**} the act of storing
ᐅᐣᑭᕒᑯᖬᐦ {**oskîsikokanân**} eye socket
ᐟᐳᐸᔪᐤ {**tipiskaw**} night or nighttime
ᐟᐳᐸᔪᐤ {**sâpopayiw**} passes right through

Since the attached photos had been sent in no particular order Dee had added, *I'm not sure what all this means, but your smart Harper. You'll figure it out.*

And figure it out he did.

At the sawn-off end of the bone with the prism, the engraving meant *day or daytime.* Halfway along, the next phrase meant *the act of storing.* Finally, the word just above the prism translated to *nighttime.*

Daylight → Storage → (for) Nighttime.

Similarly, for the second pair of bones the result was:

Light → passes through (to) → (the) Eye socket.

So, Harper told himself, *if I keep the prism at the bottom setting the bone vertically, and then tape the second horizontally, in theory, each pair should collect and store daylight, emitting it at night.*

All it took were pieces of duck tape to hold them in place and for Harper to find a spot to set up his little experiment; a spot he would remember before starting the return journey to Port Douglas.

"Where is the best place, old son?" he asked himself. "Ah. I have it."

Relics and tape in hand, he went through the side door and into the garden.

CHAPTER FORTY-NINE

With Dee intending to return to Port Douglas, Harper realized the Land Rover offered insufficient space for the copious quantities of supplies Julia had dictated to him earlier in the day. Therefore, he had to come up with a viable alternative. A trailer was his first choice, but Harper discarded the idea after considering the terrain bordering Lake Harrison. It was bad enough enduring the jolting and jarring inside a 6,000-pound vehicle. A utility trailer, one-third the weight, would be tossed around like a rowboat on an angry sea. Consequently, the contents were unlikely to survive the journey.

After much thought, Harper placed a phone call to a lake tours company based out of Lake Harrison Springs. The conversation involved a lot of financial haggling and the promise of the immediate wiring of funds. Eventually, an agreement was reached and Harper had his solution. As an afterthought, he asked if he might have his supplies delivered to their warehouse, to which they readily agreed.

Another phone call and the supplies were ordered.

By the time Dee and Federico returned it had gone 10:00 PM. They found Harper sitting on the couch, in front of the television, watching ice hockey. He waved an empty beer bottle at the Brazilian, indicating he needed a refill.

Federico politely obliged, heading for the kitchen and the refrigerator, while Dee sat down in an easy chair set to the side.

"I didn't think you were into ice hockey, Harper," were her first words.

"I'm not really, but it was this or curling. Don't you play any real sports in this country?"

"Lacrosse, cricket, rugby, soccer, to name but a few. Of course, you could broaden your mind and read a book. I have quite a collection in the study."

"So I noted. *Witchcraft, Oracles, and Magic Among the Azande* was one I spotted. *Coming of Age In Samoa* was another. How about *The Anthropology of Modern Human Teeth?* Human teeth. Please, give me a break."

Federico returned, three beers in hand.

"Not for me," Dee replied when offered one.

Harper took two. "Thanks. More for me."

The Brazilian sat down next to Harper. "What's the score?"

"Cancucks 2; Oilers 2. We've in the last minutes of overtime." As Harper spoke, Conner McDavis scored resulting in the slapping of his hands against his thighs in delight.

"At least you might have supported the home team," Dee remarked.

"I thought I did."

"The Oilers are from Edmonton; the Canucks from Vancouver," his sister-in-law informed him.

"Sorry, my bad." Harper reached forward, found the remote, and turned the television off. "However, now you stop-outs have returned, I can engage the two of you in stimulating conversation." He popped the top of his beer, and took a swig, before passing the opener to his friend. He then asked, "Did you enjoy the botany lesson, Federico?"

"I did. Dee took me on a grand tour of Butchart Gardens; a disused quarry full of beautiful floral displays. I discovered it covers fifty-five acres and has twenty-six greenhouses."

"And you visited each one?"

"Hardly. But we took loads of photographs." Federico pulled his smartphone from his pocket and selected one snapshot in particular. "Here. Take a look for yourself. We got another visitor to take it."

Harper obliged. "Ah. The loving couple. How romantic."

Dee blushed, while the Brazilian responded defensively, "Appreciate the plants and shrubs in the background, Harper; not comment on people's relationships."

"Spoken like a true knight in shining armor defending the honor of his fair lady."

"Will you two boys stop it and talk about something else? What did have to eat today, Harper?"

"For lunch; burger and fries. Dinner; a tuna sandwich. Judging how late it is, I supposed you went to a fancy restaurant?"

"We did, indeed." Federico sounded elated. "For starters we ate Alaskan salmon. Our next course was veal cutlets. Dee had cheese and biscuits for dessert. I ate profiteroles with lashings of whipped cream."

"Trumps my tuna sandwich, but I'm glad you both had a good time."

"Why, thank you," Dee acknowledged. "Speaking of cream, to show we hadn't entirely forgotten you, Harper, we picked up a carton of that ice cream the kids liked so much on the first day we met. I go get you some."

After Dee left for the kitchen, Harper asked in a low, conspiratorial voice, "Well? What do you think, *amigo*?"

"About what? The hockey game? I only caught the end of it?"

"Dee; you knucklehead."

With a flushed face, the Brazilian replied. "I haven't given her too much thought."

"Liar, liar, pants on fire,"

As Dee returned, she heard Harper's not-so-endearing remark. "Can't leave you two alone for one second without you mentally sparring." She offered Harper a large dish of vanilla-flavored ice cream layered with dark chocolate.

"This is good," he commented, mouth full. "You guys not having any?"

"After the restaurant, we are stuffed, thanks," Dee answered, sitting back down. "It will soon be time for bed, so let me ask you something. I am curious how the pair of you met?"

Seizing the opportunity to gain the upper hand, the Brazilian blurted out, "In prison. Guantánamo Bay Detention Center, to be specific."

Don't say another word, Federico, Harper commanded, telepathically. Unsure his friend would comply, in damage-control mode, he forcibly took over the conversation. "Enough with the phony story we used to tell in Cuban bars, *amigo.* Remember, this is Dee we are talking to."

The Brazilian was not done. "But ... "

Neither was Harper.

"Ouch! My head. I've suddenly started a migraine, big time."

"What's the matter, babe?" Dee asked, concerned.

She's calling you babe, Federico, Harper noted to himself. *Quiet the pair of lovebugs, you two are becoming.*

"Shall I fetch you a couple of aspirin?"

"No thanks. I'll be fine. I could do with another beer, though."

"Beer and migraines don't mix." Nurse Dee told him.

"That's a no, Federico. You can get yourself a glass of water if you're thirsty."

"Play nice, Harper."

"Whatever."

Dee tried another tack. "These drinking establishments you allude to; were they in Havana?"

On and on. This is like the Spanish inquisition, Harper thought. *I need to put a stop to this.* "They were, but that is for another evening, sister dear. We have a busy day tomorrow. I, for one, am ready to say good night."

"Me, too," Federico responded, the idea inserted into the Brazilian's mind. "But first let me help you with the dishes, Dee."

"That's not necessary. There are so few of them, that I can load the dishwasher on my own. But thanks anyway, babe. Sleep well."

Babe, for a second time in a couple of minutes, Harper thought. *She's love-sick for you, my friend.* "Sweet dreams, buddy. May your snores be with you?"

"Harper, stop it!"

"I'm only stating the truth."

Harper, you wouldn't know the truth if it bit you in the butt, Federico reflected.

Walking out of the room, the Brazilian could have sworn he heard the phrase, *I heard that,* at the back of his mind, but dismissed it as wild imagination.

CHAPTER FIFTY

HARPER WAS IN THE BATHROOM, CLEANING HIS TEETH, WHEN HE thought he heard his satellite phone ring. Returning to the bedroom, sure enough, there was a missed call. Not Julia. *The Collector*, perhaps? He redialed the number.

"Harper, we need to talk."

"Is that you, Dee? Why the phone call? I'm only a flight of stairs away."

His sister-in-law scoffed. "I hardly think it appropriate to be seen entering your bedroom. Whatever might Federico think?"

"Our Brazilian friend is already resting in the arms of Morpheus," Harper replied, "making sounds like a buzz saw that can be heard all the way to Montana. So you have no worries there."

"Nevertheless, it's best you come downstairs. I have a question for you."

Curious, Harper agreed.

He found Dee sitting at the kitchen table. Nodding, she indicated he should sit opposite, at the same time filling two shot glasses with *Grey Goose* vodka.

Her brother-in-law complied. Immediately picking up his glass, "*Za vashe zdorov'ye*," he toasted.

"You speak Russian?"

"Hardy." Harper laughed. "But I did spend time with the crew of a Russian submarine, back in the day. Drinking vodka, twenty thousand leagues under the sea, if I remember correctly."

"You know, Harper, I'm never sure if your stories are true or total BS. Sometimes I wonder how Julia puts up with you."

"That thought has crossed my mind, from time to time. Do you think we should contact the Vatican and nominate her for sainthood?"

"I didn't invite you down hear to listen to more pithy jokes, Harper. I want to ask about Federico."

"Why don't you ask him yourself?" was the response. Harper took a quaff of vodka. "I'm sure he won't mind you disrupting his beauty rest."

"Because when Federico began talking about Cuba, you cut him off. I want to know why."

"Yes, I did," Harper agreed, "and for good reason."

"I'm listening," Dee assured him, draining her glass in one swig

"What our mutual friend said about GITMO is true. He was detained there after having been captured in Afghanistan. Claimed he was embedded as a war correspondent. Unfortunately, he carried no credentials." Astounded, Dee's eyes opened wide. In return, Harper smiled. "But fear thee not, fair maid. Sir Knight came to his rescue."

"How?"

"I have my ways? Can't say more. All very hush-hush."

"Top secret; just like the episode when you helped the Brits, I suppose."

Harper nodded his head, allowing Dee to draw her own, be it false, conclusion.

"I still don't understand. Earlier, this evening, why did you so harshly draw the conversation to a close?"

Lowering his voice, Harper explained, "There is something you should know. After Federico and I became close friends, I was invited to stayed at the apartment he and his girlfriend *were* sharing. Karmina was her name." There was a pause, to bring emphasis to what he was about to reveal. "I use the past tense, because Karmina went missing. Much later her body washed up on a beach in North Carolina; a thousand miles away."

"Oh my gosh. That's terrible. Did she get washed overboard from a ship or a yacht?"

"Your guess is as good as mine. The FBI became involved, that's all I know." Another snippet of disinformation, but Harper succeeded in shutting his sister-in-law down.

"I can see why you didn't want Federico talking about Cuba. That's very noble of you. Harper."

"For two years Federico has been brooding over her loss. However, since arriving in B.C., I've been doing my best to cheer him up; encouraging him to move on with his life." Harper tried to project a self-effacing look of concern. "Which I believe, he has. He's into writing a novel. Taking the whole thing very seriously to boot."

Dee smiled. "I know about the novel, but he won't let me see the manuscript."

"Give *tu amigo* time. Whatever you do, don't ask about Karmina. To do so might trigger a tailspin into depression."

"Agreed. Good talk. Harper. I'll let you get back to bed."

"Thanks. See you in the morning."

As her brother-in-law got up to leave, as an afterthought she asked, "Tell me, Harper, when talking about Federico, why did refer to him as *tu amigo?*"

Offering more of a smirk than a smile, Harper answered, "Because he is *your* friend, is he not?"

Before Dee could respond, Harper left the kitchen.

She could hear him climb each stair. After the first three, he stopped and shouted out, "Sleep tight, sis. Dream of taking a fishing boat trip with *tu amigo*. He'll be quite the catch." There was a brief laugh, and then the ascent resumed. Dee shook her head, again wondering how Saint Julia put up with the man. Regardless, to the tune of Wagner's Wedding march, Harper was now singing,

> *"Here comes the bride,*
> *All dressed in white,*
> *Where is the groom?*
> *He's in the dressing room."*

He must have reached the landing, for Dee heard no more.

Standing up, having stowed the liquor in the cabinet, she collected the glasses. As she did so, Dee began humming to herself,

"Dah, dah, da-dum.
Dah, dah, da-dum.

Dang it, Harper. I'll have that tune in my head for the rest of the night."

Once the dishwasher was loaded and turning it on, Dee reached into the dresser cupboard and removed a cardboard box containing board games. Next, she took the box into the hallway and placed it on the bench that was also a full-height mirror. She looked at herself, turned sideways, and pushed on her tummy.

"You've still got the figure, girl, to get a man's attention," she told herself. "On a fishing boat, wearing a pretty summer dress, who knows who one might catch."

Reproaching herself for the vanity trip, she returned to the kitchen to complete her final chore; removing the trash bag from the bin under the sink and depositing it in the garbage can set in the side yard. After replacing the can's lid, Dee turned towards the kitchen. As she did so, a light shining from inside the Land Rover caught her attention.

She muttered under her breath as she made her way toward the vehicle. "Harper, I'm not your servant. You'd forget your head if it wasn't permanently attached to your neck"

Opening the rear door, Dee was astonished at seeing the source of the illumination. Held in place by tape, the four bones had been set together to the form of two uppercase 'Ls'. From the vertical's top emanated a dull glow, but from the horizontal toe a bright white light reflected off the vehicle's aluminum siding.

It took but a moment to realize the significance of what she was witnessing. After rushing into the house, Dee stood at the foot of the stairs and shouted, "Harper! Federico! Get yourselves down here, ASAP. I've got something *really* important to show you."

CHAPTER FIFTY-ONE

JULIA WAS ALERTED BY SHOUTS FROM THE TWO OLDER CHILDREN AS they called her to come look across the lake.

As a Houseboat approached, Dee was frantically waving. Harper too, once he had killed the engine and exited the wheelhouse. The vessel's momentum allowed it to drift nearer the shore.

"Roger Harper, is this another of your harebrained enterprises?"

"Don't be so judgmental," her husband protested, with mock indignation. "I've brought enough provisions to last the winter. If we relied on the Land Rover, it could only bring enough for a month or so."

There was a splash as Harper threw the anchor overboard, judging it was time to stop the boat before it grounded on the beach.

"Where is Federico?" was Julia's next question. "Didn't forget him, did you?"

Harper laughed, knowing his wife was joking. "Nah. He's taken the long way home, driving the Land Rover along the west side of Harrison Lake. Not something I would recommend, by the way. My backside was so sore after the outbound journey, I had to sit on a cushion for days."

For a few seconds, Oliver and Spencer giggled at Harper's remark, before the boy shouted, "Did you bring us any presents?"

"Something the two of you will need," his father answered.

"What's that?"

"School books." Harper grinned.

Julia was not so sure. Homeschooling was not something she had planned. However, when her sister said she was able to stay until the New Year, doubts were cast aside.

"I hope you bought pull-ups for Ophelia?"

"Yes, Jules. As well as a side of beef, a whole pig, frozen chicken and more. Another perk of the houseboat is its large chest freezer."

"And champagne," Dee added, "to celebrate that we have recovered the relic."

The houseboat was left moored near the house that evening. Tomorrow morning Harper planned to dock the craft at Port Douglas wharf, and ask Morning Star if he could borrow her truck to ferry the supplies to the Book House.

Little was said over the evening meal, Harper eating as though he had not been fed for a week. However, once Ophelia was put to bed for the night, Julia, Oliver, and Spencer listened to the account of how *The Collector* had declined Harper's proposal to buy back the relic, and the resulting counteroffer if he recovered a painting stolen by her spendthrift brother.

Dee kept her silence with regard to the men's late-night jaunts or the episode inside the storage unit.

Harper's narration continued, heavily edited, to exclude messing with Lockward's head, preferring to say the lawyer gifted it back to the original owner.

"Why would he do that?" Oliver asked.

"His wife encouraged him that it was the right thing to do," his father replied, leaving out how the sweet-talking was furtively enforced.

"Quite right too," Julia declared. "That's what I would do, once I was told it had been stolen in the first place." She picked up her fluted glass. "A toast to the oil painting and the artifact."

"A toast to the painting and artifact," the two other adults echoed.

"Can we have some Champaign?" Spencer pleaded.

"You kids are not old enough to drink alcohol. Stick with your soda," Harper responded. "But I do have a surprise up my sleeve."

"What's that, Dad? Tell us, please."

"Not this evening."

"When, then?" Spencer asked.

"Be patient. All in good time."

CHAPTER FIFTY-TWO

"I'M GLAD FEDERICO ARRIVED BACK SAFELY," JULIA TOLD HER husband, as the pair snuggled together in the master bedroom of the Book House. "What took him so long to get here?"

"Someone had tried to take an RV along the trail, got stuck, and blocked the track. Like the good Samaritan he is, Federico used my satellite phone to call for assistance, and then waited for the rescue service to arrive."

"The guy must be exhausted. Has he gone to bed?"

"He told me he was going to take a hot bath," Harper replied. "However, I prefer a quick shower and the comfort of soft pillows and a mattress to ease my aches and pains. You, of course, are my nurse."

Julia closed her eyes to the shadows cast across the room by the moonlight, murmured in agreement, and nestled closer. Except for the sound of frogs croaking and crickets chirping, that came through the screened open window, all was quiet

For a while, neither spoke. Then Julia asked, "Roger, what's bothering you?"

"Why do you say that, Jules?"

"For starters, you keep sighing. Is there something you need to tell me?"

"You know me too well, honeybee." There was a brief pause while Harper raised his head, supporting it with an elbow, in order to look into his wife's eyes. "I have a confession to make."

Julia smiled. "I've worked that out already. You're been ... What do lawyers' say? ... economical with the truth." Harper's eyes opened wider. About to speak, Julia put her finger to his lips. "What you said about Alistair Lockward gifting back the painting to the original owner is not entirely accurate, is it?" Again, Harper tried to speak. Again Julia shushed him with her middle finger. "You used your mind reading ability. That's the only logical explanation."

The next ten minutes were taken with Harper relating the entire course of events from telepathically eavesdropping on the conversation between *The Collector* and the Porsche owner, to tricking the lawyer into believing his house was on fire.

Shifting uncomfortably, Harper concluded with, "Are you mad at me?"

"If I were mad at you, Roger, you'd be sleeping in another room. I understand. Caught between a rock and a hard place, you needed to acquire the relic and return it to the reserve, and the only foreseeable way you could do so was by recovering Norell's oil painting." Julia, reached up, pulled Harper's head nearer, and kissed him on the lips "The question is, how do we put things right, as far as Mr. Lockward is concerned?"

"I don't know, honeybee. You're the brains in this family."

"Sweet talking me, huh?" Julia smiled. "Returning the original to the lawyer is not an option. Let me think." After a few seconds, Julia asked. "What's the Emily Carr painting worth?"

"Not sure," was the reply.

"Ball-park it, Roger. One million; one-point-five?"

"Could be higher. Like land, they are not making any more."

"Two, then. Or three? Why don't we settle for US$3 million?"

"Okay," Harper agreed. "Where are you going with this?"

"We make a donation. Not to Lockward, though. If he were told the painting in his office's conference room is a reproduction, he would be devastated. You said he tried covering up a shaking hand. I'm guessing he is in the early stages of multiple sclerosis, Parkinson's, or some such ailment. If we can find out which one, you can donate three million dollars to the respective research foundation, in Mr. and Mrs. Lockward's name."

"That sounds like a fair compromise. How do we find out which one?"

"Ask me in the morning. Roger. Goodnight."

Harper, taking that as the queue their conversation had ended, settled in, closed his eyes, and continued listening to the frogs and insects until he fell asleep.

———

"Roger."

"What, Jules?"

"I'm worried."

After sneaking a glance at the bedside clock, Harper asked, "About what, honeybee? I thought you said we would sort out the donation in the morning?"

"We will. There's something else." Julia cuddled even closer. "Do you believe in ghosts, Roger?"

"It's just gone midnight. Is that the witching hour?"

"Just answer the question, please."

"I would have to say no, not having seen one myself. However, Olly claims to have spoken to the spirit boy, Running Bear. Morning Star too, according to your sister." Harper sighed. "Mind you, I do recall the story Federico relayed of how he and Dee found a young girl trapped in a deep pit. When she ran off, the couple visited Morning Star's cabin. There was a photograph above the fireplace, suggesting they had saved her daughter. The caveat was the ages didn't match unless they had rescued a ghost."

"Which brings me to believe there have been other bizarre goings-on around here, while you've been away."

Harper turned to face his wife. "What do you mean? Are you telling me the house is haunted?"

"I'm not sure, but items in the kitchen have been moved around, food taken from the refrigerator, and I've heard creaking sounds coming from the attic."

"That could be Oliver or Spencer. Midnight snacks, I expect. Kids are always hungry."

"Creaking from the attic at three in the morning? I checked their bedrooms, and both were asleep."

"Did you look in the loft?"

"And if there really was a ghost, what would I do then?"

"Call Ghost Busters," Harper responded, which earned him a dig in the ribs.

"Ouch."

"You're not taking me seriously, Roger. Something else comes to mind. Chance's journal, which had been left on the library desk, disappeared for two days before it mysteriously returned."

"The kids again. You know how they like to play practical jokes."

"No, I asked them. They could see how upset I was. I think they would have owned up if they had. Oh! I've just remembered another incident. Early yesterday morning, the generator cut out. Not having a clue how to fix it, I walked over to Morning Star's place, to see if she might help. She drove Ophelia and me back in her truck, which was nice of her. However, when we arrived, the generator was running again. Weird, huh?"

"It sounds as though you might have befriended a benevolent ghost who is mechanically inclined."

Another dig.

Wrapping his arm around Julia, Harper apologized, "My poor baby. I'm sorry I wasn't here with you. "

"You're here now. That's the main thing. Perhaps all this nonsense will stop."

"I expect so," Harper agreed. "Let's get some sleep. Tomorrow I need to bring the supplies to the house."

Again, the room lapsed into quiet.

Ten minutes later, after shaking Harper awake, Julia spoke again. "There are other things I forgot to mention. The other day, Olly and Spencer told me they had seen a moving light shining outside during the night, At the time I didn't believe them. But yesterday morning I took Ophelia with me on a walk along the lakeshore south of here, and I had this uncanny feeling someone was watching us."

"From where?" Harper asked.

"The cover of the trees. Once or twice I saw movement."

"Probably an animal."

"Animals don't stalk humans, Roger. Dee taught me that. Even brown bears will leave people alone if they or their cubs are not threatened. No, somebody was deliberately sneaking around."

"Did you turn around and come home?"

"Not immediately. I hear a bird cry, coming from the long grass. Not a warning, but a distress call."

"So, being the Girl Scout that you are, you investigated. I know you, Jules. When it comes to injured creatures, you cannot resist seeing if you can help."

Julia gave her husband a gentle squeeze of affection. "It was a young sparrow. A common garden sparrow, would you believe? It had a broken wing."

"So you brought it to the house, played Florence Nightingale and it's recuperating in the outhouse? Am I right?"

"Mm-hmm. The older children and I made a nest using an old wooden crate. Spencer helped me splint the wing. Olly's been digging for worms and feeding it regularly. I went online and found out that in three weeks the sparrow should be as good as new. Tomorrow morning, you can take a look yourself."

"I will, and I'm sure all three of you will be rewarded in Heaven. For now, no more talk about ghosts, stalkers, or injured feathered friends. Can we please get some sleep?"

CHAPTER FIFTY-THREE

IT WAS EIGHT DAYS AFTER HIS SLEEPWALKING DREAM THAT Lockward returned to his law office. Greeted in the reception area by junior partner, Nicole Tremblay, the usual platitudes were exchanged, hoping Alistair was fully recovered and ready for the two clients scheduled that morning.

"Raring to go, Nicky. I should have been back to work days ago, but Kay insisted I wait until the start of a new week. Anything of note, I should be aware of."

Pausing before walking towards the break room, Nicole answered, "As a matter of fact, there is. OnFriday afternoon, I received the strangest of phone calls, from another law firm that has an office in Vancouver. Ellis Davis, one of the partners, said he represented the Harper Foundation, and that Mrs. Harper had instructed him to make available three million in US dollars for medical research. The donation would be sent in your and Kay's name. Any idea what that is about?"

"Can't say I do," was the reply, but Lockward instantly corrected himself. "Unless Mrs. Harper is the wife of Roger Harper. Some days ago, the gentleman came in and asked about becoming a Canadian citizen. I got the impression he was a man of means, although I never imagined he had three million to give away."

"More like $3.8 million in Canadian currency. Anyway, in confidence, Davis told me that Harper is quite a philanthropist and likes to support good causes. Amongst others, research into finding a cure for Parkinson's disease was proposed."

"Why Partkinson's, I wonder? I trust you did not reveal anything about my medical condition?" Alistair Lockward sounded anxious.

"Lord no. I think he was fishing. However, I did suggest, that if his client wished to make a charitable donation, he wire funds to us, which we will hold in an escrow account until you decide which charity to support."

Lockward, sounding relieved, followed up by asking about the redecoration of the conference room.

Nicole Tremblay smiled. "Completed over the weekend Take a peek, before you go into your office."

As Nicole went to make herself coffee, Lockward set his briefcase on the receptionist's counter before scurrying along the corridor. A loud shout was heard, shortly after he had entered the room.

"Praise the Lord. I didn't take the painting home after all."

"Not waiting for the security firm to retrieve the paintings from storage, I picked them up myself, first thing this morning." It was the receptionist, having followed the lawyer, who spoke. "With the janitor's help, we put them where they belong. The new color scheme provides an ideal backdrop, wouldn't you agree, Mr. Lockward?"

"Yes. Yes," but Alistair was but half listening. He walked around the long table and stood in front of the paintings. Emily Carr's oil on canvas *War Canoes* was left of center.

"Is there anything else, sir?" the receptionist asked, before leaving.

"No thank you, my dear."

Alone, the lawyer spent another fifteen minutes with his cherished artwork. Much of that time he was trying to determine whether or not there was something different. *Did the canoes seem more vibrant in color?* He could not decide. Notwithstanding, Lockward left the room a re-energized man, wishing his wife could derive the same satisfaction.

CHAPTER FIFTY-FOUR

ROGER HARPER RECEIVED THE PHONE CALL HE HAD BEEN PATIENTLY waiting for, informing him that the planned surprise was finished and ready for transportation. He agreed to send payment, two banker's drafts, by courier. The first would cover the cost of materials and labor. The second, made out to a haulage company, was for the use of a *Freightliner* truck, equipped with a twenty-seven-foot flatbed and knuckle boom crane.

The next morning, at first light, after everyone in the Book House had eaten breakfast, snacks were packed to tide them over until lunchtime, together with an assortment of outdoor clothing to cover both rain and shine.

From the house, the Land Rover transported the party to the wharf at Port Douglas. Boarding the houseboat, their destination was the southern end of the larger lake. Morning Star, hearing the shouts of excitement from the two older children as they cast off, came out of her cabin, wondering what was causing the commotion.

"Roger, is taking me to a spa and then to a posh restaurant for lunch," Julia yelled in explanation. "If you are running short of supplies, we can purchase them for you before we return."

"If you come across those fancy jars of moisturizer, you can buy me a half-dozen. I'm running short," the caretaker replied before laughing at her own joke. "I'll keep an eye on the house while you are gone."

"Thanks," Julia yelled as the vessel began picking up speed.

Oliver, standing in the bow, used his telescope to search the tree line. Spencer stood by with her camera, now fitted with a telescopic lens, in case he spotted Sasquatch. The two women moved to the upper deck. After applying liberal amounts of sunscreen, they stretched out on loungers. Federico had joined Harper in the wheelhouse, where he was conscripted to baby-minding duty.

"Why me?" the Brazilian asked. "Ophelia is your daughter."

"Good practice. Remember, I told you, one day you might start a family of your own."

Changing the subject, the Brazilian asked, "It's too early for a beer, I suppose?"

"Yes, *amigo*, but there's a Thermos of coffee in that hamper. You can pour me a cup."

They reach the canal that joined the smaller lake to its big brother. From there it was plain cruising, reaching the Hot Springs shortly before eleven-thirty.

Once on shore, Harper handed Julia and Dee tickets to a local spas, with a promise to meet up for lunch at one of the lakeshore restaurants. He even produced a menu, allowing them to peruse the various courses as they were being pampered.

"Come on kids, follow me," he instructed, heading for the harbormaster's office.

Feeling left out, Federico asked, "What about me?"

"You're coming with us, buddy, unless you feel the need to get a facial. Anyways, you'll want to be amongst the first to see what we are going to take back to Douglas."

The group set off. Ophelia, wide-awake, pointed at a group of passing hikers wearing brightly colored headgear.

"Hat." She kept repeating, "Hat. Hat."

"Yes, hat. Good job, baby girl." They passed a black miniature poodle. "Look, Ophelia. Dog."

"Dog," she echoed, as the animal barked at a passing car, which in turn prompted her to say, "Car."

"Another delight of parenting, Federico. Teaching a toddler to talk."

"Beats changing diapers, for sure. Can't we have an ice cream or something? I'm getting hungry."

"Yeah. Ice cream," Oliver and Spencer agreed.

"Okay, but not before I've spoken to the harbormaster."

Minutes later the official took the group to an out-of-the-way jetty, used exclusively for boat repairs.

"There you are, sir. Never seen the like before; not floating on the water, that is. When do you want to pick her up?"

"After we've eaten. Let's say around 2:30."

The officer took his leave. The Brazilian and two older children stood there speechless.

The toddler again pointed. "Car."

Oliver laughed.

"No, Ophelia, that's not a car," said Spencer.

"Okay, everyone. Time for ice cream, as promised. One condition, though. Over lunch, none of you are to breathe a word about what you've just seen. I want it to be a surprise for Jules and Dee."

CHAPTER FIFTY-FIVE

LAST-MINUTE SHOPPING DICTATED THE LATE DEPARTURE OF THE houseboat. Humdrum items for the most part. Julia bought herself a narrow-brimmed sun hat, white in color, which lacked practicality or panache. Spencer and Oliver shared a 5,000-piece jigsaw puzzle depicting a cluster of totem poles, similar to ones to be found in Stanley Park. Ophelia left clutching a cuddly toy; a moose wearing a Canadian Mountie uniform. Even the two men were not left out. Federico purchased a tee-shirt featuring a bright-red maple leaf, while Harper sported a wannabe commodore's cap complete with gold oak leaf embellishments on the visor. Which left Dee, the prime reason for the delay, who had spent an inordinate amount of time in a women's clothing store. Finally, when she emerged carrying a large paper carrier bag, she refused to reveal the contents, saying it was something reserved for a special occasion. Despite repeated pleadings, the mystery remained a secret to all and sundry. Consequently, by the time Harper began steering the houseboat cautiously through the canal leading to Little Harrison Lake, the sun was setting behind Robertson Peak.

Federico, who was watching the stern shouted, "Stop!" An action more easily said than done, as inertia continued to carry the craft forward. The Brazilian desperately pulled on one of the pair of towropes, causing the first of two rafts to slew to starboard. Narrowly missing the embankment, he yanked on the second rope, managing to expeditiously line up the so-called surprise with the man-made channel.

The two women and older children watched from the top deck, loudly applauding Federico's adroit maneuvering.

Seemingly for no reason, Dee whispered, "If Morning Star asks about the relic, say nothing."

"I don't understand," Julia replied, confused.

"I'll tell you later when we are back at the house. Just promise me, not a word. Okay?"

As the houseboat entered Little Harrison Lake, Julia stood in silence, trying to work out the significance of her sister's strange request. Meanwhile, in what remained of the twilight, Harper held a straight course. As soon as the Brazilian confirmed the second raft had cleared the channel, the pilot spun the wheel hard, lining up with the wharf and caretaker's cabin.

Dee broke the silence between the two sisters by revealing, "There is something I forgot to tell you yesterday. I answered a call on your satellite phone from Ellis Davis; the guy who transferred the title for the Book House into our names. I couldn't find you so he asked me to convey a message."

"I was expecting his call," Julia confirmed. "Was it about donating funds for medical research?"

"I'm not sure. He told me, as per your instructions, the wire transfer was complete. Held in escrow by immigration attorneys Lockward, Marks, and Tremblay. Apparently, Mr. Lockward has been out of the office for the past week, but Davis was assured the money would be used appropriately. I am confused. Is Harper attempting to buy back the Carr painting?"

"Nothing like that. Roger noticed Alistair Lockward has a tremor in his left hand. Considering how helpful the man has been, we decided to make a donation to a medical foundation on his behalf. Simple as that."

Dee responded with a quizzical look.

"There's something else?" Julia inquired.

""Er ... I'm not sure. Throughout the conversation, Davis kept referring to you as *Ms*. Harper. Please thank Mr. and *Ms*. Harper for their generous contribution. Don't forget to pass on the message to *Ms*. Harper. I don't recall Davis addressing you like that in his office."

"It's code," Julia realized. "*Ms*. stands for *MS*. The funds will be going toward multiple sclerosis research."

Dee decided it was not polite to ask how much money was donated. Instead, she concentrated on watching their approach to Port Stanley. Julia, on the other hand, was pondering how Ellis Davis had determined where exactly the funds were going. Letting her imagination take over, she speculated that he too shared the telepathic ability of her husband. *Nonsensical of course,* she concluded. *However, wouldn't it be something, if Ellis were able to read minds over the telephone?*

———

Standing on the shore, Morning Star waved the lantern she was holding aloft. "I'm glad you are back safe," were the first words she called out. "Occasionally a remaining log, felled by the timber company, drifts into the middle of the lake and gets carried by the current. You certainly don't want to end up hitting one of those in the dark."

"We must remember that," Harper shouted in reply, as he steered the houseboat so it was parallel to the dock. At the last moment, he swung the wheel hard left, causing the vessel to veer to port.

"Casting off now," Federico bellowed. The two ropes splashed into the water, permitting the item in tow to continue in a straight path. There was a loud grinding sound as the leading raft grounded on the beach. The houseboat continued in a lazy circle. Upon reaching the wharf it was quickly made fast, allowing everyone to disembark and gingerly walk along the rickety planking until they reached their greeter.

"Well, I never," Morning Star blurted out. "This is a blast from the past. Wherever did you find it?"

"That's a long story," Dee replied as the men made sure the totem was securely moored the dock. "Please don't tell us you cannot accept this gift"

"Without the stones, I'm not sure."

"Yes; you can." A man stepped out of the shadows. It was Morning Star's cousin, one of the few who still resided on the reserve.

"Yes. You must accept the gift." Her cousin's wife joined them on the quay.

"I agree," another said.

Four more of the clan stepped into view.

"*Myeengun*, *Ziigwan*, what brings you here," Morning Star asked, a little confused.

"The caw of the raven perched in a high tree, "*Myeengun* replied.

"The whispering wind, blowing through the tall grass," said another.

"Last night, in a dream," an eighth person responded as she stepped into the light from the lantern the caretaker held.

Two elders joined the gathering. "We were told a replacement totem would arrive this evening."

"So many. Nobody told me," Morning Star proclaimed, sounding annoyed that she had not received the message.

The first man laughed. "You are here are you not, dear cousin."

"Without the artifact, the totem alone will not restore prosperity to the tribe."

"You know this for a fact?" her cousin's wife asked.

"No. Even so..."

"Enough with your protests *Wâpanacahkos* [Morning Star's tribal name]," an elder admonished. "At the southern boundary to the reserve a hole has already been dug to receive the replacement *ojibwe* [totem]. The occasion calls for a great celebration. Tribes up and down the Frazer valley will be invited to attend. All of you on the boat will be our guests of honor."

"That's very kind of you," Julia replied. "We accept." For good measure, she gave the caretaker a hug. "Cheer up, Morning Star. This is not a time to look so dejected."

The elders and other tribal members turned and drifted into the night.

"One question, Morning Star, before we say goodnight." It was the Brazilian who spoke. "How are you going to lift the totem out of the water and set it upright in the ground?"

Pushing aside her melancholy mood, amidst squeals of laughter, the caretaker replied, "Me personally? I'm not. There will be plenty of volunteers before the ceremony. It's a great privilege to take part in the raising of a *ojibwe*."

"Unless of course, one has a giant crane up one's sleeve," Federico proposed. "I know you too well, Harper. That's just the kind of stunt you would come up with."

Harper walked up to his friend and placed a hand firmly on his shoulder. Straight-faced he told him, "You know that's a great idea, my friend. Unfortunately, I have it on good authority that using a crane on a First Nations reserve is against the local bylaws."

"Sorry, I didn't know." Crest-fallen, the Brazilian added, "It was just a suggestion."

Dee, who had been standing next to Federico, spoke. "Don't take it so personally, *mi amigo*. There's no such regulation. Harper is teasing you. It's just a bit of fun." She gave him a hard kiss on the cheek. "There. Do you feel better now?"

"Again, please." Federico pointed to his lips.

"Don't push your luck, *compañero*." Harper cautioned. "A lady has her reputation to protect."

Everyone, including Federico, laughed.

CHAPTER FIFTY-SIX

A NEW DAY WITHIN THE LILLOOET-HARRISON BASIN. OFTEN mistaken as ducks, black and white Common Loons, heads buried in the water, were feeding on crayfish. Half a dozen Western Painted Turtles, who had hauled themselves onto a log, basked in the sun. A ground squirrel was marshaling her litter of seven kits away from a solitary skunk whose tail was held aloft in a threatening manner. Birds twittered to one another from the trees. *God's in His Heaven; all's right with the world.* One person, however, would disagree.

———

"Is that a good idea?"

Although the voice was familiar, Morning Star jerked in surprise as she traversed the planking she was using to bridge the gap between the landing stage and the moored totem pole. "Enough with your unsolicited advice, Bear Cub. You nearly made me fall into the lake."

"But you didn't," the ghost-spirit replied, suddenly appearing on the quay.

The caretaker looked in his direction, before inching her way onto the totem itself. Once there, with teetering steps, she gingerly proceeded towards the raven's head carving.

"Now what are you up to?"

Ignoring the question, Morning Star muttered, "Ah! I thought so. There's black tape over the bird's eyes." Knees bent, arms outstretched, she attempted peeling away the protective covering.

Running Bear shouted at his friend, "Leave well alone, *Wâpanac-ahkos*. Do not interfere with the relic."

"I ... I was only going to take a peek, that's all."

"Not true. You were going to remove it, and we both know why. Relic or no relic, my time here is coming to a close."

The old woman waved a hand of dismissal, still trying to reach the tape.

"Enough, I say." The boy had moved to stand on the bole of the totem.

Morning Star stood to her full height, turned, and scoffed. "You're going to stop me, ghost-boy? I don't think so. I'm a shaman, remember. I could walk right through you as if you were made of thin air." She laughed. "That's a good one. Thin air. That's all you are. Thin air."

"Air, maybe, but not so thin."

Out of nowhere a strong westerly wind suddenly began blowing off the lake, causing the two pontoons to rock back and forth as they wrestled with the mooring lines. In sympathy, the totem itself pitched up and down. So violent the movement became, the caretaker lost her balance. With a resounding splash, which caused the ducks to take flight, she hit the water.

Upon surfacing, she exclaimed, "You idiot, Bear Cub. You know I can't swim."

Regaining her feet, she realized she was standing in three feet of water. While wading to the shore, Morning Star thought she heard the faint sound of laughter. She looked around, but no one was there to witness her misadventure. The noise repeated, this time as vibrations from the cab of the disused log loader. It was the vestige of what was now an abating zephyr announcing its departure.

Still bemoaning her early morning bath, the older woman entered her cabin. "There you are, you little weasel. Look what you've done." The boy laughed. "And stop sitting on my table. It is where I eat."

Running Bear, like a blur, crossed the room, stopping beside the stove. In turn, this earned him a further reprimand as Morning Star made to boil a kettle. Another swift movement and the ghost-spirit stood beside the tapestry hanging on the back wall of the cabin.

As the caretaker shuffled toward the bedroom, she told her *otôtêmimâw* [friend], "No thanks to you, I need to get into dry clothes."

By the time the shaman returned, the kettle was boiling. Without speaking she threw a mixture of dried fungi and herbs into the teapot. Two teaspoons of finely-chopped dandelion leaves were added to make the taste tolerable.

"How can you drink such glop?" Running Bear remarked, as he watched hot water being added to the concoction.

"If you must know, it's to steady my nerves and to ward off a chill." Taking a large teacup from the dresser, she sat down and waited for the tea to brew. Still in a sour mood, Morning Star added, "*Now,* what's you problem? Your standing there grinning like a Cheshire cat."

"I thought it funny," was the reply, "seeing you splashing around in the lake."

"I could have drowned if I had been standing at the other end of the totem. Would you be laughing then?"

"Drowned? Unlikely. I'd have called on a water nymph or a whale to save you."

"There are no whales in Little Lake Harrison or the bigger one for that matter." The caretaker poured herself a cup of tea and began blowing across the rim to cool the drink.

The boy's head turned slightly to take in the needlepoint on the tapestry. "Your embroidery says different, as do the cave paintings."

Morning Star did not respond to the remark. Instead, she took a tentative sip from her cup. "Ugh."

"Ha, ha. Told you that brew would taste revolting."

"You're a herbalist now, I suppose."

Adopting a crestfallen look, it was the boy's turn to say nothing.

However, *Wâpanacahkos* had been friends with her bear cub for too long to sustain their oral jousting. Consequently, she spoke about the cave paintings. "Mere childish pranks, as was telling tourists we owned a gold mine."

"But our ruse worked. Earned us a few dollars in pocket change, as I recall."

"Until your father wanted to know where the money came from."

"Don't remind me," the boy answered. "He was so mad with me, I had to groom the horses for a month."

Morning Star offered her near-toothless grin, as she remembered her friend constantly complaining at the time. "But all in all, we had a good time, wouldn't you agree?"

"We did then and again now." The boy turned once more and pointed with his finger. He spoke about *Wâpanacahkos'* decision to add the airplane to the mural. "And now your dream is fulfilled. Strangers have arrived from far away. The one called Harper has strange powers, which he used to recover the relic. We are blessed."

Morning Star continued sipping her tea. "Don't forget the two women. The younger sister is very perceptive of our customs and culture. She understands the significance of the prayer flag, for example."

The spirit-boy chuckled. "I would have stayed with or without the flag, we both know that. What do you think of the older girl?"

"Spencer? She's very resourceful. Sent her dog to get help when the boy fell down the slope."

Running Bear knew that the dog left of its own volition, but did not wish to trample on Morning Star's supposition. Rather, he continued, "Spencer reminds me of you at her age."

"She has a playmate. I didn't."

"I know. I'm sorry. Blame Hayes for that. But, imagine if we had been born sixty years later; we could have been like them. I've been watching the pair. That winged bird used to explore the area is amazing."

The caretaker picked up the teapot and replenished her cup. After another sip. she responded, "The winged bird, as you call it, is a drone." Morning Star smiled. "Think of all the mischief we could have gotten up to using one."

Both laughed, except from the woman it was more of a snort.

"What's the matter? Has the tea got up your nose?" Running Bear wondered. "What is in that brew? Smells like liberty caps. Am I right? Another name for magic mushrooms, I believe. What else? Wavy caps and diviner's sage?" The spirit boy whistled through his teeth. "I'm surprised you have not poisoned yourself."

The caretaker shrieked with laughter. "It will take more than a few mushrooms and herbs to kill off this old crow."Notwithstanding, Morning Stat shook her head, trying to clear the fog. "But I fear I have consumed too much."

"Then I shall take my leave. Promise me, no more climbing on totem poles, even if they are horizontal."

"I promise," the caretaker replied, but her words were lost to the empty room.

Hosting herself off the chair, Morning Star swiveled to survey the room. The tapestry became the focus of her gaze. *The whale. The airplane. The paddle steamer.* Repeating the word "Paddle steamer" out loud jarred her memory of the boat trip to Hot Springs with Blue Jay. "When was that?" Unable to recall the date, she picked up the photograph from atop the mantelpiece and read the notation written on the back. "Blue Jay would now be fifty years old if she had lived." There was a deep sigh. " By now, I could have been a grandmother; a great grandmother even."

Adjusting the frame to face front, about to replace it on the shelf, Morning Star noticed a bracelet laying next to the print. *Where did that come from?* she wondered, picking it up; holding it firmly between her fingers.

Flashes of white light blinded her eyes, to be replaced by moving images of a young girl tripping along the lakeshore, singing to herself. "Blue Jay. Where are you going, my baby girl?" The image change to the edge of a forest. The sound of an animal in distress. Twigs snapping as Blue Jay hastens towards its cries.

A clearing. Moss-covered ground. The girl walks forward. She stops at the edge of a pit. She leans over. She speaks. "Poor little fawn.

Where is your mommy? Come here. Let me lift you out." Blue Jay lies on the ground. Arms outstretched, she reaches forward. The baby deer backs away. "Don't be scared. I won't hurt you. Hold on. I'll come to you."

"No, no, Blue Jay. Don't do it," Morning Star cried, as the image morphed to her daughter starting to descend into the pit using an overhanging vine as support.

"No," Morning Star screamed, Dropping the bracelet, in an instant, the visions are cut off.

———

Hours passed. Morning Star had been sitting on the floor, knees drawn tightly to her chest. Her eyes now red, her face stained with tears, an indescribable pain welled up in her chest.

There was the sound of someone on the porch. The caretaker looked toward the door. It did not open. "Who's there?" she asked. "Bear Cub is that you?"

No one answered.

Using the edge of the table as leverage, Morning Star hauled herself to her feet. With faltering steps she walked to the window. Pushing the drapes aside, she looked through the begrimed glass. Fleeing movement by the lakeshore caught the caretaker's attention. Just as quickly, an eerie stillness returned. *Spencer*, she decided. *No. Wrong color hair.* Stepping outside, she called, "Blue Jay, it's mommy. Show yourself."

"It's your imagination, *Wâpanacahkos.* She is not here." Running Bear was again standing beside her. "Like me, it is time for *Kwîhkwîsiw* to leave. Ghost-spirits no longer have a place where a sacred relic protects the community."

Morning Star wept as Running Bear placed his arms around her waist. "I cannot endure the pain of losing both you and Blue Jay." For the first time in sixty-two years, she felt a palpable touch as they embraced.

"We both love you *Wâpanacahkos,* but you know that already," the boy told her. "Someday, soon, we shall again be together."

"No one wants to know the date they will die, Bear Cub."

The ghost-spirit laughed. "Always the pragmatist, now and when we were young. I'll say no more."

After a long silence, enjoying the moment, Morning Star perceived her childhood friend had drifted away. That said, a phrase came to mind; to be found carved around the base of the totem:

That which is held within your heart will never leave you.

CHAPTER FIFTY-SEVEN

Spencer was staring at the oil painting that hung on the wall in the Book House library. Something was different, but she was unable to identify exactly what. "Come here a second, Olly," she asked. "Take a look at this."

"A man and a boy reflected in the water. What's the big deal?"

"It's changed," Spencer told him, lifting a hand to touch the canvas.

"Don't," a gruff voice from behind advised. "The paint is still wet."

Both children jumped. Immediately turning around, mouths open, they gazed in astonishment at a man with a weathered face, an unkempt beard, sporting a worn leather jacket.

Oliver was the first to react. "My dad's in the next room. He's got a gun."

"By now, your parents are at the reserve watching the people arrive for tomorrow's ceremony. I saw them leave thirty minutes ago. The pair of you as well. along with the other adults. Why are you back here?"

"I forgot my camera," Spencer informed him, "but I can't find it anywhere."

"You it left on the coat stand in the hall," the interloper told her.

"I looked there, already."

"Then perhaps it's here," the intruder suggested, producing the item previously hidden behind his back.

"Give it here, this instant," she demanded, boldly snatching it away.

"You must be Spencer," the stranger told her. "A feisty little thing, aren't you? And you must be Oliver. You have the Norton chin, just like your mother."

"We can't see *your* chin," Spencer instantly responded, but then the implication of what had just been said dawned on her. "Wait a minute. You're Chance Norton. You're supposed to be dead."

"A ghost. Stunning," Oliver decided. "Mom was right. This house is haunted."

Chance laughed, at the same time pinching the back of his hand. "I don't feel dead, sorry to disappoint. I didn't mean to startle the two of you. You interrupted me putting the finishing touches to my oil paint-ing. I had to duck out of sight, in a rush."

"Mom and Aunt Dee were told you are dead. We came all the way from Georgia, that's in the USA, to check this place out."

"I know where Georgia is, Olly. I spent many years in the States, before moving to Canada. Tell me, what do you think of *this place*, as you call it, although I prefer the Book House?"

"Wicked" Oliver answered. "Lots of nooks and crannies. We are discovering things all the time,"

"Especially in the attic," said Spencer. "There's a rocking horse up there. The saddle's a bit worn, but it works real good."

"And an old train set, made from tinplate," Oliver added.

"All belonging to former occupants. Apart from the books I purchased in Hartzell and my journal, most of my personal belongings I removed before you guys arrived."

"You left the invisible writing and the engraved clue on the letter opener," Oliver reminded him.

"I had to plant a hint or two, otherwise the mystery of the stolen bones might never have been solved," explained Chance. "Say; I'm hungry. Any possibility you could rustle up something for me to eat?"

"I could make you a cheese sandwich," volunteered Spencer, "and a glass of milk."

As the three walked to the kitchen. Chance asked if they had anything stronger than milk. Oliver was reluctant to offer him alcohol without his dad's permission. Chance settle for a mug of tea.

Once seated around the breakfast table, Spencer asked again about her grandfather's faked death.

"Happenstance, that's all," she was informed. "An unexpected opportunity presented itself, while I was canoeing on the Frazer River. After going down some rapids, I can across another canoe that had capsized. In the shallows was a body, much the same age as me, and of similar build. Sorry to say, his face was unrecognizable having smashed into some boulders. By leaving my wallet containing my driver's license on the corpse, the authorities assumed it was me. I had already written a will leaving this property to Julia and Dalia, and, as I hoped, they came here to check it out."

"That makes no sense," Spencer argued. "Why did you want them to visit the Book House?"

"Having successfully tracked down the buyer, despite my pleading, he adamantly refused to part with the relic. It took Roger's remarkable talents to get the bones back."

"Dad doesn't like being called by his first name," Oliver announced. "Remember that when you meet him."

"You said *remarkable talents*," Spencer repeated. "How did you reach that conclusion?"

"One time, when I was in England, I read in the national newspapers that Harper had been instrumental in recovering stolen artwork and other valuables, including some of the crown jewels. It was rumored he would receive an award from the Queen herself, but, without explanation, he disappeared."

"Mom and I were on the steps of St. Paul's Cathedral when he was arrested," Oliver told him. "Deported to the States, Mom was told, but he never reached there."

Chance shook his head. "A sorry business indeed, leaving Julia in somewhat of a bind. Not only did she have to look after you, Oliver, but she was expecting your sister, Ophelia. So, I put myself in her place, and asked where she might go. I concluded your mother would most likely stay with your Great Aunt Cordelia in Savannah, Georgia."

Chance finished his mug of tea with a loud slurp and asked for a refill. Then he continued, "Once I saw you had arrived there safely, I kept tabs on my sister-in-law's house for a while. A few weeks later a courier arrives carrying a funeral urn and a wreath. Checking newspaper reports, it seems your father, Oliver, had died attempting to rescue inmates from the American detention camp in Cuba."

"Aunt Julia never told us about receiving any ashes," Spencer confided.

"Probably, she didn't want to upset ya'll. Good job, too, as a few months later Harper turns up alive and kicking. A bit like me turning up now," Chance added with an impassioned chuckle. "Never did find out what Harper was doing in Cuba, though."

"He was working undercover, helping find local people who had been kidnapped. Turns out a mad scientist was linking their brains together with electrodes, trying to make a human computer. Dad stopped all that."

"You must be very proud of your father. And my hunch was right. Harper and his friend tracked down the artifact in Vancouver and persuaded the collector woman to give it back. Lord knows how, but he did it."

"Grandpa, will you attend the raising of the new totem?"

Chance felt a sudden skip of a heartbeat. He had never been called *grandpa* before. "Unlikely," was the hesitant reply.

"Are you going to wait here until the others get back?"

Again a pause. "Best not. I don't want to open old wounds with my daughters."

Chance got up from the table.

"We shall have to tell them you were here," Spencer enlightened him. "They are sure to ask why we didn't return to Port Douglas."

"I wouldn't want either of you to lie on my behalf. No doubt Julia and Dalia's response will be the same as your Great Aunt Cordelia. The old biddy never had a good word for me, always saying I could never stay in one place very long. Called me a *rolling stone*, she did. I guess she's right."

Heading down the hall toward the front door, Chance stopped. "Give that painting a day or two for the fresh pigment to dry. It would be a shame to smudge it with your fingerprints."

Remembering the addition Chance had added, Spencer asked, "Why did you paint in the boy standing next to the man. Only his reflection in the water was there before."

"That's for me to know, and you to work out, missy." Which left Oliver and Spencer standing on the porch, once more open-mouthed, as Chance headed for the cover of the forest.

CHAPTER FIFTY-EIGHT

"COLD, HALF-FULL MUGS OF TEA, AND BREADCRUMBS ALL OVER THE kitchen table? What have the pair of you been up to?" Julia demanded.

"We had a visitor," Oliver answered. "You're never going to believe who?"

"No time for guessing games, son," his father responded. "Your mother and I were getting worried."

"Grandpa Norton." the boy announced. "He explained how he faked his death in order to encourage you to come here and recover the relic."

Dee inquired, "Is Chance here now?"

"He left a short while ago," Spencer responded. "Chance told us he shouldn't stay around incase he upset you and Aunt Julia."

"Typical," Dee remarked. "He abandoned my mother and me when I was five years old, and now he cannot stay to say hello. I can't remember much about him, except that he liked to draw and paint."

"The reflections painting in the library was painted by Grandpa," Oliver volunteered.

"I knew there was something familiar about that painting. The scrawny tree can be found in John Trout Lake Park, Vancouver. I used to play on the nearby swings, as a child."

"That was the reason Grandpa came into the house. To paint in the missing silhouette of the boy on the embankment."

"We asked why," Spencer interjected. "He replied, *That's for me to know, and you to work out*. Does anyone understand what he meant?"

There was silence, until Federico spoke. "I believe Chance now believes that with the return of the bones the boy no longer needs to remain a spirit."

No one could think of a better explanation.

"How long do you think Chance has been hanging round?" Harper wondered.

"Ever since we arrived things have mysteriously been moved in the house. More recently, I had a strong feeling I was being watched when I rescued the injured bird."

"I bet Chance was watching Olly and me, when we went on our adventure to the top of the hill," Spencer decided. "Although, if he saw Olly slither down the slope, why didn't he come to the rescue?"

"Saw the dog go for help, I expect," Federico suggested.

"More likely he wanted to keep his little, 'I am dead', secret under wraps,"Dee surmised.

"True," Harper agreed. "Assuming he was there and help had not arrived, I'm sure Chance would have stepped in. Olly is his grandson, after all."

Julia scoffed. "That's taking the charitable point of view. Cordelia said that Dad always was a free agent, coming and going as he chose."

"Do you think we'll see Grandpa Norton again?" Spencer asked.

"If he does return to the Book House, I for one won't be here to meet him," Dee informed the group. "I received an email late yesterday evening, asking me to return to the University. Apparently a member of staff has been hospitalized. They want me to stand in for a while. I plan to leave a day or two after the First Nations festivities. Sorry to spring the news like this, but there was never going to be a good time to tell you."

"Then we will have a farewell dinner this evening," Julia decided. "Roger, go and pull some steaks out of the freezer. Federico, you can make sure the barbecue lights okay. You kids can set the table on the front porch. Everyone got that?"

"What are you going to be doing, Mom?"

Julia smiled, "Dee and I are going to kick back, share a bottle of wine, and talk about old times. Any objections?"

Before anyone could protest, Dee called out, "Two votes in favor. Four abstentions. Motion is carried."

CHAPTER FIFTY-NINE

REPRESENTATIVES OF THE *KIK'WAT* TO THE NORTH, THE *SKWAH* TO the south, and tribal bands in-between gathered at Port Douglas. Come nightfall, the *potlach*, or gift-giving feast would begin. Morning Star explained that the lavish demonstration of generosity was the traditional way of celebrating the raising of a new or replacement totem pole.

As the feasting began, drums and rattles were used to make music, which provided the accompaniment for songs. The songs, in turn, were the background for dances. A large bonfire illuminated the proceedings.

The opening pair of dancers, dressed in costumes made of straw, flapped their arms as they moved. Both wearing headdresses depicting large beaked birds. they slowly circled the fire. As the sounds increased other members of the troupe joined in, responding to the hypnotic rhythm. Soon the majority of attendees were on their feet swaying to and fro, Hoops of laughter and squeals of delight accompanied the frivolities.

A loud drum roll interrupted the proceedings, a signal it was time to raise the totem. Some pulled on ropes, while others pushed simply by lending weight with their shoulders. Locals and visitors, young and

old, the pole was slowly raised. Once straightened, and fixed into position with rocks and dirt, loud cheering and clapping erupted
throughout the crowd.

Copious quantities of food and drink were consumed as the cele-
brations continued with fervor. Nevertheless, over time the flames of
the fire dwindled, eventually diminishing to a dull glow of smoldering
embers. The music ceased.

"Time to return to the Book House," Julia announced. "Gather up
the picnic blankets and head for the Land Rover. I'll bring Ophelia."

Dee, Federico, and the older children left. Harper, however, stood
his ground, for complete silence had overtaken the gathering. One of
the clan separated herself from the assemblage and began a protracted,
high-pitched, ululation. It was Morning Star.

Moments later, two men stepped forward. Each began pulling on a
thin cord of twine, which snaked up to patches covering the raven's
eyes. In unison they tugged. As the coverings fell away slivers of bright,
white light shone from the sockets.

Save for Morning Star's voice, not a sound was heard. The crowd
watched as the older woman pulled an eagle's feather from her headband.
With exaggerated strides, she circled the *ojibwe*. Pausing between
mesmeric twists and turns, she pointed the feather north, then south, east,
then west. *Wâpanacahkos* called on *Sisiutl*, the supernatural three-headed
serpent. Unlike six decades earlier, when the rite centered on the death of
a young boy, that evening the focus was on good fortune and prosperity.

The ritual continued until the lone dancer sank to the ground
exhausted. Shortly afterward the gathering dispersed, and Harper
ushered his flock to the vehicle.

———

Back at the Book House, Julia carried Ophelia in her arms, the two-
year-old being sound asleep. The older children, after making half-
hearted protests for they were truly tired, readied themselves for bed.
Roger Harper, feeling the effects of too much adult beverage, slumped
into a rocking chair on the front porch and closed his eyes. Conse-

quently, he did not notice that a few minutes later, his sister-in-law and Federico had occupied seats nearby. Using notepads that rested on their laps, both began writing up the events of the evening. Fifteen minutes later, having ensured all the children were in bed, Julia joined them, curious as to what was being penned.

"I'm writing the conclusion of my novel," the Brazilian explained. "The ceremony, music, and dancing adds color to one of the final chapters."

Julia smiled encouragingly, and then asked, "When will I get a chance to read it?"

"Soon. I'm hoping the ending will take the reader's breath away."

"What about you, sis?"

"The *potlach* ceremony was fascinating," Dee replied. "I've read about them in textbooks, but witnessing the real thing is something else. Not wanting to forget, I was jotting down questions to ask Morning Star."

"What sort of questions?" Julia asked.

"The gift-giving, for starters. It requires great wealth to be so generous. I'm wondering how the local band could afford to be so extravagant."

"Don't tell me, Dee, you are going to publish a paper in some academic journal."

"That's part of the things I do, Harper. I am an anthropologist after all."

"I thought you might have fallen asleep, Roger," Julia remarked. "Earlier, I was talking to *Ziigwan,* Morning Star's cousin. She told me the elders distill potato mash with birch sap. It makes an alcoholic drink more potent than vodka. You certainly were knocking it back."

Ignoring the reference to the amount he had consumed, Harper replied, "No, I'm wide awake. Although my head is still buzzing from all the shouting and people jigging about. Mind you, I must admit, it was quite a gathering of the local tribes."

"Yes, it was," Julia agreed. "I'm happy we played a part in restoring the relic to its rightful owners."

"Talking of generosity, that was a magnanimous gesture of your part, Harper, paying for the new totem and getting it transported here."

"It was the least I could do, Dee. Jules and I like living here. It's our way of giving back to the community."

"What about you. sis? Are you going to come live with us?"

"On a permanent basis, no. The university won't grant me indefinite leave of absence. I'll come visit in the vacations, for sure."

"Good," Julia responded. "What are you planning to do, Federico?"

"That depends," was the reply.

Harper cut in. " *Depends*. What sort of answer is that?"

"At this time, I'd rather not say. It's personal."

"Personal, hah?" Harper offered a piercing look. "Federico, is it my imagination? I do believe your face has turned bright red." He snickered. "You're blushing."

CHAPTER SIXTY

HARPER, WHO WAS SITTING, GAZING ACROSS THE LAKE, HEARD THE screen door behind him slam closed. He turned his head to see his sister-in-law steering Ophelia, practically unassisted, towards him. The infant giggled as she rushed the last few steps into her father's outstretched arms.

"That's my girl," he said, as he lifted his daughter onto his lap. "Why has Aunt Dee brought you out here?"

"Julia's orders," Dee replied, on Ophelia's behalf. "The pair of you are to spend some quality time together."

"Is that so? I'm already busy, keeping an eye on Oliver and Spencer, who are kayaking."

Dee held a hand to shade her eyes from the glare of the sun. "Those two dots halfway across the lake, you mean. And what are you going to do if either one gets into trouble."

"They won't," Harper replied dismissively. "Besides they are both wearing life preservers and are strong swimmers."

"I hope you're right," was the response as Dee removed a blanket from a canvas bag that had been looped over her left arm. She spread it out on the wooden decking. "There. Now you and Ophelia can play without getting dirty."

"Play what?" Harper said defensively, wondering what was in store.

A cardboard box was the second item removed from the bag. Deposited on the blanket, Dee removed the lid. "You can help your daughter with this wooden jigsaw puzzle."

"I'm not very good at jigsaw puzzles," Harper professed.

"For heaven's sake. It's only twelve pieces. The pair of you best get started, otherwise I'll report you to the boss."

"Okay, okay. Come on, Ophelia; let's show Aunt Dee how clever you are."

Dee sat herself down in the chair Harper had vacated. Immediately the dog, who had been lolling on the grass a few feet away, came over and nuzzled her into stroking its head.

"And why aren't you with your mistress, Shadow?" she asked.

Three pieces of the puzzle in place, Harper looked up. "Last time the mutt went on the water, he fell off the front of Spencer's kayak big time, Olly told me. Now you're a dedicated landlubber, aren't you boy?"

Shadow, whined in protest at having his secret revealed.

Dee patted the dog's head once more. "Never mind. Could have been worse. Harper might have given you the kiss of life." She laughed.

"That joke is worse than one of mine," Harper told her. Then, returning to the task in hand, he asked his daughter, "Where does this piece go, honey?"

Seemingly without effort, Ophelia chose the right place. Same for the next, and the next; in quick succession.

"Smart girl. You clearly have your father's brains."

"*You* are *clearly* cheating, Harper," Dee told him.

"Not me," her brother-in-law replied, holding both hands in the air as if that was proof enough.

"You get inside people's heads, Harper, with your mind-reading funny business."

For the moment, he ignored the accusation, helping Ophelia complete the puzzle. Then he responded, "I don't know what you mean."

Ophelia, grabbing the corner of the blanket, pulled. The jigsaw pieces scattered in disarray.

Dee scoffed. "There. That's your daughter's way of indicating you should stop telling porky-pies." Harper opened his mouth to protest but Dee cut him off.

"Do you remember the evening of the first day we met? Over dinner, I had the distinct impression things were being held back from me, and every time I attempted to ask, the probing question just slipped away. That was you, Roger, with your mind trick, wasn't it."

"My mind trick? Come on, Dee. You have been reading too many science fiction novels."

"Have I? How about the time you walked the streets of a Vancouver suburb, looking for the person who bought the native artifact from Hayes? Did you knock on every door, *Roger*? No. You stood outside and probed the occupants' minds. Didn't take you long to come up with the answer, did it?"

Harper about to protest; again Dee cut him off.

"Then there's the fact that Morning Star deliberately lied about the nature of the stolen relic. She led everyone to believe it was fashioned from jade. At first, you too were sucked in, but not for long. You, *Roger*, figured it out. You took a quick trip into her head and found the truth."

Harper, seeking distraction, began turning puzzle pieces right-side up. Ophelia, deciding this was a great game, promptly turned then back again.

"Please stop calling me Roger. You know I don't like people, other than Jules, calling me by my first name."

"If you want me to stop calling you Roger, *Roger*, start telling me the truth."

"All right. I admit it. Did Julia tell you?"

"Have a little faith in your wife, Harper. She is not one to betray a confidence. It was your *amigo*. He told me how you tricked your way past the guards who tried to block your escape from Guantánamo Bay. Further confirmation you can get inside people's heads." There was a pause and a moment of realization. "Where is Federico, by the way?"

"Oh. He's at the dock. Loading empty fuel drums onto the house-boat, ready for the trip to Harrison Hot Springs. Either that, or he has eloped with Morning Star."

"Enough with the jokes, Harper."

"Why are you blushing, Dee?"

"Stop it Harper, or, as soon as Julia finishes washing her hair, I'll tell her you are being mean to me. As a child you experienced being bullied, so you know what it's like. That is something Julia *did* tell me. The time you and your so-called friends went scrumping apples. They got caught by the farmer; you didn't. *Roger the Dodger*, they called you, all through high school."

It was Harper's turn to be red-faced.

"I'm thinking you evaded the farmer by subconsciously getting into his brain. I believe you possessed an innate aptitude to read people's minds. I haven't yet figured out how your natural ability was amplified, but I suspect that was connected to the oil rig episode."

Harper raised a eyebrow, neither confirming or denying the assertion.

From a distance, they heard the toot of the approaching Rover's horn.

"Here comes your *amigo*, Dee." Harper offered an all-knowing grin. "And don't deny you have a soft spot for Federico. We've already established I can read minds."

CHAPTER SIXTY-ONE

AND SO IT WAS. DEE HAD SAID HER GOODBYES TO JULIA, HARPER, the children, and Morning Star. Federico carried her baggage on board the houseboat and waited for his passenger to join him.

"Be safe, sis," Julia called, as Harper cast off the mooring lines. With the Brazilian at the helm, they were underway.

"What's with the snazzy summer dress your sister is wearing, Jules?" her husband inquired. "You don't think Dee is intent on getting her hook's into Federico do you?"

"Don't tittle-tattle, Roger. You sound like a washer woman with nothing better to do but spread gossip."

Unaware of Harper's remarks, Dee watched from the bow as the boat made its way toward the southern end of the smaller lake. She kept a close eye on the clearance either side as it negotiated the narrow channel. Within minutes they had entered Harrison Lake itself.

Having previously read up on the lake's geography, she knew Harrison Lake was the largest lake in the southern Coast Mountains of western Canada. Occupying a former glacial valley, it covered an area of approximately ninety-five square miles. A non-stop journey to Harrison Hot Springs would take approximately five hours. From the resort Dee would continue her journey to Vancouver by bus.

In the meantime, the Brazilian remained in the wheelhouse, as Dee moved to the top deck. She spent a short time scanning the water for birds, but without binoculars she only spotted a pair of herons and a flock of Canadian geese; the latter busy grazing the lakeshore grass, preparing for their migration south. Ten minutes later, Dee decided to check up on her pilot.

"Everything okay," he asked as his companion approached, offering an awkward smile.

Dee nodded. By way of conversation, she inquired, "Is your novel finished?"

"Apart from a spellcheck, yes. I worked until the early hours to get it done."

"Did you bring the manuscript with you?"

"I did. You can read it, if you like."

"It would be my pleasure, Federico. Do you mind if I go back to the top deck? It's a little quieter there."

A nod of assent, another awkward smile from the author, and Dee left to return to her lounger.

Hours later, having passed Echo Island, Dee heard a change in background noise as the boat's engines were shut down. Moments later there was the splash of an anchor being tossed overboard, leaving the stationary vessel bobbing up and down in the slight chop. The sound of footsteps on the decking caused her to look up. The Brazilian was carrying a picnic hamper in one hand, two glasses and a bottle of wine in the other.

"Are you ready for lunch?" he asked, sitting down at the nearby table. As he poured the wine, Dee moved to sit beside him, setting the manuscript to one side.

He waited until Dee had taken the first bite out of her sandwich before asking, "How is the reading going?"

"I've just finished the penultimate chapter," she replied.

"Really. You *are* a fast reader. What do you think of it so far?"

"Needs a little editing here and there, but overall it's pretty good." Dee took a sip from her wineglass and bit into a raw carrot. "You know, once I've written something, I find it helps to read it out loud. Would you like me to do that for the final chapter?"

Federico, once again, nodded his head. Dee did not seem to notice the flush of pink skin exposed above the collar of his neckline.

CHAPTER SIXTY-TWO

MORE WINE, A SHORT WAIT WHILE SHE FINISHED THE SANDWICH, then she began:

"Shortly the sun would rise, bringing warmth to an otherwise crisp morning. In preparation for the short jaunt that was to come, the occupants of the Land Rover were bundled in sweaters and windcheaters.

The party reached the cabin, home of Morning Star. She was standing beside her dilapidated truck, waiting. By way of greeting she waved, before climbing into the cab. Turning on the ignition and headlights, she made a slow turn, taking the track that followed the head of the lake. She crossed the Old Courthouse Creek bridge, slowing as she looked in her rearview mirror. The brights of the Land Rover could be seen bobbing up and down as its suspension wrestled with the uneven terrain.

Morning Star turned north, following the same route the older children had taken on their first adventure unaccompanied by adults. Like a young foal following a mare, the Land Rover stayed close at all times.

Having ascended part-way up the hill, they arrived at the edge of a large clearing where a ruin of earthen mounds huddled together in the center. Morning Star stopped her truck and turned off the lights. On cue an orange-red hue broke on the horizon, signaling the new dawn. After opening the truck's door and stepping out, she waited until the occupants of the other vehicle had done the same. Her brisk two words were, "Follow me."

Julia, carrying Ophelia, Dee, Federico, and the two older children did as directed. No one spoke, unsure what to expect. In the distance an owl hooted. The sound of feet shuffling through the grass spooked a jackrabbit, sending it scampering for cover.

Spencer tugged on Oliver's arm to gain his attention. She mouthed, *"We've been to this place before."*

Nodding an understanding, the youth mouthed back. *I know. This is where we ate lunch.*

After a short distance Morning Star stopped, half-turned and instructed," This is close enough, wait here."

The older woman resumed walking. Sixty feet farther she stopped at one of the flat-topped, mounds. Morning Star pulled out a small trowel, previously hidden in the fold of her waterproof jacket, and carefully began to dig.

"Wherever have you been?" Julia asked of as Harper quietly joined the onlookers.

"I had an errand to run," he confessed.

"You are worse than a child. Next time use the

bathroom *before* you leave the house," she whispered. "Fortunately you didn't miss much."

Once the depth reached six inches Morning Star stopped, looked towards the eastern horizon, and smiled in satisfaction.

She produced a silver bracelet that she allowed to slip from her fingers into the hole.

For a few moments, there was silence. Then, as the sky morphed into blue, the woman removed an ancient wampum from around her neck. After lifting it high to allow the sun goddess to snatch at the threaded ring of elk teeth, she placed it with the bracelet.

Spoken in her native tongue, Morning Star began calling on the two spirits of Bluejay and Running Bear to depart this place; to head toward and over the mountains, to cross the sea, to rise into the heavens.

Then, save for the far-off call of a pigeon, for a short while there was silence.

Morning Star wiped aside tears from her eyes, before tenderly stroking soil to cover the two objects. Returning to the group the older woman forced a smile and then spoke. "With the agreement of the tribal elders, it is my privilege to welcome you all as honorary members of our clan. For retuning the relic, I say *kinanâskomitin*, which means in my native tongue, thank you. I am forever grateful."

"*Thank you* for the permitting us to witness this final sacrament," Dee replied. "We are truly privileged."

After the ceremony everyone returned to their respective vehicles. The Land Rover left first.

"Heart wrenching," the older sister concluded,

as they began the drive back to the Book House. "Does anyone disagree?"

"With respect, Aunt Julia, I do." The statement came from Spencer, who was sitting in the back seat with her cousin. *"Why do my brothers mourn? Why do my daughters weep? that a young man has gone to the happy hunting-grounds."*

"That's very profound, young lady," Harper responded. "What made you think of that?"

"It's the quote from James Fenimore Cooper's *The Last of the Mohicans*."

"Which makes a fitting elegy for us to remember Running Bear," Federico suggested.

———

As Morning Star settled inside her truck, two items left on the passenger seat caught her attention. The set of keys was less puzzling once she realized they were the ones misplaced around the time she borrowed the Land Rover to drive to Tipello. The other item was a folded newspaper; a copy of the *Vancouver Sun*. Scrawled across the front page were the words:

Page 2 will interest you.

Looking inside she read another message, this time in the margin:

May your Bear Cub rest in peace.

And opposite the headline:

LOCAL POLICE PUZZLED AFTER FINDING VAGRANT IN SHAUGHNESSY SUBURB OF VANCOUVER WHO CLAIMS THE INJURY

**TO HIS LEFT SHOULDER HAD BEEN CAUSED BY A VEHICLE
LUG NUT.**

It took the elderly woman only a few minutes to read the article, which referred to a man with a black widow spider tattoo on his neck. From the marking alone, Morning Star knew the man was undoubtedly William Hayes; the son of Running Bear's killer. However, it was another half-hour before she drove back to her cabin, the time spent gazing through the truck's windshield as the sun slowly rose higher in the sky. Tears of sorrow, tears of joy, ran down her cheeks, but none could wash away the hurt she felt deep in her chest.

CHAPTER SIXTY-THREE

DEE STOPPED READING.

"Not over the top, is it?" the Brazilian asked, apprehensively.

"It's fine. Do you have a tissue?" she asked. "Thanks."

It took a moment for Dee to blow her nose, and then a long awkward silence endured, as the couple stared at each other.

Eventually, Federico's voice broke the tension. "More wine?"

Dee shook her head, her attention drawn back to the manuscript, now closed, face-up, on the table. "There's no title," she declared, noticing only the name of the author on the cover sheet.

"I was hoping you might suggest one?"

"Assuming Running Bear no longer needs to show himself in our world, how about ... " Taking a moment to pull a pen from her handbag, Dee wrote:

The Boy Who Wasn't There.

"What do you think?"

Federico didn't answer.

"You don't like my suggestion?" she sounded disappointed.

"No. No. It's a great title. Better, by far, than anything I might come up with."

"So why the glum look?"

After another uncomfortable silence, Federico replied, "You haven't read the last page."

"I thought I did." Dee was becoming even more puzzled.

"Why don't you check?"

Picking up the document once more, she turned to what she considered the end. Federico with a hand gesture indicated she should flip the manuscript over. Eight words, handwritten in capital letters, were centered on the back sheet:

I LOVE YOU DEE.
WILL YOU MARRY ME?

Thirty-three words were written in reply:

I love you too, Federico. So, yes! Without reservation yes!
I want to spend the rest of my life with you, because that which is held within my heart will never leave me.

CHAPTER SIXTY-FOUR

Two months had passed since Dee and Federico's wedding. The happy couple were residing in Vancouver, while the Harpers and Spencer remained at the Book House.

On the front porch, Ophelia and Shadow were playing tug with one of the dogs toys. Seated, Julia was sketching on her iPad. The two older children, with Harper's assistance, were removing the kayaks from the water. The sound of a vehicle's horn cut into the activity. Everyone looked up to see a bright red Ford F150 approaching; the sun reflecting off the chrome trim. Morning Star was driving.

She pulled up in front off the house, turned off the ignition, and climbed out. Shadow, tail wagging, was the first to greet her. Julia and Ophelia followed.

"Nice wheels," Spencer declared, moving toward the vehicle.

Oliver and Harper were right behind.

"Christmas come early?" Harper asked, jocularly.

"Seems so." Morning Star punctuated her response with a broad grin. "I went to the Post Office in Tipellol and found a set of truck keys and a note inside my mailbox." She pulled a scrap of paper from the band around the rim of her hat, and began to read aloud:

> "Many sincere thanks, Morning Star, for all your help.
> We appreciate you keeping a eye on the house while
> we were in Vancouver. Please accept this gift as a
> token of our appreciation."

There was a pause. "You shouldn't have."

"Does that mean you don't want it?"Oliver asked. Without waiting for a response, he added "In that case, I get first dibs."

"Your too young to drive," his mother responded, tousling his hair.

"It's mine then," Spencer asserted.

"So are you, young lady," Harper reminded her. "The new Ford is a present to Morning Star from all of us. That old truck should have been consigned to the scrapyard year's ago."

"No arguing," Julia added, definitively. "Come inside. I'll make some tea."

"I've some mail for Harper and Julia. One of the kids can fetch it from the front seat.

The pair raced to the truck and open the door. Spencer lost.

"A letter addressed to Mom and a parcel for Dad," Oliver announced, handing each item to its respective recipient. ""What ya got, Dad?" Oliver asked.

"I expect it's the digital camera, with a zoom lens, that I ordered online. I'm starting a hobby; photography." Harper grinned. "And you, Spencer, may borrow it, providing you ask first."

"Deal," the girl acknowledged, following up with a high five.

Everyone, except Julia mounted the stoop.

Realizing his wife was still standing by the pickup, staring at the letter, Harper stopped and walked back. "What is it, honeybee?"

"Here. See for yourself." Julia handed over the opened envelope.

"Addressed using an old fashioned typewriter, with no sender's name. Hmmm. Bolivian stamp. Postmarked Santa Cruz. Interesting."

That's where mom and dad are," Spencer excitedly shouted. "Are they coming here? Tell me they are."

Julia did not reply. Between sobs, all she could do was wave the enclosed photograph, which Harper took from her. The image showed a church with a brick facade. Standing in front was a woman and a man, both smiling, arms around each other. His wife's cousin Hope and her husband George, Harper realized. On the reverse, written by a shaking hand, were two sentences:

Help us, we're begging you.
The priest will know how.

———

THE END

———

PLEASE POST A REVIEW

We hope you enjoyed reading *The Boy Who Wasn't There*. Please post a review at the source of purchase and on GoodReads. You will be helping others decide whether or not to read the book, and hopefully make us better authors in the future.

Thank you.

JGR & BR

www.ingramcontent.com/pod-product-compliance
Lightning Source LLC
Chambersburg PA
CBHW020312200626
46814CB00006BA/2213

9 781944 108151